LOVE & OTHER LIES

Book 3 Professional Players Series

LYNDSEY GALLAGHER

CHAPTER ONE

KERRY

The commute to the office is the same every day; the bus is late and it's always ridiculously packed. Finding a seat is like finding a needle in a haystack and being groped, touched, or breathed on by strangers is the norm. This morning I'm lucky enough to find a seat wedged between a mother clutching a screaming toddler and a man with a bristly looking foot-long beard, which reminds me of Roald Dahl's *The Twits*.

I've never been a fan of facial hair. Tattoos, on the other hand, do something inexplicable to me – but that's another story.

A flashback of that old program *This Is Your Life* flashes through my head, where celebrities are publicly presented with a huge leather-bound book containing their most glorious moments – the highlights of their career. Right now, mine would amount to finding a seat on the bus, making the best coffee for my ungrateful boss and successfully filing all ten fingernails at a desk I hate. My biggest achievements have to be my friends. I, Kerry Walsh, am friend of the stars, close confidant of famous radio agony aunt, Abby Connolly, and drinking buddy to famous beauty brand owner, Emma Harvey-soon-to-be-Harrington.

It's hard to achieve big, when you don't know what you want, or where to start. Not only do I lack ambition, but I lack direction, much to my parents' dismay. My initial dreams ruptured inside me a long time ago. So, I'm the party animal friend – always fun on a night out, and nearly always a liability. It's a role I fill well.

The red faced toddler to my left stops crying long enough to pull my hair, before wiping his chubby little hands across the back of my office-issued navy blazer. His mother glances at him briefly, before continuing to scroll through her phone.

Alarm bells sound like a church gong, as a hurling noise threatens from my left. I pray it's a false alarm, but one quick darting glance proves me wrong. The child sprays the remnants of his Weetabix all over the bus. Leaning towards the man on the other side of me, I take a chance with his facial hair, rather than the vomit. Eventually, the toddler's mother puts the phone back into her pocket and her face tightens in an apologetic wince at the mess. I note she doesn't appear to have a changing bag with her. Opening my hand-bag, I scratch around my accumulated junk for a pack of baby wipes. Don't be fooled into thinking I have a baby – I just tend to get myself into messy situations.

Gratefully, she takes a handful and passes the packet back to me. 'Thank you so much.'

I push them back into her hands. 'Keep them, just in case.'

It's a relief when I reach my stop, three streets away from Grafton Street. I hop out into the cool May morning, grateful it's not raining, for once. Dusting down my blazer, I scan for any stray lumps of sick, satisfied there are none.

The cobbled street paving is uneven and my four-inch

heels click precariously as I negotiate the cracks. Heels are essential when you're as short as I am. I still get asked for ID on a night out – at thirty-one.

A quick glance at my wrist confirms what I already know. I'm late. I'm supposed to be in at nine am, contracted to the early shift. Most of my colleagues work from ten until six, but I get to finish at five if I open up the office.

My overbearing boss, Annie Scherzinger, is going to wreck my head when I get in. I'm already on my final warning. Annie is a plastic paddy with an American accent, meaning she's of Irish heritage but was raised in the states before returning home thirty years ago to start an au pair agency. Built like a brick shithouse, but with a penchant for floral tent-like outfits, it's no wonder the staff nicknamed her Arnie.

The familiar ringtone of my iPhone sounds from my handbag. I reach for it without looking down, bobbing and weaving between the fellow commuters of Dublin City. Caller ID says unknown, but I know exactly who it is. My boyfriend is in the British Army. Ninety per cent of our relationship is conducted over phone calls and FaceTime, which actually suits me fine. I like my independence, the nights out with the girls, and while he's away I'm under zero pressure to settle down, buy a house, or commit to any of the other mundane aspects of adulthood. Basically, I'm like a female version of Peter Pan, but in a Tinkerbell sized package.

I push the green button, then balance the phone between my shoulder and my ear, while I fumble around in my handbag for my work keys. 'Craig.'

'Good morning, gorgeous. Did you sleep well?' Craig's familiar Scottish voice hums through the receiver.

'Not too bad. How about you?'

'Not great. It's so hot here; the humidity is unbearable.'

He's on a six month tour of Syria and won't be back until at least the end of summer.

'Huh, we definitely don't have that problem here.' Summer in Ireland's been non-existent so far this year. To lift everyone's spirits, I promised my work gang I'd host a beach party in my apartment, complete with piña coladas and Hawaiian garlands. I can't promise the weather, but I can deliver the atmosphere. Party planning is one of my few fortes.

'I miss you,' Craig's smooth voice echoes across the crackling line.

'I miss you too.' I reach the grey front door of my office building. I needn't have bothered with the keys, someone's beaten me to it. I send up a silent prayer it's not Arnie, her moods are as turbulent as the Irish Sea.

'Listen, Kerry, I've got some news.' I am listening but I'm also scanning the building as I enter, peeking around each corner before taking my chance rounding them, in an attempt to dodge Arnie's frowning face and yet another verbal warning. I'm eighty per cent sure if she was going to sack me, she would have done it by now. But there's a slim chance she just might. I hate the place, but like everyone else who works here, I have bills to pay.

Peeping around the corner, I scuttle towards my station on reception like a crab. Six other desks are placed behind mine, situated in a small open-plan area, but so far the room's empty. I dump my bag onto my messy desk and collapse into my chair.

'Kerry?'

'Sorry, I'm here.' I take the phone into my hand and click my cramping neck. 'I was just walking into work. No sign of Arnie's hefty hide thankfully, but the door was unlocked so someone's here.'

Craig clears his throat noisily. 'I was saying, I've got some news.'

'Well, go on.' I'm guessing he's been promoted. After ten years in the military, it's about time. Says me who's never been promoted in my life – I've never stuck a job long enough for it to be a possibility.

'I'm getting out.' His deep Scottish lilt projects the words like a brag.

'That's great, honey. How long for?' I wasn't expecting to see him until at least August. I'll have to sweet talk Arnie for some time off. When Craig gets leave, we usually spend the week on a beach somewhere in Spain, drinking cocktails, over-eating and having frantic, hurried sex.

'For good.' Excitement taints his tone.

'What?' I bolt upright so fast I almost tip over my chair.

'For good, baby.'

A well-timed cough masks my shock. 'For good?'

I open the top drawer of my desk, pull out a bottle of once-sparkling water and take a huge gulp to lubricate my rapidly drying mouth. Scratching around for two paracetamol, I swallow them in one.

Last night's glass of wine with my work buddy Mags, had turned into three. She's a bad influence on me, though I do have a reputation to uphold, after all. Abby, Emma and Karen call her Metallic Mags, not only is her hair so platinum blonde it's practically silver, but they also say she leaves a bad taste in their mouths. I told them to wash it out with wine, Mags is grand. They're just at different stages in life, that's all.

Craig speaks again, before the silence can be deemed awkward. 'I filed for discharge three months ago. I didn't want to get your hopes up, so I didn't mention it. It was approved yesterday.' Excitement oozes from his every syllable.

Maybe I'd be excited too, if it wasn't such a shock.

'Wow. That's unreal, I mean it's…' I can't actually think of the right words because I honestly don't know what they are, what this means for us. After eight years of a long-distance relationship, as mad as it might be, we've never actually discussed the future.

'You better calm down on the nights out, Kerry, we'll have to start saving for that country house we've been talking about.' He chuckles.

Country house? We never once spoke about a country house, though now I think of it, he used to joke about buying an old house in the Scottish Borders and renovating – well, I thought he was joking. It seemed like such pie in the sky, not for a second did I think he meant it.

'I, wow, I mean it's just such a surprise. I had no idea you were thinking that way.' I take another gulp from the bottle and wonder why I'm so shocked. Somewhere deep inside, I must have had some inkling this would happen at some point?

'Imagine, we'll be able to be together every single day.'

I swallow down the rising panic and thankfully Annie/Arnie barges into the office before I have to answer.

'Is that a personal call, Kerry, or is it a potential client you are discussing my hefty hide with?'

Fuck.

'Craig, I gotta go, call me later.' Dropping my mobile into my bag, I rearrange some papers on my desk into a semi-respectable pile.

Arnie shuffles across the room towards me. The ankle-length pleated skirt she wears does absolutely nothing to flatter her.

'You're late again, Kerry. It's the fourth time in two weeks.'

'Sorry. The bus was late.' I smooth down my navy blazer

and re-tuck my company shirt into the scratchy material of my waistband.

'You should have taken an earlier one! It really isn't good enough, Kerry. You know, there are plenty of people who would be grateful for a role within this company.'

I swallow my snort as she takes a step closer, leaning over my desk to invade my personal space. Her overpowering musky, floral perfume hangs nauseatingly in the air between us, and as her right hand reaches for my hair, I'm frozen to the spot. What on earth is she doing? Talk about too close for comfort. She wouldn't get away with it if she were a man. Hell, she might be yet, that skirt could be hiding a multitude of things. And her perfume's choking me.

'Is that vomit in your hair?' Her calloused hand yanks at the left side of my head.

'Ouch.' Several hairs are ripped from my scalp and I stand, startled, as she dangles a knotted lump of something horrific in front of my face accusatorily.

'Kerry, did you even look in the mirror this morning? Employees of this company must take a bit of pride in themselves. When you walk around the streets of Dublin wearing a shirt emblazoned with At Your Service Au Pairs on it, and vomit hanging out of your hair, what kind of message do you think you're sending out?'

That little brat on the bus got me after all! I should have kept the wipes for myself.

Her cheeks are flushed with rage and her nostrils flare dangerously. I've only seen her this mad once before; Steve, the maternity cover stand-in, had been caught with his trousers down with one of the new girls that had just arrived from Spain. He received an instant dismissal.

'Ar-Annie, I'm sorry. There was a child on the bus and he—'

'That's exactly it, isn't it, Kerry? There's always something, or someone else to blame; if it's not the traffic, it's a child. You need to start taking responsibility for your actions. You're constantly late, thrown together, or hungover. Even when you're physically here, you're mentally miles away. You're unpresentable, unprofessional and careless, and now you're demonstrating a complete lack of personal hygiene and commitment to my company.'

I raise my hand to speak, as if asking the teacher for permission to go to the toilet, but she completely ignores it.

'You leave me with no choice, Kerry. I'm going to have to let you go. Friday will be your last day. If you leave quietly, I might even give you a reference.' She turns on her heels, her pleated skirt swaying as she sashays back towards the office to the kitchen, probably for a protein shake and two dozen eggs for breakfast.

As if she can read my mind, she glances over her shoulder and shoots me a parting glare. 'We'll see how petite you are when you've had four children.'

Fuck. I sink down into my faux leather chair and close my eyes. It's not even nine o'clock and I've managed to get the sack from the job that I hated, and my boyfriend's just announced he's being permanently discharged from the military.

I should probably be over the moon but for some reason, from where I'm sitting, it's hard to even make out the outline of a single star. It might finally be time for me to find that missing sense of direction.

CHAPTER TWO

NATHAN

'Hey, Millie.' My five-year-old daughter charges at me, excitement shining in her topaz eyes. I lift her into the air, revelling in the squeals of laughter that erupt from her tiny ribs as I swing her round in circles.

'Nathan, stop please. She's only just had breakfast and I do not want to see it again. It was hard enough to get her to eat it the first time round.' Clodagh, my ex, huffs and folds her arms across her lilac cashmere sweater. It could only be cashmere – this woman developed expensive tastes the second I made the national team.

Wednesday's my favourite day during the week. Clodagh drops Millie off first thing in the morning, until Friday, and every second week I get to have her until Sunday. It's an arrangement we just about managed to settle out of court.

Becoming a father at the mere age of twenty was never part of my plan, but I wouldn't change it for anything in the world. It was unfortunate that things didn't work out between Clodagh and me, but thankfully we managed to agree on a routine which seems to work well for all of us. As much as I'd love to have Millie more, I'm caught with a strict training schedule and a good few away games – it's a juggling act at the best of times.

My career with the Irish rugby team has really taken off in the previous six months. Marcus, our current captain, probably has two seasons left in him, if that. Rumours are circulating that Coach is already weighing up potential candidates for his successor, and I have my eyes ferociously fixed on that particular title. My chest silently constricts at the prospect, imagining the honour holding that position would bestow. I'm prepared to do whatever it takes to make it a reality.

I place Millie gently on the steps and watch as she runs through the front door, no doubt in search of Barbie, my yellow fluffy Labrador. Do you have any idea how embarrassing it is to bring a dog called Barbie to the park? It's so bad, I'm almost tempted to employ a dog walker, solely for the purpose that I never have to call her name out in public. But the dog was for Millie, so the name was hers to choose. Barbie is four times the size of Millie, and ditzy and blonde like her namesake, but she's more than happy to carry Millie around on her back, as Millie pretends she's a unicorn.

Clodagh clears her throat, forcing me back into the moment. Lingering outside the front door, she shifts her weight from one foot to the other, squinting at me. Her coral painted lips open to say something, then close again.

'What is it? Is everything okay?'

She scratches at her neck and I notice tiny raised marks of a rash, a tell-tale sign she's worked up about something.

'I was hoping to talk to you. Maybe inside?' She gestures to the open front door and I take a step back to let her pass, curious and mildly concerned at her request. Normally, she refuses to come in, claiming it's too hard.

My immediate thoughts stray to Millie's health. She's asthmatic and wheezes a lot but the paediatrician said it's something she'll grow out of. She doesn't sound particularly bad this morning. I didn't detect that rattling sensation from her chest when I had her in my arms, but maybe there's something I missed.

'Coffee?' I'm buying time, unsure I want to hear what she has to say, but simultaneously desperate to know.

'No, thank you. I'm leaving,' she says, pulling out one of the eight heavy chairs that rest under a solid oak table. The dramatic glance she shoots me bears a hint of defiance, a dare to challenge her, as she slips into the seat.

I'm confused. If she's leaving, why is she sitting? 'Leaving for work?'

'No, I'm leaving the country,' she confesses in a low enough tone for Millie not to hear from where she's rubbing Barbie's upturned tummy.

Adrenaline pulses through my veins and my jaw locks into a tight grimace as I process what she's telling me.

'You're taking Millie away from me?' Nothing normally rises me. An ability to remain focused, cool and in complete control is essential on the pitch, but right now, panic churns in my stomach sending my words hissing out like a seething snake.

'No. That's what I want to talk to you about. She can't come with me, not where I'm going.' Clodagh looks up at me from under elongated eyelashes and sweeps her blonde hair back from her face. It's a gesture I've seen a million times since we were seventeen.

My jaw relaxes and sweet, soothing relief floods my tensed limbs, replacing the rapidly evaporating apprehension. Though the relief is short lived, once the reality of what Clodagh is telling me hovers thickly in the air before firmly settling in. She glances around the house; the home we once shared, and unshed tears brim in the bright whites of her eyes. She would move back in the morning, if only I'd say the words. But I can't. I won't. It's not fair to any of us.

'You want me to take her? Full-time?' I pull out the chair next to Clodagh and drop into the seat.

'It's only for a few months.' Piercing blue eyes silently plead with me.

'Where are you going?' I can't imagine her leaving our daughter to swan off to another country on a whim. Ok, she struggled for the first two years but things got easier once Millie started playschool. The pregnancy was a shock to both of us, barely more than children ourselves, and certainly not the best suited life partners. But I thought we'd adjusted to the situation well, given the circumstances.

'I've been offered the chance to sing on a cruise ship. You know it's been my dream since I was young.' I do know that, although I haven't heard her speak of it in a long time. I've known it from the very first day we met, when I sat next to her in Mr Shay's history class and she told me that she wouldn't need to know anything about Oliver Cromwell where she was heading. We had big ambitions at that class-room table all those years ago, desperate to escape the council estates we were dragged up in. Out of both of us, I never would have expected it would be mine to come to fruition.

Our different, but equally humongous, ambitions were one of the things that initially united us, until hers had to be put on the backburner. She didn't make the cut as a singer and her application for stage school was also unsuccessful. Then she fell pregnant before she could try again. Mother-hood then took the obvious priority and the cracks in our own relationship emerged, great big perforating ones, which no amount of Polyfilla could cement over.

I bite my lip, considering if Clodagh could actually leave Millie when it comes to the crunch. Could she really offer up sole care to me? In a flash, I realise she probably could. Clodagh has always been a tad cold, almost resentful even. I hoped, with time and space, those feelings would fade, that the joys of motherhood would come to her. Financially, she doesn't have any concerns. My job provides plenty for both of them. She goes to work because she can't stand being at home full time.

If she's serious, what does that mean for me? I adore being with my daughter; I'd have her here all the time, if it were up to me. The only trouble is, I'm not here all the time. And if I'm ever going to make captain, I have to put the hours in, practice relentlessly, and play professionally to prove that I'm worthy.

How can I care for Millie and still provide the life I do for her, in addition to pursuing my own ambitions, when half the week I'm away training or on tour?

'When I applied last month I never seriously thought I'd make it. It's only for a few months.'

'What about Millie?' I ask.

'I thought you'd jump at the chance to have her all to yourself for the summer – you fought so hard for access.' Her throat bobs with a swallow. I wonder now if she regrets making me jump through hoops to see my baby girl, or if she wishes she'd just handed her over at the time and saved herself this conversation. Either way, I'm not going to let her find another alternative – there's no way I'll allow her to take her away from me, to take her with her, or worse again, leave Millie with her mother who can't stand me. No way.

'Of course I'll take her.' Even as the words exit my mouth I wonder how the hell I'll manage. The only help I have is my own mother. And as funny and wonderful as she is, she's not the most reliable woman in the universe. She thinks absolutely nothing of bringing Millie to the bingo, to the pub or to the bookies, claiming it did me no harm.

Clodagh clasps her hands together. 'I can't believe this is really happening. I'll miss her so much, but if I don't go now, I'll always wonder. We were so young when we had her. I wouldn't be without her, but this is something that I have to do for myself.'

'And what happens if you love it? If you decide not to come home?' I wonder out loud.

'I'll be back,' she repeats adamantly. 'I wouldn't have even considered going in the first instance, apart from you and I both know that Millie would rather be here with you anyway. She is a daddy's girl, through and through. Every day she asks if it's a *daddy day*.'

Clodagh's words pierce my heart. The underlying implication in her resigned tone is obvious; it's my fault we're not the typical, traditional nuclear family, and she's right. Ultimately, it was me that called it a day, she was so far gone from me, I had no choice. We weren't happy. All I had to do was broach the subject of us splitting up and she upped and left, taking Millie with her.

Would she have put this idea out of her mind altogether if things had been different between us? Am I costing Millie her relationship with her mother? My skull aches as the questions consecutively implode between my ears.

'When do you leave?'

'Saturday.'

'This Saturday?' Incredulity drips from those two words.

'Yes. I haven't told her yet, but kids have no true concept of time at her age. She'll think she's at yours more because the summer holidays are approaching next month.'

Shit. I hadn't factored in that there wouldn't even be any

school for nine weeks. Ireland seem to have the longest school holidays in Europe.

As Millie races towards me with a hair tie in her hand, demanding a French plait, I realise I'm going to need to enlist some professional help, for her sake as much as mine.

CHAPTER THREE

KERRY

The lazy rhythmic beat of a summer soundtrack pumps from the dusty speakers of my ancient docking station. My hips sway from right to left, taking up a life of their own as I sip a Hawaiian cocktail concoction I'd free poured from bottles of Archers, vodka and Malibu. Eight of my colleagues are wedged into my tiny studio apartment drinking beer and wine. Former colleagues, come Friday.

On a whim, I'd decided to throw myself an impromptu leaving party; the Hawaiian beach party I promised to my work buddies. Fake palm trees, squashed in soil-filled pots, are crammed into every corner. Paper lanterns hang from the wall. The place is roasting, not exactly a tropical heat, more like I've forgotten to turn off the heating for the last three days and then squeezed bodies into every square foot, but it's all fitting with the theme.

Now I've gotten over the shock, it's almost a relief to be let go. On Monday, I'll ring the temp agency and get something sorted for the following week. Office jobs are ten a penny in Dublin. At least I have a roof over my head.

I'll miss the girls in the office and the au pairs that we place, but frankly I hate being tied to a desk, eight hours a day, five days a week. Annie/Arnie saved me from having to resign from yet another unsuitable position. Over the years, I've had quite a few, still unable to find my true calling in the real world. Which wouldn't necessarily bother me if I didn't have a mountain of bills to pay, and parents I feel I have to avoid like the plague.

Squinting at my mobile, I check for messages from my girls, Abby, Emma, Karen and Fran, in case they've changed their minds and are on their way. I'm not holding my breath; my closest clique have begun the dreaded inevitability of swapping cocktail parties for candle parties, and bottles of Martini for bottles of milk. I resign myself to the fact they aren't coming the second my phone vibrates in my hand.

Withheld number again.

'Craig?' I step out of the tiny living room-cum-kitchen-cum-bedroom and into my four foot bathroom. Good job I'm only five foot four – and that's in decent pair of heels – because even I can't swing a stick in here. It's not for much longer anyway, I guess Craig and I will probably rent something bigger in the city. Or maybe we'll go travelling; I quite fancy the idea of swanning round the world, earning a few quid waitressing or pulling pints in bars along the way.

Closing the door behind me, I sink to the floor, only realising now how much the alcohol has affected me.

'Kerry, where are you?' That familiar soft accent hums across the thousands of miles of land and sea that separate us.

'I'm at home. Got a few friends round. We're having a beach party.' I don't tell him that I effectively got the sack after our last conversation, not wishing to give him any future ammunition.

Glancing down at the cheap multicoloured garland that hangs lifelessly around my neck, I realise what a sorry state I'm actually in. Perhaps the sooner he gets out of the military the better? Because apparently I need someone to keep me in line.

A low chuckle echoes in my ear and he pauses briefly before saying, 'Things are going to change when I get back to you.'

I'm fairly sure it's intended as a joke, but he accidentally stumbles on my newest fear. A nervous energy ripples through me, and fine hairs stand to attention at the base of my neck.

'What are you wearing?' His tone is low and husky.

'Not a lot, actually.' I'm not lying. A luminous yellow bikini top clings to my non-existent cleavage. The itchy protruding fake grass of a hula skirt, purchased by Mags, sits skewed across my midriff. I might not have much in the boob department, but my friends assure me that my small waist and curvaceous bum prevent me from being mistaken for a child, or a troll, even with my condensed height. All good things come in small packages, right?

'Send me a picture...' It was a definite order, one I would have found sexy once upon a time, but now, if I wasn't so drunk, might trouble me.

'Will do.' I rest my head in my hands.

'Are there any guys there?' Jealousy inches into his voice, one of the few traits I dislike in him. One time in Majorca he punched a guy who looked at my bikini for longer than he deemed appropriate. At least he cares, I suppose it's better than not giving a shit at all.

'No. There are no guys here.' A heavy sigh falls from my lips.

'Good. Now, behave yourself and don't drink too much more.'

'I won't and I will. No, sorry, I meant I will and I won't!'

I disconnect the call as he says, 'Love you.'

Fists begin to hammer on the door, but standing up proves more challenging than I anticipated. It's nights like these I miss my true friends. The ones who've swapped the spontaneous weeknights out for Sunday brunches in some sophisticated and child-friendly venue. Abby, Emma, Karen, and even Fran at this stage, all know when I'm teetering on the edge. They'd have stopped me drinking hours ago. That they should even have to at my age, is a thought I squash to the back of my mind before it can take root and grow wings.

The pounding on the door increases. I use the handle to hoist myself from the sitting position, unlock it and sway back out, leaving Mags to boldly relieve her bladder with the door wide open. Mags has zero shame.

In the living room-cum-kitchen things are spiralling out of hand. Two of the office juniors are throwing sausage rolls into the air and attempting to catch them with their mouths, unsuccessfully, I might add. Chunks of papery pastry dust the floor, alongside empty bottles and cigarette ash. To my horror, someone has knocked over the hamster cage, sawdust lines the table and the metal door is open. Fluffy is no doubt running free somewhere. I pray I catch her before the downstairs cat does.

Someone turns up the music, just as it occurs to me that I have two elderly neighbours above, and a single mother below. At that precise second, the front door bursts open and to my horror, in storms my landlord, Mick the prick; his belly busting out of his too-tight shirt. Narrow, thunderous eyes shoot arrows at my bare belly, then to the scattered sawdust, then the mess on the floor, before finally landing on the ancient docking station, of which he yanks the chord out, in an impressively swift movement for a big guy. The silence is more deafening than the music.

'What the hell is going on in here?' he roars.

I stare dumbfounded at him as the cocktails lurch threateningly, in my stomach.

Apparently, it's a rhetorical question because he continues without an answer. 'I've been knocking the door for forty-five minutes solid. I had to ring my pregnant wife to bring me the spare keys.' I flinch, as he dangles them aggressively in front of my face with his stumpy fingers.

'I've received complaints from four separate neighbouring flats about the noise level radiating from here. You stated on your rental application that you were a professional, yet this looks like a piss-up fit for freshers' week.'

I take a step towards him and raise my hands in an attempt to regain some sort of control over the situation. Bad enough I'd lost my job today, I can't jeopardise my home as well. Affordable accommodation is almost impossible to come by in this city.

As I struggle to find the words to justify the current messy state of affairs, a rush of vomit wooshes uncontrollably up my throat. Before I can clamp a clammy hand over my mouth, the cerise cocktails explode out of me, cascading unceremoniously onto his once shiny black leather brogues. I look at the floor, my hands, then at Mags who lingers, wide-eyed with horror, in the doorway of the bathroom, anywhere but directly at his fuming features.

Mick turns on his heel in disgust, removing an old-fashioned handkerchief from the pocket of his navy cords and wipes his hands distastefully. 'I want you out by Sunday.' He glances back pointedly, scrutinising the chaos, and repeats, 'Sunday,' with a finality that refuses to be bargained with.

Shit.

CHAPTER FOUR

NATHAN

Today's practice was an intensely gruelling mud-fest. Following a torturous ten kilometre run around Carton House in the lashing rain, the shrill sound from Coach's whistle permits us to hit the locker room.

'Eddie, is it the unseasonably damp drizzle that has your balls shrunk to the size of peanuts, or is Emma wearing them around her neck since you put a ring on her finger?' Marcus bellows across the open showers, as Eddie lathers his naked torso in soap. I snigger along with the rest of my teammates. Banter is par for the course with this gang, if you can't handle it, it will handle you.

'Fuck you, man! Shelly's had you by the balls for years.'

Drying myself with one of the hotel-crested towels, I glance at the sleeve tattooed on my arm. Each weave, each line, each imprint holds a significance; a line for every game, for every point and try – an otherwise unmarked triumph.

'Fan mail, lads.' Coach gestures to a small pile of letters abandoned on the bench of the changing room. Who would even bother to write a letter in this day and age, when email, Facebook and Twitter provide a much simpler and often more effective way of personally reaching their idols? Still, there are some crazy bastards out there, nothing surer. Eddie, generally considered by the women of Ireland to be the team looker, is forever getting sent lacy scraps of indecent underwear, much to the disgust of his new fiancée. Sometimes the garments have even been worn.

'One here for you, Nathan.' James flicks through the pile, flinging it out with disinterest. We're contractually obliged to acknowledge the odd one, sometimes select a mascot, or do a good deed from another. It reflects well on the team and it's an opportunity to give something back to the community, a thank you for all the support.

Dressing hastily in my rush to get back to Dublin, to Millie, I shove the envelope in my pocket. My phone begins to ring in my kitbag. Searching through damp training gear and half empty bottles of water and shampoo, I eventually manage to locate the damn thing as it rings out. It's Millie's school. Glancing at my Garmin, I wonder what they want. Before I can dial back and find out, it rings again.

'Mr Kennedy?' A deep voice booms across the phone line. The specific disapproving manner in which he states my name immediately transports me back to my own classroom days.

'That's correct.' I clear the frog from my throat with a cough.

'This is Mr Smith calling from St. Magdalena's National School. I presume you are on your way to collect Millie?'

Fuck. I'm actually an hour away. Collecting Millie is the one job I'd asked my mother to do. She's probably in the bookies betting on the horse racing, the dogs, or anything else she can gamble my money on. No matter how much I give her, she'll never stop trying for the 'big win' despite the

fact that we've already had the 'big win' with my job. She'll
never have to work again, never know a day of hunger again.
She'll never have to put up with being treated like shit, now
so far removed from the inner city slums of Dublin's most
notorious council estates on which she raised me, yet she
can't stop wandering back there.

'I'm so sorry, Mr Smith. I was under the impression
Millie's grandmother was collecting her, but we must have got
crossed wires somewhere along the line.'

Mr Smith sniffs in a disbelieving manner, like he's heard
every excuse under the sun and doesn't care, as long as he gets
to go home at half three with the rest of the teachers.

'This is the second time this has occurred in a matter of
months,' he reminds me, unnecessarily. It's a fact I'm well
aware of and the reason I've been contemplating employing a
nanny, even before Clodagh's announcement yesterday.

'I'm sorry.'

'If this continues to be a recurring problem I'll have no
choice but to—'

I interrupt him before he can issue whatever stuffy threat
he's about to utter. 'I can only apologise again. I will be there
in forty-five minutes if someone can wait with her until then.
And I will of course make a substantial donation to the new
outdoor sports facility that you're fundraising for.' I send up a
silent prayer that the traffic is kind and disconnect the call.

'See you tomorrow, lads,' I shout over my shoulder,
jogging out towards my BMW X5.

It's not quite rush hour and the traffic is mercifully light.
My mind wanders back to my mother, who can be so good, so
kind, so loving and yet so irresponsible, thoughtless and easily
distracted.

With the car in automatic cruise control, I chance dialling
the first au pair agency on Google.

'A1 Au Pairs, Sharon speaking, how can I help you?' a high-pitched voice sings down the phone and I lower the volume of my hands-free.

'Hi, Sharon. I need an au pair.' Duh.

'Is it a full-time position you are looking to fill?'

After Clodagh's revelation, it is.

'Yes, please.'

'Live in? Or live out?'

'Erm...' I'm still not entirely comfortable with the thought of a complete stranger living under my roof, but it would make things far easier. 'In, I guess.'

'And when are you thinking?'

'Now. Like this week, or as soon as possible.'

The singsong voice offers a tinkling little laugh. 'I'm afraid we have a waiting list of approximately eight to twelve weeks at the minute... Many of the girls are preparing to go back to their own families for the summer. Can't blame them.'

Shit.

'Never mind. Thanks anyway.' I disconnect the call and my heavy sigh steams up the windscreen. Scrolling down to the next agency on my screen, I glance up at the motorway ahead, then down again before hitting dial. The call is answered on the second ring.

'Good afternoon, you have reached Caring Hands Au Pairs, how may I help you?' The gritty voice of a middle-aged man reverberates around the sound system of my car, sending a chilling shudder through my spine. I hang up immediately. Call me sexist, but if the name isn't creepy enough, the fact it's run by a man is an immediate non-runner.

Third time lucky. I dial the next agency listed on the Google search. It rings for almost two minutes, then just as I'm about to hang up, someone picks up.

'At Your Service Au Pairs, Kerry speaking.' A silky smooth voice echoes through the sound system, oozing boredom, like its owner is counting down each and every second until five o'clock. I wouldn't blame her, I'd hate to be a slave to the typical nine-to-five.

'Hi, I'm looking for an au pair.'

'No, really?' Sarcasm drips from her tone.

Instead of being annoyed, bubbling laughter stirs within my chest. I grasp the steering wheel with both hands to stop myself veering off the road with unexpected convulsions. She sniggers along with me – my laughter is apparently infectious.

'What kind of customer service is that?'

'The kind you get from a woman whose last day in this crappy, dingy office is tomorrow.' Her voice seems to pick up slightly at the prospect.

'Well, in that case, you've got nothing to lose. Tell me truthfully, is this the right agency to find a suitable au pair for my energetic five-year-old daughter?'

She pauses for a second, as if in contemplation. 'Honestly, it's not bad. The girls are great, their English isn't hectic, but they all come with Garda vetting and first aid training. The manager's a bit of a pain, but you're not likely to meet her anyway. She has no childcare qualifications, mind you her managerial ones haven't done her much good either, perhaps she might actually be better suited to braiding hair or playing with Barbies.'

A flicker of hope ignites inside me. Her comment about the Barbies is eerily close to the truth. Though I assume she means the doll and not a six-stone ditzy Labrador; Kerry has intuitively hit the nail on the head, instinctively knowing what I need. Maybe, just maybe, I might get lucky, but the English could be a problem.

'Hmm. I've just spent six thousand euro on private speech therapy classes for my daughter, so what I need is someone with excellent English. I can't have all that work undone with a Polish twang or an American drawl.' I'm contemplating aloud to myself, more than anything.

'Six thousand euro? Did you win the fucking lotto or something? I'd want a fucking finishing school in Switzerland for that!'

'Something like that.' I chuckle, fully appreciating, though not judging, why she might benefit from one. It's a known fact people who swear are more honest.

'Any other requests?' The trace of a smile in her voice hints she's mocking me, but with another thirty minutes left of my drive back to Dublin, her wry humour and blunt honesty is intriguing, if not entirely constructive. I decide to indulge in a bit of fun.

'Kind, obviously. Intelligent. Third level childcare qualification essential. Sense of humour would help, if she's going to be living under my roof. An ability to cook would be advantageous. Honest, of course, that's essential too.' I reposition my numb bum in the seat and stick my tongue out at the speaker, waiting for Kerry's onslaught.

'Mary fucking Poppins is what you're looking for, pal. Good luck with that! In fact, if you find her send her my way, I could do with a spoonful of sugar myself!'

The convulsions start again as the laughter splutters out. If I met this girl in the real world, I'd definitely ask her out. Not that I'm in any position to be starting anything, but everyone needs a bit of adult fun from time to time.

'Okay, I think I'm going to have to put out a private ad or something. Or get a recommendation from someone I know, because quite frankly yours is the third agency I've phoned and so far I've been laughed at, scoffed at and ridiculed. It's been fun, but less than helpful if I'm honest.'

'What's the rush anyway? Did you send the last au pair on the first flight back to Paris when she burnt your toast? Or were your slippers not left warming by the fire when you arrived home from a long day at the office?'

Before I can reply through my sniggers, she continues.

'No wait, I know, your wife ordered her to leave after seeing her strutting around barely clothed in front of you, accidentally brushing her pert, braless breasts against you in the corridors?' She actually snorts with laughter at the last notion.

'I don't have a wife. Single dad. Hence the reason I need help.'

'Oh shit, sorry to hear that.' Her tone takes on a newfound seriousness, and a reassuring kind of warmth sweeps through me at her unexpected sincerity.

A long pause follows, but for some mad reason, I still don't want to hang up, don't want to end this conversation. There's something about this girl that's familiar. Or maybe it's just that I can relate to her honesty. Or maybe, it's the unknowing Barbie and braiding reference? Whatever it is, she's sparked my interest. Not that I can afford to be interested in much with my commitments.

Before she can hang up, I blurt, 'So, where are you moving to, when you escape the dingy office?'

'That is a very good question. If I knew the answer, I might even tell you.' Her low, sensual laughter echoes around the car. The clarity is unreal, she could almost be sitting next to me. For a split second, I wonder what she looks like. I knew a girl called Kerry once, briefly. I would have liked to have known her better, but it wasn't to be.

Seconds pass, she seems in no rush to end the conversation either. I'm probably passing the rest of her boring afternoon, the way she's passing my commute.

'So, are you going to be a lady a leisure for a while?' I ask, switching lanes to let Marcus pass. He followed me out of the hotel and has been sitting on my tail for the last thirty kilometres. He smiles and gives me the middle finger as he passes.

'I wish.' Another tinkling laugh escapes her lips. 'I'd want to find somewhere fast, the bills won't pay themselves. I'm sure a temp agency will have me sitting behind another crappy desk in under a week. Plus, I have to find somewhere to live. There will be nothing leisurely about it.'

'Why don't you look for something else, if you don't like being behind a desk?' An inappropriate image of a brunette bent seductively over a desk springs to mind. I squash it before it can grow wings.

'It's not that easy.' Kerry sighs. I imagine her breath rushing out of full lips and wonder again what she looks like, more than a little intrigued by her honesty, honeyed voice, and humour.

'Well, what kind of qualifications do you have?' Why do I suddenly feel like I'm interviewing her or something? I hope she doesn't hang up.

She laughs again, louder this time, as though I've said something really funny, but I have no idea what.

'That's the *really* funny bit...I have a first class honours degree in early education.'

'What? Why are you answering phones then? Why aren't you out minding children, doing what you trained to do?'

A heavily weighted pause turns the atmosphere awkward. Perhaps I got too personal?

'It's a long story...but ultimately, I couldn't mind other people's babies once I discovered I can't have any myself.' The bubbly, girlish tease has left her tone and I could kick myself for putting my ridiculous size twelves in the shit.

'I'm so sorry. I shouldn't have asked; it's none of my business.' I'm baffled the conversation took such a rapid turn, though I shouldn't be. She was honest from the first line that came out of her mouth and I'd deliberately kept her on the phone, kept her talking.

'No worries. Life goes on. I don't know why I even told you that, it's not something I ever bring up. I haven't even told my best friends, or...' She clears her throat and I hear the distant rustling of papers from her desk. 'Never mind.'

'If you want me to take down your details I can pass them on. Whoever takes over next week will get in touch to see if we have anyone that might suit what you're looking for. It might not be Mary Poppins but we could work something for you. Placement usually takes three to four weeks; I can start the ball rolling today.'

'Three weeks? I kind of need someone now.' My lip catches between my teeth as I bite back the craziest idea I've ever had. The one that's now relentlessly pushing to the forefront of my mind, internally jumping up and down, silently shouting and screaming at me to voice it.

'Three weeks would be the absolute quickest. I'm sorry.'

I inhale a long deep breath and blow it out slowly through my nose, trying to decide if what I'm about to ask is the stupidest, most insensitive thing I've ever come out with, or if it is the perfect solution to both of our problems.

Swallowing hard, I squash down the irrational niggle of nerves. If you don't ask, you don't get.

'Kerry, please excuse me if you think I'm an insensitive prick, but if I put the phone down and don't ask, I'll always wonder.'

I hear the gentle sound of her lips smacking together, then she says quietly, 'If you're about to ask me out, you should know I have a boyfriend.' Is that a lingering trace of regret in her tone, or simply wishful thinking on my part?

'I wasn't going to ask you out.' Although the thought wasn't a million miles from my mind.

'Oh my god, I'm such an idiot, forgive me. I just thought, seeing as we've been on the phone for about twenty minutes longer than necessary and neither of us seem to want to hang up, maybe that's where you were going. I'm such an idiot! Sorry. I'm absolutely mortified!'

The smirks tugs at my lips as she continues in a nervous babble.

'I'm the kind of person that goes out to a restaurant and when the waiter places my dinner in front of me and says "enjoy your meal", I say "you too". I have no filter. I'm liable to come out with anything.'

Her embarrassment only endears her further to me. I decide to come straight out with it, as soon as I can control the laughter erupting from my belly again.

'Kerry, I don't know you, but I'm pretty sure if I met you on a night out, I might ask you out. You sound kind of hot.' I don't mention that I wouldn't expect it to go much further than that. Once women hear I'm a separated father, they tend to run a mile. Now my title has officially changed to 'single father', the possibility of any woman taking me – us, I should say, – on, permanently, is a pipe dream.

'Only kind of? Shit, I'll have to work on that. You don't sound too bad yourself, but I wasn't joking about the boyfriend.'

'He's a lucky man. Seriously though, I have something more important to ask you.'

'Oh.'

'Is it just babies that you have an aversion to minding? Or is it all children?' I bite my lip, hoping once again that I haven't pushed her too far, but I have a gut feeling I can't ignore – like I was meant to get talking to her on her last day. An inexplicable feeling that someone with her sense of humour could fit effortlessly into my dysfunctional family. The degree in childcare and her perfectly neutral Irish accent is simply an added bonus.

She pauses for a second, then her breathing quickens over the phone.

'Mostly babies.'

'Would you consider minding my five-year-old daughter

Millie?' Kerry's laughter would be a dream to have around my too-big house. And her brutal honesty about her vulnerability inclines me to believe she's trustworthy.

I barely breathe while she contemplates it.

'I don't even know your name,' she says.

'It's Nathan. I promise I'm not a serial killer. Come to the house and meet me, meet Millie, and see what you think. This could be the perfect solution to both our problems.'

She hesitates for a few seconds. 'I might be able to help you out short-term.'

'You're not looking for a long-term position?'

'No, I have a... I have other commitments at the end of the summer.'

'Well, what about for the summer then, say three months? We could call it a trial position, but you never know, you might like us and decide to stay on.'

'I can assure you, I won't. Oh shit, there I go again with my big mouth, sorry! What I meant to say is that I'm sure I'll like you, but realistically I could probably only do the few months.'

'Sometimes things change.' I can only hope.

'No babies?'

'The only other baby I have is a six-stone Labrador called Barbie.'

'You said you were looking for someone to live in?' Her tone suggests this could be a dealbreaker. The boyfriend could be an issue. I doubt I'd like my girlfriend living in another man's house. But she did say she's looking for somewhere to live and I need live-in help, there's no other way around it.

'Yes.' I'm barely able to swallow while I wait for her decision.

'Give me your address and I'll be over at midday on Saturday.'

Could it really be *that* simple?

A nervous excitement ripples across the inside of my stomach, and worryingly it has equally as much to do with meeting the intriguing Kerry in person, than simply having found a suitable minder for Millie.

CHAPTER FIVE

KERRY

'You did what?' Karen's eyebrows shoot so high that they disappear underneath her thick, dark fringe. Her girlfriend, Fran, sits next to her looking equally surprised but purses her lips together, opting not to voice it in the same manner.

After twenty years of friendship, I'd imagine there's nothing in the world I could do to surprise Karen. When it comes to me, she's seen it all − like the time my chicken fillet slipped out of my bra onto the dancefloor and I had to kick it into the nearest dark corner, while the guy I was kissing was still trying to cop a feel of my suddenly three sizes smaller boob.

'It's just for a few months, until Craig is released from the army and we get a place together.' I take a sip of my cappuccino and glance around at the shoppers, some wandering aimlessly around Liffey Valley, others bustling by with serious intent. I wish I had some serious intent. Sometimes I feel like I'm wandering aimlessly through my entire life, waiting for something. Craig maybe? Or something else?

The thought of his return is something I should be looking forward to, but instead I find myself trying not to dwell on it. Change always terrifies me. What if when he gets home we can't live together? What if, ultimately, we want different things? I cringe internally, knowing that I've had eight years to tell him I can't have children, yet have never actually managed to broach the subject. I didn't lie, just omitted the truth. Whenever he's been on temporary release from the military, our time together is always a whirlwind of adventure. We've never discussed too far into the future.

'It's madness, Kerry, even for you,' Karen announces, dragging me back into the present moment.

'What if it's fate?' Fran says quietly, placing a hand lightly on Karen's thigh and offering a meaningful glance. Karen and Fran are big into fate, convinced an old fortune teller brought them together, after she died. Excuse me if I don't buy into it. I'm delighted they found each other, but it was probably just luck. Right place at the right time. And I'm convinced that this short-term summer position is simply a stroke of luck too.

Imagine, the day after I lose my job and my home, I get offered both, and with the freedom of not being tied to a desk or a lease. And my new boss sounds like a hoot. At least I won't have to pretend to be anything I'm not because he pretty much got most of it on the phone yesterday. It almost sounds too good to be true, but then again the thought of minding a five-year-old girl does concern me slightly. I can't even mind a hamster – I never did find Fluffy.

What if Millie hates me?

I remind myself it's only for three months. And it's the answer to all of my current problems, though we didn't discuss a salary yet. I know au pairs don't earn a lot, but at least I'm avoiding paying Dublin city rent prices.

'Whatever it is, I'm going to be late if I don't leave now.' I stand, pushing my chair back with a screech on the shiny tiled floor and kiss both of them on the cheek.

'Call me later,' Karen urges as I waltz off, raising my head as high as a short girl can, in an attempt to portray a confidence I don't feel.

Half an hour later I'm strolling the symmetrical tree-lined streets of Ranelagh, aka Dublin central suburbia. The houses are enormous and notoriously expensive; Victorian and three storeys high. The schools are supposed to be the best in the city. Nathan, the single father, must do well for himself. I wonder exactly what it is that he does so well? Perhaps he's a banker? Or maybe a solicitor; funny on the phone, probably geeky in the flesh – buck teeth and inch-thick glasses. Not that there's anything wrong with that look, but I prefer the full-bodied, hunky type myself, throw in a few tattoos and I'm liable to openly drool.

He said it was number sixty-five and I'm currently at sixty-three. Taking a deep breath, I power walk the final few metres as fast as my short-girl legs will carry me, trying to quell the rising panic. What if he's a psychopath and he's lured me here to murder me?

I mentally scold myself for being so daft. He's a single father, with a dog called Barbie, and he's simply stuck in a rut. Although, it doesn't look too bad from where I'm standing. Walking up the stone coloured paving towards an emerald-green front door, I inhale and exhale deliberately slowly trying to steady my increasingly hammering heart.

My phone vibrates in my pocket. Unknown caller. I decline the call. I haven't told Craig about any of this. Only that I was sick of my desk job and hoping to start nannying. Coincidently, I didn't admit I'd been pretty much evicted too. Twice now, he's suggested I need to slow down on the nights out. He might be right, but I'm not ready to hear it. Some people like to exercise, personally, I prefer to let off steam with a few drinks and a dance.

The front door opens before I can touch the brass knocker. The hammering in my heart intensifies three-fold. Instinctively, I take a step back at the sight of my potential new boss. A tiny o forms at my lips, and the air rushes out of my mouth in an awkward typical Kerry 'fuck'.

Not only is he way younger than he sounded, devastatingly good-looking, with the face of a fallen angel and the body of an athlete – but he actually is a fucking athlete! One that I met before, many moons ago, and drunkenly fucking kissed! This *cannot* be happening to me! It's like a bad movie.

Recognition flickers on his unjustly handsome face. Rugby players are supposed to have broken noses and cauliflower ears, yet the man before me looks like he could be a poster pin-up for a trendy Ralph Lauren aftershave. His hair is shorter than I remember, the blond surfer curls have been replaced with a cropped cut that frames his face and shows off his symmetrically handsome features. A white t-shirt clings to his ridiculously ripped torso, revealing muscular arms both covered with full-sleeve tattoos. I wipe my lips with the back of my hand in a less than ladylike gesture.

Rubbing an enormous hand over the blond stubble that dots his strong jawline, he stares at me, with a glint in those striking cobalt eyes. He doesn't even attempt to hide the smirk curling at his full boyish lips, and I mean boyish, because that's what he is – at the age of only twenty-five – yet somehow, he radiates this aura of indisputable masculinity. It's not even the sheer size of him, it's the quiet solidness to his presence, commanding an unhealthy amount of my attention.

'You.' Is the only word I can utter. I'm not sure if I'm mad at him, or mad at myself for not even considering the possibility. Abby said he had a daughter, but not for a second did I think...

What are the chances of pretty much agreeing to move in with the only man I ever drunkenly kissed when Craig and I were on a stupid break? And a famous rugby player, six years younger than me at that.

At the time, Craig had been under serious strain, following seven months in Afghanistan. He'd said the long distance was too hard, that he'd rather concentrate on what he was doing over there and not worry about me. I wasn't entirely surprised. It was the longest we'd ever been apart and the phone calls had become less frequent and increasingly strained. It was September, just before my friend Abby's wedding in Croatia. I didn't want to put a dampener on things by announcing I'd been dumped by my boyfriend of seven years by text message. And though I was hurt, I couldn't bring myself to miss him straight away, like other women might miss their boyfriends, as I was so used to him constantly being abroad. With the wedding and a week in Croatia to distract me, I wasn't as cut up about it as I otherwise might have been.

After the holiday, I arrived home to an enormous bouquet of white roses on my doorstep with an apology note from Craig, pleading a moment of madness. He was discharged on a two week release after that. We picked up where we'd left off, except I felt as guilty as fuck, but he was none the wiser.

I chalked it up to my own moment of madness – too much sunshine and tequila. I convinced myself I didn't need to confess because technically he'd dumped me. I persuaded myself he wouldn't gain anything from the knowledge; Craig's jealous at the best of times. Telling him might alleviate my guilt, but it risked inflicting unnecessary pain on him and unleashing untold aggro. So I decided to say nothing.

Nathan's a friend of Abby's husband, a fellow teammate

on the Irish rugby team. I was foolishly flattered by his advances that week. I'm not the type of woman a famous athlete might go for. They usually prefer the likes of my stunning friends, with long hair and legs up to their armpits, not a five-foot, flat-chested gnome. After Craig's rejection, attention from a man like Nathan did wonders for my battered ego, temporarily of course.

Never in my wildest dreams did I expect to see him again, let alone agree to move into his house and mind his daughter. Shit.

'Me.' Nathan shrugs, bringing me back to the current predicament. His tone is almost apologetic but the devilish glint in his stare isn't remotely remorseful.

Now what?

He steps back inching the door wider open, a silent invitation to enter, but my size-four feet are rooted to the spot, the blood still rapidly draining from my face. I haven't had this much of a shock since George Michael came out.

Before I can decide to turn on my heels and run for my life, a little girl wearing a Disney Princess gown ploughs down the steps and leaps into my arms. Tiny arms squeeze me with an innocence I'd love to bottle. Her silky yellow hair smells like sunshine and strawberries as it tickles my face

'Kerry? I've been waiting for you!' Little fingers clasp the back of my neck, as she tilts back to squint inquisitively at my face in the way that only a child can get away with. She behaves as though she's been waiting for me her entire life. A twinkle of hope glitters in her brilliant blue eyes – eyes she inherited directly from her father.

'Will you be my new best friend?' Her wholehearted enthusiasm melts my own heart, even as it sinks further into the pit of my stomach.

CHAPTER SIX

NATHAN

Millie drags Kerry into the house, desperately excited to show off her toys, starting with her favourite, a stuffed monkey called Captain Barnacles. Seeing as I have no clue how to handle the situation, I allow Millie to take the lead. Filling the kettle up with water, I flick it on.

'Tea or coffee?' I call across the open-plan kitchen to where Kerry's sitting cross-legged on the floor, while Millie gathers up her dolls for a 'tea party'. From the look on Kerry's face, she would probably prefer something stronger.

'Coffee, please,' she says, as Millie makes herself comfortable in Kerry's lap.

At least she didn't run because I really do need the help. Though that doesn't mean she won't the second my bossy daughter permits her to stand again. I switch on the coffee machine.

'Millie, will you get the treat tin for Kerry?' It's the only way I know how to move Millie, and it works; she leaps from Kerry's lap and skips into the utility room. She'll need to use the step to reach up high enough to get the tin of multi-coloured lollipops and Freddie Frogs, which might buy me thirty seconds.

Kerry stands and crosses the room slowly, like she's walking the green mile. The colour still hasn't fully returned to her face. She's every bit as beautiful as I remember, more so if possible. She's got the girl-next-door look going on, understated, oblivious of her own appeal and excruciatingly sexy. Enormous steely grey eyes peer up at me from her tiny height, almost tentatively as she approaches. She wedges her hands into the back pockets of her jeans, resting them on her bum. Lucky them. Hovering three feet in front of her, I take a step closer.

'If it's any consolation, I had no idea it was you.' I pull out two mugs and drop a teabag into mine.

'Dad, I can't reach the tin!' Millie wails from the next room.

'Use the step!' I'd normally run to help her but I'm stalling for time.

'Seriously? What are the chances?' Kerry helps herself to the mug I'd left out for her and crosses the kitchen to wait by the coffee machine, putting a safe distance between us.

I follow her, leaning over her tiny frame to reach the coffee capsules which are stored in a jar a foot above her head.

'I'll have to move these lower if you're going to be living here for the summer.' I'm testing the water and she seems to know it. She takes a step back again, resting a hand casually on the counter, but there's nothing casual about the chemistry that's still crackling between us – it's been nine months, but it's still electrifying.

'Let's not get carried away now, handsome. You know I can't accept the job, not now.'

'You think I'm handsome?' I probably should be more

concerned about her declining the position, but I'm stupidly flattered. Plus, I'm going to offer her an obscene amount of money to work for me, and not just because I like her. Millie never throws herself at anyone the way she threw herself at Kerry. Her mam's departure this morning obviously hit her hard, though she put on a brave face. There's no way I'm letting Kerry leave now too.

'Huh! You know I do, otherwise we wouldn't be in the awkward situation we find ourselves in.' She selects the darkest coloured capsule, the strongest coffee I have. She means business.

'Look, I wasn't joking. I need you.' I'm more than happy to lay on the guilt. She needs this job as much as we need her, she practically spelled it out for me on the phone the other day.

'Daddy, help me reach, pleeeeasssseeee!' Millie's scrambling around in the utility still.

The daddy guilt grips my insides. I go in and lift her up to reach the precious tin. The second I set her feet back on the floor, she races through to Kerry and opens the tin in front of her.

'Take a lolly.' She points to the fluorescent candy sticks we buy in bulk. The pink ones are her favourite.

Kerry peers into the treat tin, her fingers skim over the wrappers and I hold my breath. Millie is a great girl, but she's an only child and she never shares the pink ones with anyone. 'Hmm, I like the pink ones the best.' I wait for the protest but it doesn't come.

'Ha! Me too!' She hands Kerry two lollies and takes one for herself. If I was in any doubt, which I'm not, this reinforces what I already suspected – Kerry is the right woman for the job.

'Put the tin back now please, Millie.'

The second she's out of the room I turn to Kerry, as her

fingers battle to unwrap the lolly. I take it out of her hands and do it for her, like I've done for Millie a hundred times.

'Kerry, I need you. Millie loves you. I'll pay you five grand a month and you'll have your own floor of the house. Do the three months and see how you feel after that. We'll forget about that...incident. I promise, I'll forget it ever happened.' I'm lying. I can't forget it ever happened but I'll do my best to pretend.

Kerry's enormous eyes widen further. She's saved from answering immediately by the pink candy she's sucking indecently, but it's an offer no one in their right mind would refuse. Yet, from the deepening line on her otherwise flawless forehead, I wouldn't put it past her. The boyfriend is a pain in my ass and I've never even laid eyes on him.

Millie returns faster this time. 'Kerry, do you want to see your new room? It's pink, like mine!'

Conflicting emotions dance in Kerry's pupils as they dart between Millie and me, seemingly torn. Seconds pass, before she shrugs in a reluctant acceptance. She takes the lollipop from her mouth and points her index finger to my chest. 'Fine, I'll do it, but no funny business.'

A slow grin spreads across my face. It's going to be a long hot summer, and I'm not talking about the weather. But I'll keep my hands to myself. Shagging the nanny never ends well. Look what happened to Jude Law.

CHAPTER SEVEN

KERRY

Sellotaping the final piece of cardboard closed, I count the boxes that surround me. There's eight; that's the entirety of all I've accumulated in the three years I've lived here. Like the job in the agency, this studio apartment was supposed to be a stopgap, until I got something more suitable sorted, until I eventually made my mind up what I was going to do with my life. The trouble is, I never quite got round to it. I'm aware I can't keep drinking like a student forever, but I've never had a reason to stop.

The empty hamster cage mocks me from the corner of the room and I glance out the window at the street below, eyeing all that I'm leaving behind. Tourists swarm the city like ants, but then again, it is Temple Bar, one of the most popular areas in Dublin. The buzz of being so central, the feeling of being in the thick of it, is something I've grown to adore. I love being able to merge with the crowd, swarming unidentifiably in a flock. Having grown up in a small coastal suburb, the city centre always offered more choices and a sense of independence from my overbearing parents.

Ranelagh will be quiet in comparison, though I'm there to work, not for fun. The idea of living with, and working for, the one man who has the potential to ruin my future is not something that's sitting easily with me. If Craig finds out that Nathan and I kissed, he will lose his shit completely and I wouldn't blame him. Ok, we were on a break at the time, which was his decision, not mine, but if the shoe were on the other foot, how would I feel? Squeezing my eyes tightly shut, I try to picture Craig living with another woman but I just can't summon the image. In fact, the only thing I see any time I close my eyes in concentration is Nathan Kennedy in that tight white t-shirt, with his adorable daughter peeping out from behind his toned legs. I need to get a grip, it's just a little lust. Craig's been gone too long this time.

My mobile rings for the fourth time that morning and it's only eleven o'clock. Unknown caller again. I decide I'd better answer it. I take a deep breath, knowing I have to tell Craig I'm moving. It all happened so fast, I haven't had the chance. Ok, truthfully, I've been putting it off because I'm not sure what he's going to say about it.

'Hello?' I perch on the edge of a box and take a sip from a bottle of sparkling water.

'Good morning, sleepy head. I tried calling you earlier, I take it you were having a lie-in.' Craig sounds like he's a million miles away, but then again, he probably is.

'Sorry, I was busy. I didn't hear the phone ringing.'

'And what exactly has my girlfriend so busy on this fine Sunday morning?' His tone is jovial but I don't doubt he wonders. A flicker of sympathy lights inside of me. It must be hard being away all the time.

'It's not fine here, it's actually lashing down.' I bite my

lower lip, wondering why I feel like I'm about to tell my parents I was caught drinking in the playground.

A wince pulls at my face and I blurt, 'I'm moving,' before I wimp out. 'I accepted a nannying position for the summer and it's live in, so I'm here packing up my measly few belongings.'

'Seriously? You've been talking about leaving that office job for ages, I never genuinely thought you would do it. Well done, Kerry,' he says and my shoulders sag with relief.

'Yes, well, I thought it was about time.' Another lie; it's becoming a bad habit.

'Is it just for the summer?' Concern creeps into his voice, as if he's beginning to realise this may affect his return, and the plans I wasn't even aware 'we' had.

'Yes, I agreed to do three months. You know the school holidays are coming and it's difficult for working parents to get childcare. It'll save on rent for the summer as well.' That should please him. Craig's always banging on about saving for a rainy day.

'Well, it sounds like you've got it all sorted, Kerry, I'm impressed.'

'Thanks, I think...' I'm unsure why but the fact he didn't think I had it in me feels like an insult.

'So, where's the nannying job? And what are the family that you'll be working for like? I hope they're not exploiting you? You know, some of those families have four kids and pay peanuts, even if you are saving on rent.'

I clear my throat while I think of how to word this without setting off alarm bells in his head. His temper is notoriously quick to flare. There have been times when we've rowed and it's been a relief he's on another continent.

'The house is in Ranelagh. It's nice. The family seem lovely and it's just one little girl to mind. She's called Millie; she's five. I met her already and she's a dote, energetic but lovely. The pay is actually better than what I was getting at the office, and that's without considering I won't be shelling out on rent.'

Craig lets out a long, low whistle. 'Sounds like you've landed on your feet, babe.'

'I just fancied a change.' Still, I omit to mention it was pretty much forced on me.

'What do the parents do?' He asks the question that I've been dreading. I deliberately keep it vague, not wishing to lie to him any further than necessary.

'The mother is a singer and the dad's into athletics. Apparently they're both away a lot.' Hopefully he'll assume they're away together. I cross my fingers behind my back, as if it makes my lack of honesty any better.

'Wow, sounds fancy. Are you sure you won't be tempted to stay on afterwards? Don't forget I'll be out at the end of August and we have plans.'

Considering he hadn't mentioned these plans until last Wednesday, I've been hearing a lot about them since.

'I won't. But we need to talk about these plans... It's all been so sudden and we need to make sure we're on the same page.' I pick at my chipped nail varnish while I wait for him to reply.

A low chuckle echoes through the phone line. 'Of course we're on the same page. We've been together eight years; I'm pretty sure we both know what we want at this stage.'

Well one of us does, apparently...

There's a rustling sound in the background. 'Babe, I've to go, sorry. Good luck with the move. Sorry I'm not there to help you.' His tongue clicks against the roof of his mouth, a habit that I've grown used to over the years. Before the phone disconnects he adds, 'But don't worry, I'll be there to help you with the next one.'

That's what worries me.

The phone goes dead. I glance at the lock screen photo of Craig and me, taken in Majorca, two years ago. We're both clutching a bottle of Budweiser and our smiles extend all the way to the crinkling corners of our eyes.

It'll be ok, I promise myself, sucking in a lungful of air. I'll do my job, mind Millie, keep my head down, and my distance from her ridiculously attractive dad. When Craig gets out, everything will fall into place. I love him; everything will be perfect once he gets back.

CHAPTER EIGHT

NATHAN

I spend the day dusting, hoovering and making sure Kerry's accommodation is perfect for her. It's essential she's happy here, essential for Millie. A final glance round the predominantly pink guest room reassures me it's pretty fabulous, even if I do say so myself. Clodagh had the entire house decorated by an interior design company when we first moved in. She thought we might fill it with little girls. It turned out we had very different ideas about our future, and that's one of the reasons why we no longer have one – together that is.

I could have given in, given her what she wanted, but I'd known deep down for several years that things weren't right between us. We were childhood sweethearts who would have gone our separate ways, had she not fallen pregnant. The sleepless nights and the pressure of parenthood only highlighted the cracks in our relationship.

'She's here!' Millie bounces excitedly up the stairs, two at a time, with Barbie close on her tail and Captain Barnacles clutched under her right arm.

'Well, open the front door then.' I trained her not to open it until I say it's ok. It's not the Jehovah's or people selling stuff I worry about. At the end of the day, I'm a sports celebrity, whether I like that aspect or not, and there are a lot of crazy people out there. That's why I recently installed discreet CCTV over the front door. Millie's privacy and safety is of the utmost priority to me.

Reaching up onto her tiptoes, Millie's fingers yank the latch open to reveal Kerry, surrounded by several cardboard boxes. She looks stunning in tight blue jeans and a red chiffon shirt. Her lips are painted the same shade as her top and the flat pumps she wears on her feet. Without her heels, she looks sweet sixteen and ready to be kissed. I remind myself she's off limits. Apart from the obvious fact that's she's Millie's babysitter, and new best friend, she also still has a boyfriend, wherever he may be. I hope he's not going to cause me any problems.

A taxi is parked on the main road in front of the house. The driver balances another box on his hip. 'This is the last one.' He huffs, setting it down at the bottom of the concrete steps.

'Here.' I hand him a fifty euro note in thanks, swatting Kerry's money back at her.

'I could have collected you. Don't you have a car?'

'I never got round to taking lessons.' A pink tinge rises from her neck to her cheeks.

'We'll have to rectify that. I'll teach you.' Before she has the chance to accept or decline my offer, Millie drags her into the kitchen and through to the lounge area, towards the doll's house and twenty dolls. I watch her swaying figure disappear as the enticing exotic scent of her perfume teases my nostrils.

Carrying the boxes upstairs, I place them in Kerry's room for her to unpack when she's ready. Jogging back down the stairs, I put my hand in my jeans pocket to fish out the front

door key I had cut for Kerry. An envelope falls out, floating to
the floor in front of me. Stooping over, I pick it up, fingering
it as I walk towards the kitchen and the sound of Millie
bossing Kerry around already. It's the one I stuffed into my
pocket when I left training in a rush during the week. I
meant to wash these jeans but thankfully hadn't yet got round
to it.

Kerry glances up at me but continues the tea party game
that Millie instigated. I lift the lid on the casserole dish that's
simmering on the stove. It smells good, probably because I
laced the diced beef in red wine and garlic. I stir it with a
ladle, before returning my attention to the envelope.

My full name is scrawled across the front in spindly writing. I slice it open with a knife to see it's a letter composed of
mismatched words cut out from various newspapers and
magazines.

You think you're so great, but no one is invincible.

The line sends a tremor of unease across my spine but
before I can overthink it, I crumple it in my hands and slam
dunk it into the waste bin in the utility room. It comes with
the territory, unfortunately. We get a lot of fan mail, but on
the flipside we get the odd hate mail too. When we narrowly
lost the Six Nations to France two years ago, we were
bombarded with abuse from disappointed fans, most of it
online. I hate social media. I never use it myself.

'So, do you want the full tour?' I want her to feel at home
here, to know every part of the house is hers to use while she
lives here. I'd hate to think she felt she had to sit in her
bedroom.

'Sure. This place is amazing.' She gazes around at the high
ceilings and Victorian architecture. A wide coving with intricate detail lines the corners of each room.

'Well, you've seen the kitchen and living area. There is a

sunroom through there.' I point her towards the back of the house where double doors open up on to the neatly trimmed lawn. I have no interest in gardening, one of those robot lawn mowers does all the work for me.

'Wow. Nice garden.' She opens the door and sticks her nose out. 'I love the smell of freshly cut grass and rain. It reminds me of my childhood.'

'Where did you grow up?'

'Here in Dublin. Well, Dalkey. My parents still live in the house I grew up in.'

'Do you get to see much of them?'

'Not if I can help it. They live in the dark ages. My father believes a woman should be at home, raising a family. And if she's not, she better have a damn good career to justify why not. He's a judge and by god, does he judge, especially his daughter.'

'Wow. He sounds intense. What about your mother?'

'He is. My mother's the quiet, mousy type.' She arches an eyebrow. 'I know what you're thinking...the apple didn't fall too far from the tree, right?' A wry, seductive chuckle leaves her lips.

'Of all the words I'd use to describe you, quiet and mousy would be the last that spring to mind. You must be doing your best not to fall into that category. I'd say Abby Connolly would have a field day with you.' Callum's wife is a shrink, albeit a radio celebrity one these days.

'Any siblings?' I ask, as she follows me back through to the living area.

'This is starting to sound like an interview, I thought I'd already got the job?' She nudges me, then pulls away just as quickly, seeming to remember herself.

'Just curious. I'm an only child. I used to wish I had a brother. Now I've got fourteen, all wearing matching jerseys.'

'What's behind there?' She points to the door I'm hovering in front of. I never bring women in here. It's my private sanctuary. But she's not any woman.

The key's tucked on top of the doorframe, out of sight. I reach for it, swallowing back my snigger. I won't have to worry about Kerry spending too much time in here, not unless she snuck a pair of stilts in. Although, she's one of the few women I'd welcome in here, hell, I've even fantasised about it a hundred times in the last twenty-four hours.

'I can read you like a book. You think it's the first time I've been laughed at for being short?' That elbow nudges into me again, harder this time.

'I'll have you know, I think your height is absolutely adorable.'

Careful, Nathan, don't frighten her off before she's even begun.

'Huh.' I unlock the door and she steps inside. I make one more quick check on Millie, who's still engrossed in the dolls, before following her in. When Clodagh moved out, I turned 'the good sitting room' into a man cave – a relaxation suite, complete with jacuzzi, steam room and sauna. I'm contemplating putting a swimming pool in the garden too, I've not had the chance to call anyone out to price it yet.

'Wow.' Her granite glinting eyes match the shade of the Colourtrend paint on the wall. They sparkle as she takes it all in. 'Is that a hot tub?'

'It is, fit for eight people.' I pull back the cover to show her.

'And do you regularly have seven other people in there with you?'

'Now who's interviewing who?' I bite back another snigger.

'Do you have many women over?' Her hand flies to her

mouth, covering it before it can run rogue again. This time, I can't swallow down the laughter. The convulsions erupt from the depth of my stomach and echo round the double height ceiling. To her credit, she joins in.

'What's so funny? I thought you sports stars were all the same?'

'Hello, you're looking at "Daddy Day Care" in the flesh. When I'm not watching YouTube videos on how to braid hair, I'm making hot chocolate with marshmallows and singing "Let It Go". You're going to be hearing a lot of that song, so you better get used to it. Besides, what kind of father would I be if I traipsed umpteen different women through here? What kind of an example would that set for my little girl?'

'True.' She nods in approval.

'That's not the best bit.' I place my hand on the small of her back, nudging her forward towards handmade sliding doors at the far side of the room.

'There's more?'

I slide them back into the wall to reveal every man's wet dream – my own personal bar, six metres in length, also hand-made from the best mahogany I could source. I even have Guinness on tap. Not that I get to use it much, but one day I plan to. A cinema size screen's built into the opposite wall for anytime the lads want to watch a match together. Overhead shelving lines the back wall, stocked with a variety of red and white wine. Twelve bottles of Bollinger sit chilling in the wine fridge.

'Wow,' Kerry repeats again, strutting towards one of six red leather high-backed stools that line the bar.

'I don't get out much.' I don't know why I feel like I have to justify my own little luxuries to her, but she's so different to most other women I've met. Many of them want to be impressed, demand it in fact. Kerry seems like the total oppo-site, a very undemanding sort. I get the impression she'd be happy with a five euro bottle of wine and a bag of chips, and I mean that as a compliment. Most of the women I've dated are such high maintenance. But then I'm not dating Kerry, she's here to mind Millie.

'Dad?' Millie calls from the living area.

'We've been busted.' I pull back the sliding doors, cover the jacuzzi and lock the door behind us.

'Something smells good.' Kerry kicks her shoes off in the sitting area. I like that she seems to be making herself at home. I make a mental note to set some hours with her. I don't expect her to entertain my daughter twenty-four seven.

'Daddy's cooking,' Millie tells her. 'He only ever does that for the pretty ones.'

I almost choke on my own saliva. 'Don't be silly, Millie.'

'It's true!' She looks wide-eyed at me, then back to Kerry and I silently concede that she's right. I don't date often, it's not easy between my work schedule and Millie, but a few weeks ago I started seeing a model called Serena. Having cancelled the same date five times, instead of making it a sixth, I invited her over for dinner. Millie should have been fast asleep, but it didn't quite work out as planned. She woke up and wanted to join the party, eating the dessert I'd prepared from both mine and Serena's bowl.

It didn't go down well. Serena became really busy after that. As amazing as Millie is, I fully understand why people prefer not to get seriously involved with me, with us, long term. Children complicate things. Still, I was hoping Serena might be able to introduce me to a few of her modelling contacts. Loads of my teammates have side numbers with big brands, butCalvin Klein aren't exactly banging my door down right now. If it's good enough for Dan Carter, it would defi-nitely be good enough for me. A guy can dream.

Kerry stands, pats Millie's head gently, then crosses the room to inspect the dinner I'm cooking for her.

'So, you think I'm pretty?' An infectious giggle slips from her crimson lips.

'You know I do, or we wouldn't be in the awkward situation we find ourselves in.' I repeat her own line back at her and another laugh splutters from her indecently appealing mouth, reminding me what enticed me to offer her this position that day on the phone, long before I realised who she was.

'You know, we're just going to have to get on with it, get over it, and put it behind us.' She takes the lid off the dish, dips a finger in the sauce and places it in her mouth, closing her eyes in appreciation. A rush of blood goes directly to the contents of my underwear.

'I find alcohol helps. I'm partial to a glass of wine or a G&T.'

'What about a few tequilas? I think I have some in the bar out there.' I deliberately remind of her of that night in Croatia, the one that resulted in our drunken kiss.

'On second thoughts, I'll stick to water.' She sticks her pretty little tongue out at me, then returns to play with Millie.

I lay the table for three and pull out a bottle of red from the wine rack, uncorking it with a pop. I'm increasingly warming to the idea of having another adult around the place, especially one who is so attractive and funny. Since she arrived on my doorstep, wrapped up like a Christmas present, I've been reliving that kiss way more often than what is healthy for me. Or her, for that matter. The more I try to forget it, the more it rises defiantly to the surface. I need to keep my inappropriate memories, and my hands, to myself. She's here for Millie's benefit, not mine. It's one crush I'll have to get over.

Kerry's head flicks round and her eyes lock into mine as she bites back the smirk stirring on her lips. Crushing the crush might be harder than I initially thought, though a couple of glasses of wine should be safe enough.

CHAPTER NINE

KERRY

I wake, surprisingly refreshed, not having expected to sleep so well in my new bed. The second my head hit the pillow, I was gone. A quick glance at my watch tells me it's six-fifteen. I shower and dress in jeans and a casual pink shirt, ready for the day. I'm never normally up this early. I used to set five snooze alarms just to get to the office on time, but this morning I'm excited to see Millie again.

Last night had been way less awkward than I'd antici- pated, though the half bottle of red might have helped. Nathan's cooking was delicious. Turns out he has a thing about fresh, organic food and a complete intolerance for hidden sugars, hence everything was done from scratch.

The conversation had mostly centred around Millie, who seems to love the limelight. I've only met her twice but already feel like she's been a part of my life for a lot longer. I'll have to be careful not to get too attached, not being able to have my own. If the option hadn't been taken from me, I wonder if I'd be a mother by now? Or if I'd even want to be?

Since I discovered I couldn't, a feeling of despair enveloped me and a sense of not being a proper woman lurked in every part of me.

At eight o'clock, Nathan and I had put Millie to bed together, so I could see her routine. She relies on inhalers for asthma, so I noted the number of puffs and the technique. After her bedtime story, she went down easily enough. Instead of risking time alone with Nathan, who seems to get off by tormenting me with his flirtatious remarks, I went to my bedroom, unpacked and phoned my boyfriend. Craig was distracted, but we chatted for a few minutes anyway.

This morning the house is eerily silent as I creep down the stairs towards the kitchen.

I'm on the third floor, right at the top of the house. There are two bedrooms on my floor, a dressing room with a chaise longue and a main bathroom bigger than my entire old flat.

Nathan's room is on the second floor, right across the hall from Millie's. Both their bedroom doors are closed. I push the thought of a potentially naked Nathan, lying in his bed just a few feet away, from my perverted brain. Craig's been away for a long time and I miss the sex. I'm only human.

Barbie lies in her bed by the front door. She barely glances at me as I pass by – some guard dog she is. Even though the house is ten times the size of my old studio flat, it's oddly cosy; there's a homely feel to it. Instead of being a show home, it's really lived in by its owners. I never aspired to living in a big house, but if I did, I'd like one like this – not a place that people were afraid to relax in, in case they dirtied it, like the one I grew up in.

The relentless rain lashes on the huge sash windows and I sigh quietly as I search the kitchen for breakfast stuff. Opening all of the cupboards, I familiarise myself with the layout of everything, so I'll be able to get Millie some break-fast without it taking all morning. Nathan said her school's only a mile from the house, so I figure we'll be able to walk it in twenty minutes.

I'm beginning to wish I'd taken driving lessons like my parents suggested all those years ago. When I moved to the city centre, I hadn't needed a car and never missed having one, until now. I'm not sure if Nathan was serious about lessons, but I would be mortified if he realised how uncoordinated I am. How do people watch the road, change gear, check mirrors and still manage to hold a conversation down? Plus, there's the teeny tiny fact I might not even be able to reach the pedals of the giant jeep I glimpsed in the garage!

I lay the table with three bowls and a selection of cereals, then boil the kettle to make a pot of tea, trying to block out the surrealness of the situation. For the first time in three years – bar holidays – I don't need to make that dreadful commute to work. I don't need to rush into the office and listen to the phone ringing off the hook, or deal with complaints from clients about au pairs, or au pairs' complaints about clients. I'd been so busy fretting over living in Nathan's house, I hadn't considered the freedom it would offer me.

Millie will be at school for five hours today. I figure, even if I clean the house, do the laundry and prepare something for dinner, I'll still have two whole hours to myself. It's more than I've had in years. I consider calling on Abby. She's just given birth to her second daughter and I've been putting off the visit. I wonder if Nathan's been to see them yet? He and Callum are pretty pally. A hot flush rushes through me at the thought of Nathan telling Callum about the accidental kiss. I never told a soul.

Karen enquired about my new job on the friend WhatsApp group, and though there was a little bit of teasing, no one mentioned anything untoward. The girls know I'm a

sucker for a hunky man with tattoos – Nathan would be right
up my street, if I was single, which I'm not.

I glance up to find him leaning in the kitchen doorway,
wearing only a tight white t-shirt and navy boxer shorts.

'Holy shit, you scared the life out of me.' My hands clutch
my chest to steady my hammering heart.

With his toned, tattooed arms folded across the solid
muscles of his chest, his lips curl into a satisfied smile, like
he's pleased to see me here in his kitchen. As our eyes lock,
the lust rips through me. He is exactly what I'd draw if I was
to create my own poster pin-up. Ironic that that's exactly
what he is, to some women. Shit, I'd nearly go and buy the
Irish rugby calendar now, just to be able to justify hanging his
picture on my wall for an entire month of the year.

'Sorry, you looked so content, I just wanted to watch for a
second. Is that so wrong?'

Morally, it probably is but I can't hold it against him. I am
content. I'm looking forward to making breakfast for his
daughter, and for him, if I'm honest. I'm a pretty good cook,
not that I've bothered much in the last few years, but everything I know, I learnt from the best, my mother.

The rain continues to bounce off the windows, it's the
only sound as we stare at each other across the kitchen.
There's a slight awkwardness hanging in the air between us,
though we seem to have adopted an unspoken mutual acceptance of the situation.

This is already the best job I've ever had in my life, and
I've barely even started. I don't want to fuck it up by inappropriately drooling over a man who probably wouldn't have
even looked twice at me if he hadn't downed four tequila
slammers beforehand, at my insistence I might add.

'You don't have to do everything for her, for us, you know.'
He takes three steps forward and I hand him a mug from the
table.

'What else am I doing? Besides, that's what you're paying me for.' I pour steaming hot tea into his mug, from the pot I'd found underneath the sink. His cupboards are a mess, they need rearranging – it's top of my to-do list.

'Yes, but you're not on duty twenty-four seven.' He takes the carton of milk that I'd left on the table, sloshes a generous measure in and places it back on the table, before sipping gratefully.

'I'm happy to help, to be here. Millie's a great kid.' Pouring myself a mug of tea, I pull out a chair from the table and sit. He pulls out the chair opposite and his sturdy fingers tap the table between us.

'I wondered if it would be difficult for you, you know, after what you said.' Earnest eyes gaze intently across at me, exuding a warmth I wouldn't have associated with someone his age. He's only a baby. Mind you, I hadn't realised that until after I had my tongue halfway down his throat. Craig's six years older than me. Nathan's six years younger but he demonstrates an unbelievable maturity.

Why am I comparing them? It's not healthy. But while I'm in comparing mode, the biggest thought weighing on my mind is that Craig's my boyfriend of eight years, so how come Nathan's the one I confided my biggest secret to? It should be the other way round and a sliver of guilt gnaws at my stomach.

I swallow a mouthful of tea, buying myself time, wishing I'd never mentioned it. 'It's fine.'

My shoulders shrug and I brush off his question, along with the imaginary fluff on my shirt. His eyes travel to where my fingers stroke and I feel like a complete tit as I realise I'm actually sitting stroking my tit in front of him. Heat creeps into my cheeks and I push back my chair to stand, but he grabs my hand, halting me.

'I'm here, if you want to talk, Kerry. I really want you to

be happy here. Millie adores you. And I'm relieved to have another adult around.'

'Thank you.' I rise, tucking my chair back underneath the table, before turning to the fridge.

'How do you like your eggs in the morning?' The age-old chat-up line is out of my mouth before I've had the chance to stop it. I really need a muzzle. His rumbling laugh echoes round the kitchen.

'I thought that's supposed to be the man's line?' He clutches his non-existent belly.

'It is but I borrowed it. Scrambled? Or fried?'

'Scrambled, way healthier. Thank you. You don't have to, you know, I'm perfectly capable.' He moves to stand but I raise a hand to signal him to stay put.

'Let me, Millie's going to be gone most of the day, it's the least I can do.' Especially seeing as I noticed five grand had gone into my account last night, apparently he pays in advance.

He shrugs in a reluctant acceptance, but the smile curling at his lips indicates he likes being looked after. I've never had anyone to look after before, so it's a bit of a novelty for me. I just hope it doesn't wear off in the first month.

Though I try to focus on beating the eggs, I'm aware of the heat of his eyes following my every move around the kitchen.

'I have a proposition for you,' he blurts, and I'm glad my back is turned so he can't see the grin on my face.

'I already told you, I have a boyfriend.' The flirtation rolls too easily from my tongue and a flicker of guilt rips through me. This is not a game. This is my job and he is my boss, and I'd do well to remember Craig knows nothing about this.

'Ha, I know, unfortunately. But seriously, about those driving lessons? Do you have a learner's licence?' He swirls his tea around his mug while I think about it.

It would be useful. Craig's always on at me to learn. Maybe I could surprise him by picking him up at the airport in August. He wouldn't believe it. Though that means extra time with Nathan, and those muscled tattoos, in a confined space.

Fuck it, I already live with the man – it's not like I can't trust myself, attractive as he might be – and, despite my inappropriate flirting, I love Craig.

'Would you, really? I do have my provisional licence but I never got round to properly learning.' I leave the eggs simmering on the stove and turn to face him.

'It would honestly be my pleasure.'

'Oh wait.' I slap my forehead in jest. 'Are you old enough to drive yourself yet?'

'Funny. I turned twenty-six last week, I'll have you know.' A smirk curls at his lips.

'Belated happy birthday. I should get you a gift.'

'You are the gift.' He winks at me and I laugh. He's too funny and too easy to be around.

'I warned you, I'm no Mary Poppins. I'm winging it here.' I shrug, as the smell of burning reaches my nostrils and I lunge at the pan to stop the eggs sticking. So much for being a good cook, I'm so distracted I can't even scramble a few eggs.

'She's a boring old hag anyway. She never would have stroked her boobs in front of her boss.' He sniggers, as I throw the nearest tea towel I can find at his head, stifling my own giggles. The awkwardness is rapidly evaporating. He's very easy to be around. If I didn't already know, I'd never guess he's a famous sports star. He's completely grounded and very normal, well, in some ways. Though there's nothing normal about the fire igniting deep within my core.

Millie stumbles into the kitchen, rubbing her sleepy eyes, and I automatically go to her for a hug, at the same time as

Nathan turns to embrace her. The three of us stand in the kitchen in a surprise group hug. Before I can feel too awkward again, his arm slips around my waist and pats my back.

I slink off back to my burning eggs before I can over analyse how happy that hug made me because it's a moment I never dared to dream I'd see, let alone be part of.

CHAPTER TEN

NATHAN

Two mad, busy weeks have passed with Kerry living under my roof, and the pressure to rush back from training has been completely relieved. Kerry might not be Mary Poppins but she's a million times better when it comes to my daughter. She's a natural.

I can't help but feel sorry for her situation because she would have made a fantastic mother. Perhaps that's why she doesn't talk about it, nobody wants to be pitied. I guess the boyfriend mustn't want kids either; some people prefer the holidays, the nights out and the good life. Raising a kid is hard, raising someone else's must be torture. Mam never found anyone willing to stick around long enough to help her raise me. I'm under no illusion it'll be different now I'm the single parent.

'No training today?' Kerry's already downstairs when I enter the kitchen. She looks round from where she kneels by the cupboard under the sink, rearranging five years' worth of clutter. Her ass looks unbelievable in a pair of tightly sculpted jeans. I look away before I embarrass myself by gawping. Bar the odd funny blurted flirt, she's given me no indication that she ever thinks about that kiss, or thinks about me like that. Each night, come eight o'clock, she locks herself in her room and calls her boyfriend. She mentioned he's in the army. If she were mine, I wouldn't leave her alone for a night, let alone half a year. Man, he is one lucky fucker.

'No. Friday and Saturday are rest days, before Sunday's game.' I sit at the table and fill my mug from the teapot. We seem to have established a little routine, although Kerry has started waiting for Millie to run to her when she wakes, since that first awkward group hug.

'England, isn't it?' Kerry stands and closes the cupboard door, seemingly finished for now.

'Yes. Do you want to come?' I can barely meet her eye as the words fall from my lips. She doesn't know the significance of bringing a woman to a game, but there certainly is one. Although technically, I want her to bring Millie, but I'd be lying if I denied I'm trying to impress her too. I know she's off limits, yet I can't help but test them.

'Holy fucking shit? Are you for real? I'd love to come!' She does an excited, barefoot jig around the kitchen, finishing with a jump and a perfectly timed mid-air click of the heels. Her enthusiasm is infectious. Her personality literally sparkles the same way her silvery eyes do.

'Sure. It'll be great to have you there.'

'I need to buy a jersey. Millie and I will be twins, she'll love it.'

'I have a million of them, don't buy one.' I push away the thought of her wearing my jersey, preferably with nothing underneath it. Man, I'm going to have to start dating again because I'm not doing myself any favours pining over a woman I can't have. Maybe I'll text Serena again and offer to bring her away for a night, now that I have a babysitter.

'I'll drop Millie off this morning.' I drain my cup and refill it.

'Ok, if you're sure. Is there anything else you want me to do?'

Oh man, what I wouldn't want her to do to me. She has me hot and bothered just looking at her. 'Put some flat shoes on, we're going for a drive.'

I wink and her eyes widen as she realises she's going to be the one behind the wheel.

'I'm not sure I'm ready.' Her hand goes to her throat, fingering the heart-shaped necklace she wears.

'No, sweetheart, I'm not sure *I'm* ready.' I laugh it off but there's a truth in my statement. I've never taught anyone to drive before, but it'll be useful in the winter for Millie's school runs, if I can persuade Kerry to stay on. Plus, she's done so much for me, for Millie, I want to do something for her. We've sort of become friends over the last couple of weeks and I've really come to value her, as well as fancying the pants off her. Teaching someone to drive can't be that difficult, can it?

An hour and a half later, I have to practically coax her into my garage. It's attached to the left side of the house and both my cars reside in it. I decided to start her in the BMW before letting her loose in the convertible. It'll be cheaper if it goes wrong and besides, no company in Ireland would insure her on a Porsche.

She stands at the driver's side, looking up at the doorway. Her tiny frame would look hilarious against the X5, if she didn't have such an unbelievably serious ass. I open the door for her and offer her a hand up. Her clammy hand grasps mine and I give her a reassuring squeeze as I nudge her into the driver's seat.

'Who gets to learn how to drive in a car like this?' Bright eyes glance around the dash in awe.

'You do.' I take the liberty of leaning over her to strap her in. She stiffens slightly but allows me to do it. The scent of her perfume hangs enticingly in the air between us. I try not to act like a complete weirdo by sniffing it.

'What if I crash?'

'You won't.' My voice oozes more confidence than I feel.

I close the door and get into the passenger side, strapping myself in before beginning the lesson. She readjusts the seat so she's practically sitting on top of the dashboard. I fail to stifle my snigger and she shoots me a glare.

'All good things come in small packages!' She sniffs, indignantly.

'Not all good things...' My hands drop to my lap and her eyes follow.

She lets out a snort, but her eyes linger a few seconds longer than necessary. I shouldn't flirt with her but I can't help it.

First I point out the basics: mirrors, indicators, gears.

'Push your foot down on the clutch and press the start button.'

She hesitates for a second, doubt pinching in her eyes, then tentatively touches the button and the engine roars to life.

'Trust me, I've got you.' I take her clammy hand from her lap and place it over the gear stick, resting mine over the top of hers. The sensation of my skin on hers sends a shooting burst of electricity through my fingers. It's a battle to hide the effect she has on me. I'm worse than a horny teenager around her.

'Find your gear.' The look of concentration in her steely eyes is seriously sexy. I remind myself to concentrate or it could end very badly for both of us.

I tap her left thigh, hoping she won't sue me for sexual harassment, yet unable to stop myself. 'This one controls the clutch. Foot down, find your gear.' I manoeuvre the gear stick and her hand into first. A giggle bursts from her crimson lips. I can only assume it's nerves. 'Ok, ease your foot off the clutch gently and use your other foot to press on the accelerator.'

The car lurches forward before she slams on the brake, almost sending me through the windscreen.

'Easy!' We don't want to take out any passing pedestrians before we've even begun.

She takes a deep breath before trying again, pulling straight out into the road. I'm beginning to wonder if this is such a good idea after all. There's no oncoming traffic, which is a miracle because Kerry didn't actually pause to check.

'Stop.' It comes out sterner than I intend and I raise my hand to halt her.

She slams the brakes on again and takes her foot off the clutch without putting the car into neutral. It stalls noisily in the middle of the road. I put the hazards on, silently thanking the heavens rush hour is over.

After a detailed explanation, thorough demonstration and six YouTube videos on my phone, we set off again past the tree-lined streets of Ranelagh.

Kerry's a fast learner and as she cruises along the main road, a fraction of the tension slips from my shoulders, though I'd be stupid to get too relaxed.

'Who taught you to drive?' Kerry's eyes don't leave the road.

'My mam.'

'I would have thought it was more of a fatherly task.' It's not really a question, but I answer it anyway.

'I don't have a father.'

'Oh. I'm sorry to hear it.' Her mouth opens again, then

closes, like she thinks better of it. That's a first. A smirk tugs at my lips.

'Don't be. He left before I was born. Mam raised me alone.'

'She must be some woman,' Kerry says.

'You have no idea. She's a character alright. If your parents are as strict as you say, my mother is as laid-back as a joint-smoking surfer, except much louder. There's a pedestrian crossing ahead, slow down.'

A young mother coos over her baby in the pram, waiting to cross. Kerry frowns and looks away, staring out of the side window until it's time to move again. This time her clutch control is perfect and her frown is replaced with an accomplished looking smile.

'Wow, for once in my life, I feel like I'm completely in control.' Her shoulders straighten from the position she initially adopted, hunched over the dash, and her fingers loosen their grip on the leather of the steering wheel.

'Do you not normally then?'

'Ha! You've got to be joking. I'm used to blowing like a tumbleweed from one bar to the next, one job to the next. Sometimes I feel like I'm waiting for something, I just haven't figured out what yet.' Her teeth catch her lower lip between them; how I'd love her to do that to my lips.

Swallowing back my inappropriate thoughts, I bring up the subject we've been avoiding talking about since she moved in. 'What about the boyfriend? Chris, is it?' I know well it's not fucking Chris but the unjustified green-eyed monster inside prevents me from saying his name.

'It's Craig.' She rolls her eyes.

'Same difference. Once he's home, you think that feeling will go? The feeling of waiting for something?' I don't know why I'm asking because I'm pretty sure I'll hate the answer.

A long, low sigh falls from her lips. 'I honestly don't know.'

The green-eyed gremlin inside somersaults. Knowing she's not one hundred per cent convinced about Craig's return feels like a minor victory, though it doesn't change the fact he's her boyfriend and he is returning.

'Where shall we go?' Kerry motions to the widening road ahead.

'Let's not run before we can walk. There's a supermarket a couple of miles ahead. We could do with some shopping for the weekend.'

'Ok. Just keep me right.' She throws a quick sideways glance at me. Oh how I'd love to, if only she knew.

'I will, don't worry. Speaking of the weekend, I know we have the game on Sunday, but you don't have to spend the entire weekend with Millie, with us, if you have other things to do.' I scratch my head while I wait for her response. Last weekend she'd spent the entire weekend with Millie and me in the garden and I was grateful, but guilt-ridden.

It's such a weird situation to be in, having a woman living in my house, helping me to raise my daughter, a woman I'm not related to or in a relationship with. I'm not quite sure what the etiquette is, or where the boundaries are.

'I was going to ask you about that. Abby invited me to go and see the new baby tomorrow.' She swallows hard, before clearing her throat.

'Go, it's no problem. Myself and Millie will have a day out somewhere. I already told you, I don't expect you to mind her twenty-four seven.'

Kerry lets out an enormous sigh before saying, 'The trouble is, I'd prefer to be with ye...'

For a split second, I'm foolishly flattered. Kerry would rather be with us than her friends. Then I realise the truth of it; it's not that she'd prefer to be with us, but more that she wants to avoid having to fuss over Abby's baby. If she can't look at a stranger at a pedestrian crossing, seeing Abby with her bouncing new bundle might actually kill her on the inside.

'Do you have to go?'

'The child is four weeks old already. I really need to make an appearance. I probably sound like a total bitch, I'm not, well, I don't mean to be. It's just hard you know? That sweet, unique new baby smell, the obligatory snuggles. They yank at my heart strings, completely out of my reach. Sorry, you don't need to know that.'

'Indicate here. It's the next turn on the left.'

Silence fills the air between us but one distinct thought screams inside.

'I don't want to overstep the mark, but would it help if we came with you? I haven't seen Callum in over a month. You'd barely get a chance to hold the baby with Millie cooing over her and treating her like one of her dolls. We can say we are on our way to the zoo or something and leave after half an hour.'

We reach the supermarket and Kerry steers the car across two parking spaces, a million miles away from the front door. I suppose I did advise she walk before running. She puts the car into neutral before taking her foot off the clutch this time. The engine automatically cuts out to save emissions.

Turning to face me, she says, 'Would you mind?' Her voice is tinged with a hopeful relief. I'm not sure if it's relief we have reached our destination in one piece, or relief that we'll go with her. Either way, I'm not used to seeing her so serious.

'It would be my pleasure. But there is only one little problem. If we say we're going to the zoo in front of Millie, we will actually have to. It's one of her favourite places.'

'It's one of mine too.' She hands me the key to the car,

signifying the end of the lesson. We cross the car park together, abandoning the X5 in its terribly parked state.

'Basket or trolley?' she asks.

Worryingly, it feels like the most natural thing in the world.

CHAPTER ELEVEN

KERRY

Millie is beyond excited about the trip to the zoo, hence she's knocking my bedroom door at five-thirty in the morning. For a second, in my sleepy state, I wonder if it's Nathan. Then I realise, despite our passionate kiss last year, we've firmly transitioned into the friend zone. By that, I mean I can tell him anything, and I do, because it doesn't matter what he thinks – I'm not trying to impress him. And there's a lot of comfort in that. Though I can't deny my heart does seem to beat a little quicker in his presence, but that's just a physical thing. It's only natural, when my own boyfriend is away more than he's home.

'Come on in.' I pat the bed next to me and Millie bounds over, with Barbie close on her heels. The two of them leap onto my bed, Millie beneath the covers and Barbie sprawled widthways across the bottom.

'I'm so excited. Did you know that there's a new baby panda there? It's only a few weeks old.' Excitement shines in Millie's cobalt eyes. She is the image of her father with his strong bone structure and the same little dimple in the left cheek. It amazes me that even five-year-old girls are excited by the prospect of babies. I guess it's nature's way, inbuilt into us to reproduce and cherish the tiniest of our species in order to survive. I have the instinct alright, but I'm like a bullock – I have it upstairs but not downstairs unfortunately.

'I didn't know that, but I love baby pandas.' I scooch over to make room for her and pull the duvet tight up around us. It's far from cold, but her pyjamas are short sleeved and it's yet to warm up in this damn city.

'Can we see some zoo clips on your phone?' I'd booked the tickets on my phone the night before and Millie had caught a glimpse of the animal pictures.

'Sure.' I put my arm around her, pulling her into me so we can both see the small screen. The website has multiple videos of the zoo keepers feeding the monkeys and tending to the smaller animals.

'I want to be a zoo keeper when I'm older.' At least Millie has some inclination what direction she wants to take in life. At thirty-one, I'm yet to decide. Though I've worried about it infinitely less since I've been living here. We snuggle under the covers with the curtains still drawn, the early morning sunlight filtering in through the cracks of the heavy material. It looks like, at long last, the sun may be making an appearance.

After an hour scrolling through cute animal videos, the screen of my iPhone changes to a photo of Craig in his uniform, a split second before it rings. Millie hits the green button before I can stop her, accepting Craig's incoming video call. His face pops up onto the screen in front of us. Surprise lights in his eyes at the sight of Millie and he breaks into a huge grin.

'Hello, ladies.' He squints further, to get a better look. For some reason it makes me uneasy, like it's an invasion of privacy.

'Who are you?' Millie's childish honesty sets him bellowing out laughter into the darkness that surrounds him.

'I'm Craig, Kerry's boyfriend. And who are you?' He indulges her with a grin.

'I'm Millie, her best friend. Shucks, I thought she was going to marry—'

The bedroom door inches open and Nathan's head appears, followed by his bare ripped torso, a pair of tight black boxer shorts and long, strong legs. I swallow down the increasing saliva foaming in my mouth. It's a good job Craig can't see what I'm looking at because he would go absolutely mental, especially if he saw the effect it had on me.

'Daddy!' Millie shrieks, leaping out of the bed and into his strong arms. He mouths 'sorry' and disappears as swiftly as he entered, taking Millie with him. Before the door can swing properly closed, Barbie jumps off the bed and nudges it open again with her nose, scarpering at the prospect of breakfast. Footsteps sound on the stairs. Nathan returns, his fingers reach for the door handle to pull it closed at the exact same second Craig says, 'You are going to make a wonderful mother one day, Kerry.'

Nathan freezes. His eyes raise to meet mine, widening a fraction. A line forms on his otherwise smooth forehead. I look away. Bad enough he knows my deepest darkest secret, but now he knows I've been lying about it too. Well, technically I didn't lie, it just never came up. A bit like how I also never mentioned I'm living with one of Ireland's newly single, most eligible men, according to the *Tatler* magazine I leafed through in Emma's salon last week.

The door closes with a click and I revert my eyes back to the phone.

'She's adorable,' Craig says. He's right but I'm barely

listening. For some reason, I'm more concerned that Nathan thinks I'm a liar, than the fact that I have never admitted the truth to Craig, in eight years. What does that say about the situation?

'Kerry, are you still there?'

'She is adorable, for sure.' I shake my head, shaking off the niggling thoughts I don't have the luxury of addressing.

'So how many will we have?' His voice drops to a low, seductive murmur, as though he's imagining the process of making them. Instead of turning me on, it sends a ripple of anxiety through me.

'We never talked about having kids, Craig. I didn't even realise you wanted them. The only thing we've ever talked about is where we're going to holiday next.' It's the truth.

'Of course I want kids. Doesn't everyone?' He shrugs, like it's a given. If only it were that simple. A sinking sense of dread fills my empty stomach, churning like the stormy Irish Sea on the wildest of days.

It's a rare moment where I'm at a complete loss of words. Thankfully, Craig makes up for it as he launches into a full weather report for Syria and how he beat four of his soldier friends in a game of poker the previous evening. Eventually he seems to realise I'm quieter than normal.

'You ok, Kerry?' He leans forward again and a close-up of the top half of his face fills my screen.

'Yes, I'm just tired,' I lie.

'I hope they're not working you too hard. I'm all for you getting a bit of practice, but if their daughter's in the bed with you at six-thirty in the morning I can only imagine you're having a hard time of it.' His voice fills with concern and his hazel eyes glint with a warmth that reminds me why I was attracted to him in the first place, all those years ago.

'No, that was a one off. We're going to the zoo today and

the excitement is unreal.' I don't mention that Nathan is coming too.

'That sounds lovely. Listen, babe, I've got to go, no rest for the wicked. I'll call you later.'

'Be careful.' I blow him a kiss and hang up, relieved that today is not the day I have to admit my truths, though that day is certainly coming.

CHAPTER TWELVE

NATHAN

We arrive at Callum's house in Dun Laoghaire just before midday. I didn't ask Kerry if she wanted to drive and she didn't offer. It wouldn't be right with Millie in the car. The huge motorised gates swing open and I cruise up the asphalt driveway to park in front of granite, paved steps. Callum opens the heavy-looking front door, the newborn child in his arms and the toddler clutching his legs.

'Congratulations, man.' I glance around at the secluded, manicured gardens overlooking the Irish Sea. They moved in three months ago and although I've seen him at matches and been on a couple of nights out too, I hadn't made it out here, until today.

Kerry slips out from the passenger seat and goes straight to Millie's door, unbuckling her from the child seat. Abby appears behind Callum to welcome us.

'Come on in, guys.' Smiling, she beckons us in, her floaty dress swaying in the breeze that blows directly off the sea. She does not look like a woman that had a child four weeks earlier. It was months before Clodagh would have anyone round to see Millie. She really struggled to adjust to having a baby, we both did, barely more than children ourselves. We both grew up very quickly after that, there was no other choice.

Kerry grabs the huge bouquet of flowers and the presents we'd bought on the way over. She clutches them to her chest, mounting the steps to the front door. Peering in at the tiny sleeping child in Callum's arms, she makes all the appropriate noises, before handing the goodies over to her friend and throwing her arms around her. My heart bleeds for her. Millie bounces two steps behind her and Kerry automatically takes her hand, instinctively knowing she's there without even glancing down.

'Come in,' Callum repeats, as I try not to stare open mouthed at the obvious natural bond between my au pair and my daughter.

Inside, the place is tastefully decorated with greys and chromes. It's very stylish; I'd expect nothing less from Callum Connolly. He must be making a bomb on sponsorships and advertising.

We enter a sitting room with a double height ceiling, enormous windows and panoramic views of the sea. It is pure class.

Kerry sits on a plush velvet couch and loudly asks Abby, 'How's your vagina?' I wince internally at her crassness, but I can't stifle the giggle.

'What's a vagina?' Millie climbs up onto Kerry's lap and snuggles in, as if she's known her her entire life.

'It's a foo foo,' Kerry says, before mouthing 'sorry' across the room with a helpless shrug. I can't complain, her blunt-ness was one of the reasons I hired her.

'Did you not drink enough water either?' Millie asks Abby, who lets out a snort. Millie had a bladder infection a few months earlier. It's almost impossible to get her to drink water, then she holds it when she needs to go to the toilet until the very last second. Man, I didn't know what I was signing up for when I came here today. Thankfully, everyone sees the funny side of it.

'My vagina is fine, thank you for asking.' Abby behaves as if Kerry's question is the most natural thing in the world. I'll never get over how freely women talk about such personal subjects. Callum looks at me and winks, I shrug.

'I had a planned section. It's the way forward. When it's your turn, I advise you to ask for the same.'

The baby stirs, releasing a cat-like cry, and her tiny hands dive out in front of her in a stretch. Callum hands her to Abby who drops the strap of her dress and places the child on her breast. The second I realise what she's doing, I avert my eyes to Kerry who is intently playing with Millie's hair, twisting it into an elaborate braid.

Callum ruffles the top of his toddler's head. 'Casey, do you want to show Millie your playroom while Mammy feeds Cora?'

I drop onto the couch next to Kerry in a silent display of support. She glances at me gratefully and I wonder for the hundredth time of the day, why she lied to her boyfriend about her inability to have children. And her friends for that matter.

'Can I offer anyone a drink?' Callum rubs his hands together, as our daughters leave the room in search of toys.

'G&T please.' Kerry's answer flies from her lips. I glance at my watch, it's just gone twelve. We could be in trouble if she starts too early, her alcohol consumption in Dubrovnik was borderline animalistic, but then again, maybe today she needs it.

'Tea for me, thanks. I'm driving. We're going to the zoo this afternoon.' It's a subtle reminder to Kerry, as much as anything else. She nods in agreement and Callum leaves the room.

'So, how did this all come about?' Abby gestures between the two of us, skilfully multitasking feeding the baby and entertaining us.

'Luck,' Kerry says, at the same time as I say, 'fate'.

Kerry turns to me with a smile. A grateful look flashes across her face and I'm certain it's gratitude for being here with her, not for offering her a job. I wonder if Abby knows about our kiss? I didn't tell a soul. I heard she had a boyfriend and was simply chancing my arm. I didn't expect her to actually let me put my lips on hers, and I certainly didn't expect the ripple of flames that it sent searing through my body. I squash down the memory, before it consumes me.

'Good timing and crossed telephone wires.' I shrug again, as if it's nothing. The reality is, it's everything, she's everything, and it's only been two weeks. The way she's slipped effortlessly into my life, into our lives, like she was meant to be here.

An image of her in bed this morning flashes to the forefront of my mind. The thin strap of her pyjamas dropping to reveal the taught, tanned skin of her collarbone. I force it away, turning my attention back to the conversation. Kerry is unavailable and there's not a damn thing I can do about it, well I promised I wouldn't try, at least.

'Clodagh's taken a job singing on a cruise ship and Kerry was looking for a position. It couldn't have worked out better.' Well it could have, if Kerry was single, but I choose not to voice that thought, even though it keeps popping up, refusing to stay quietly in its box.

'I'm surprised Clodagh left Millie,' Abby says, having met Clodagh a handful of times at various matches.

Even I find it hard to believe that Clodagh could have left Millie; if it were the other way round I don't think I could have done it. But it's easy for me to say that, when I could achieve my dream on my doorstep. We both found the baby days hard. Truthfully, it broke us and it's not an experience I'd like to repeat again. If I only ever have Millie, I have more than most.

'So, how is Casey adjusting to the new arrival?' I change the subject, not wishing to go over it. Discussing nappies, bottles, reflux, and sleep patterns is way more comfortable than discussing my own failed relationship.

'Casey wanted to send her back to the hospital the night after we got home. Mind you, I couldn't blame her. She screamed the house down for five hours straight. Callum and I spent the night pacing the floor trying to pacify her.'

'The baby days are difficult.' I sympathise, while Kerry stares blankly at the wall behind Abby's head. I can only imagine it must be hard to listen to, when someone's complaint is something that she can only dream of. Callum returns with a tray of drinks and various nibbles.

'We're going to hire a nanny,' Abby announces.

'Well this one's taken, for the next three months at least.' I nudge Kerry affectionately and she laughs.

'Three months? Is that all?' Abby leans forward, readjusting the baby on her chest.

'That's all she'll do for me.'

'Why?'

Kerry shifts uncomfortably on her bottom and takes a huge mouthful from the gin goblet Callum presented her with, before answering. 'Craig's coming home.'

Abby rolls her eyes theatrically. 'Where are you two love-birds swanning off to this time? Don't tell me you've finally persuaded him to bring you to the Maldives? I know it's on your list.' I bank this information for the future, just in case.

Kerry doesn't answer, though Abby doesn't give her much chance to either. 'How long's he home for?'

Kerry seems to find a sudden fascination with the chipped nail varnish on her right hand. She stares at it, not meeting Abby's gaze. 'He's getting out...for good.'

'What?' Abby's voice raises four octaves. 'That's amazing news! You must be over the moon.'

'Yes,' Kerry says, before taking another large sip of her drink.

'And what are your plans? Will you buy somewhere in Dublin? Or will you travel a bit first? You could go back and finish your Master's if he's prepared to take care of the bills for a year. Oh my goodness, this is so exciting! Maybe he'll propose?'

'Who knows, hey? Anything could happen.' Kerry's voice doesn't hold a fraction of the excitement Abby's does. She drains the remaining gin and holds it out to Callum, blatantly looking for a refill. I should probably suggest we get moving, considering our afternoon plans, but Millie is playing quietly with Casey and things are beginning to get interesting. It's becoming increasingly clear that Kerry is not entirely comfortable with her boyfriend's return. Why though, is beyond me. I can only assume it has something to do with what I overheard this morning.

Kerry swiftly moves on to another subject, discussing their other friend, Emma. She recently got engaged to one of my teammates, Eddie. They hit it off in Croatia and the wedding is booked for next year. That week in Dubrovnik has a lot to answer for. I glance at Kerry, wondering if she's thinking the same. The small smile playing on her lips hints that she might be.

Callum returns with Kerry's drink and asks about team strategies for Sunday's upcoming match. Looks like I won't be getting a further insight into Kerry and Craig's relationship today, though that doesn't mean I'll stop wondering about it.

Half an hour passes before Millie runs in to look for us. I

open my arms for her, but she runs straight into Kerry's. Instead of being miffed, I'm ecstatic, even as a niggle of worry reminds me Kerry might not be staying. I make a mental note to chat to Millie about it, before she gets too attached. Although if I get my way, Kerry won't be going anywhere.

'Are we going to the zoo now?' Millie gazes up at Kerry with obvious adoration in her bright eyes.

'Ah, you'll have one more...' Callum stands to get Kerry another drink.

Kerry glances at her empty glass, then down at Millie. 'No thanks, Callum. We've got a baby panda to find, don't we, Millie?' She stands and lifts Millie into a big bear hug, despite the fact that Millie weighs a tonne and isn't even that much shorter than her. Abby's eyes glint with a hint of knowing as she bites back the smile forming on her lips.

'Great to see you, guys. Call again soon, all of you.' Abby waves from the doorway. Callum stands next to her, each of them holding a child.

As Kerry's passenger door slams shut, she exhales a laboured gust of air. She smiles and waves enthusiastically at our friends through the window, but the second we exit the driveway she hunches forward. I pretend not to notice the heavy tear she brushes away with the back of her hand.

CHAPTER THIRTEEN

KERRY

The zoo provides the perfect distraction. Millie, Nathan and I spend hours traipsing round the various animals and another full hour watching the baby panda. The sun shines throughout the afternoon, a welcome break from all the rain, though it's still only sixteen degrees.

'Are you girls hungry?' Nathan asks, as we head out the exit towards Phoenix Park.

'Yes, Daddy, I'm a starvin' marvin!' Millie takes my hand, then Nathan's. To the outside world, to all that pass by, we must look like we're a family. I swallow the lump in my throat. In a different situation, it's not an idea I'd rule out. But I'm with Craig, and I'm pretty sure Nathan wouldn't be interested, even if I wasn't. The initial silly flirting's almost been replaced with a comfortable friendship, though there's nothing platonic about the way I feel when his hand grazes mine. I'd be a fool to think it was mutual. And a cheat to consider finding out.

'How about you?' He turns to me, a genuine warmth in his

soulful blue eyes. We've definitely transitioned to the friend zone, because I'm truly beginning to think he actually cares for me. He was brilliant at Abby's house and brilliant all afternoon, making me laugh, chasing Millie round the place. When he was stopped for an autograph by a couple of rugby fans, he introduced Millie and me as his girls.

It's been a long time since breakfast and the ice cream we had in the zoo barely touched the sides. 'I'm getting that way.'

'Who wants pizza?' He looks from Millie to me and back again, scrutinising my face.

'Me, me, me,' Millie practically shouts. I nod my acceptance. Pizza sounds great. I don't feel like cooking, tired from the day, both physically and emotionally.

'How about that new Italian restaurant, on the south side?'

My fatigue must be evident because he instantly changes tack. 'I know, how about three takeaway pizzas from Julianos', a bucket of Ben & Jerry's Cookie Dough and a movie at home?'

'That sounds like heaven. Throw in a glass of red and you've got yourself a deal.'

'Can we watch *Frozen* and eat pink lollipops?' Millie squeals in delight.

'Sure, honey.' I don't remind her we've already watched it four times this week already.

An hour later, the three of us are sprawled out on the couch, empty pizza boxes discarded on the coffee table in front of us. Millie sits between us, her heavy eyelids fluttering, until eventually she drifts off to sleep with her head on my lap and her feet on Nathan's thighs. He reaches for the remote and switches off the television. Thank god, because even though

I've heard 'Let It Go' about four hundred times this week, I still can't let it feckin' go.

Gazing down at Millie, I stroke her silky white blonde hair from her closed eyes.

'She's so beautiful. You must be so proud of her.' I glance at him, there's an envy in my tone that I don't try to conceal.

'She's a character.' He shakes his head with a smile, brushing a strong hand gently over her cheek. We sit silently for a few minutes and I reach for my wine from the coffee table, slowly so as not to disturb Sleeping Beauty.

'Can I ask you a question?' Nathan shuffles slightly next to me.

'I know what you're going to say.' I've been waiting for it all day. He was bound to call me out on my lies. Honesty was one of his requirements for his daughter's minder and now he thinks I'm dishonest.

'I didn't mean to eavesdrop this morning, but I heard you talking. I heard *him* talking.' For some reason, it's like he can't even bring himself to say Craig's name, though I know he knows it.

'It's not as bad as it sounded. I didn't technically lie to him, I just never told him the truth.' I swirl the wine around my glass, watching as the liquid stains the glass a blood red, the colour of my devilish soul.

'Is that not the same thing?' Nathan's tone is gentle. I don't detect a hint of judgement in it, but I fear he's disappointed in me. And for some reason that rips my insides apart. I take another mouth of merlot and contemplate telling him something I've never told anyone.

'When I was twenty-one I was going out with a guy who was ten years older than me. His name was Martin. I was mad about him. I thought the feeling was mutual but it wasn't. He treated me pretty badly.'

Nathan's fingers discreetly clench into a fist.

'Don't get me wrong, he didn't hit me or anything but he was unreliable. He'd arrange to meet me somewhere, then not turn up. Days would pass without a word, he wouldn't answer my calls or texts. Then, he'd call me at three in the morning and ask if he could come to my apartment. I was stupid enough to let him.'

Nathan shakes his head, his nose scrunched in what looks like disgust. He opens his mouth to say something, but I continue before he can interrupt. Now it's come up, I just want to say it once and get it over with.

'I found out I was pregnant the same day I found out he was married.'

'Oh, Kerry, I'm so sorry.' He leans over his sleeping daughter to take my hand.

'When I saw him with his wife in Dundrum shopping centre, I decided I couldn't have his baby. I considered a termination, even booked the boat to England, but when the time came, I couldn't go, I couldn't do it. The following week, I got an awful stabbing pain here.' My hand travels to the left side of my stomach, as the memory rips through me like it was yesterday. 'I was so dizzy and when I started vomiting, my flatmate called an ambulance. It turned out the pregnancy was ectopic. The fallopian tube had ruptured, along with any dreams of ever having children of my own. I only had one ovary to start off with; I had a cyst on my right one when I was three and they had to remove the whole thing. So, there you have it. That's why I can't have children.'

'I'm so sorry, Kerry. Life can be so cruel. You would have made a brilliant mother.' He's still holding my hand, his thumb tracing over the back of it and gentle soothing strokes of warmth surge through my skin.

'It was the same summer I graduated with my childcare degree. I'd intended on doing a Master's, then looking for a premises for my own crèche. After everything that happened,

I just couldn't face the thought of minding all those babies. Then I met Craig the following year. He was mad for adventure, for excitement. There was never any talk of marriage or children. He never even told me he was applying for permanent discharge. Apparently he wanted to surprise me. It was a surprise alright.'

'You've been together for eight years and never once discussed the future?' The look that tears across Nathan's perfectly even features can only be described as incredulous. I can only imagine how it must look from the outside, when even the inside is beginning to appear a little off balance.

'We never discuss much, other than what happens in our respective days. Now he's dropped this bombshell on me, like it was the plan all along. It might have been *his* plan all along, but he never mentioned it to me until a couple of weeks ago.'

'You have to tell him.' Nathan squeezes my hand.

'I know but it's not something you can just drop into conversation.'

'I can only imagine. I'm truly sorry, Kerry.'

There's nothing more to say on the matter.

'Shall we put her ladyship to bed?' I stroke Millie's rosy cheek once more, before gently lifting her into Nathan's arms. He carries her up the stairs to her bedroom, I pull out her pyjamas and the two of us change her and tuck her into marshmallow-pink cotton sheets. He drops a kiss on her cheek, then lingers in the doorway as I place Captain Barnacles next to her. Kissing her head, I quietly exit, closing her door behind me.

Normally I'd go straight to my room when Millie goes up but tonight, I tiptoe back down the stairs. Nathan must have been expecting me because he's topped up both our wine glasses. He sits on his side of the couch and I drop back into mine, silently marvelling at how comfortable I am here with him, in the space of a couple of weeks. The sound of my phone ringing in my pocket penetrates the air between us. Removing it, Craig's picture illuminates my caller display. Nathan glances at it, sighs and looks away. I do something I rarely do and decline the call.

A smile curls at Nathans lips but he bites it back. 'Movie?' He hands me the remote.

'You pick. Make it something funny, or scary, anything other than *Frozen*.'

My right hand falls into the empty space between us, still warm from where Millie had been lying. His left hand flops down to the same spot and his fingers gently brush over mine. Instead of jerking my hand back, I leave it there and he takes it fully in his and squeezes it again. I squeeze back in an unspoken exchange. I tell myself it's a friendly gesture, a bit of comfort. We both stare at the sixty-five inch screen. I don't dare look at him as he scrolls through a mountain of Netflix movies, before settling on *The Hangover*.

'Is this ok?' I'm not sure if he's referring to the choice of movie, or the fact he's still holding my hand, but worryingly, both are fine with me.

CHAPTER FOURTEEN

NATHAN

I glance up at the players' lounge where the terrace looks out directly onto the pitch. Knowing that Kerry is up there with Millie sends a current of adrenaline coursing through me. I wanted to win this match before, but now it's a need. I'm an absolute fool to still be crushing on her but it's escalating uncontrollably.

Hearing her truths last night, what she went through alone, I wanted to pull her into me and comfort her but I couldn't get past the hand-holding. She's not mine to comfort. I'm increasingly less certain she's truly Craig's either, but even if she isn't, would she want to be tied to a single dad with a dog called Barbie?

The atmosphere in the stadium is electric. Today is a test match against England. Both teams are putting on a great show, determined to demonstrate strength, speed and superiority. With ten minutes to go, the scoreboard's even: 13–13. The rain's lashing from the heavens. The pitch is treacherous with mud. I have only minutes to prove my worth to Coach, and to Kerry. Worryingly, the latter seems way more of a priority now than the first, but Marcus isn't getting any younger and he's been off his game for the entire season. He missed two conversions in the first half, something we can't afford against England.

I might be the youngest, but I am one of the fastest wingers this team has ever had and that's not a brag, it's a well-known Wikipedia fact. And the two tries I nailed in the first half further prove it. Though, I could do with getting another one now.

The English defence is tight but I manage to break through it, firing the ball at Marcus who runs hard and fast towards the white line. He's tackled by England's full-back, a giant player with dreadlocks and a jaw like the cartoon character Bananaman. England take possession again. Coach paces the sideline shouting his instructions, but at this point in the match, I tune him out. We all know what we need to do, we've been over it enough in training.

England's fly-half bombs towards the goal, his eyes glinting with a steely determination. James O'Malley tackles him. We take possession in the next scrum. The clock ticks menacingly above; only four minutes remain. The next score will be crucial. Eddie crash passes the ball to me and I run, with fire radiating through my thighs in what might be my final chance of this game. White shirts and humongous shoulders charge towards me. I hunch forward and plough through them sending two bouncing to the floor. I think another one is winded but I don't stop to find out.

With the wind behind me, I sprint to the touchline and slam the ball down over the white line. The crowd erupts, cheering and chanting. My teammates land on me as the scoreboard lights up with the updated results and the referee blows the whistle, calling for the conversion kick to be taken. There's only two minutes left of the game. Marcus locks eyes with me and nods. He thinks he can do it; his jaw's set in a determined grimace. For his sake as much as the rest of us, I hope he's right.

The stadium is silent. You could hear a pin drop. Marcus lines the ball up, takes a few steps back and runs towards it, gathering momentum. His foot connects with the ball, powerfully sending it over the posts. The crowd roars with glee. The referee blows the whistle signalling the end of the game and my teammates bunch together, slapping each other's backs. Shouts of congratulations fill the field, melting into the cheering crowd.

The rain has even stopped in time for the WAGs to run to the side of the pitch. Marcus's wife, Shelly, leaps into his arms with relief in her eyes. Eddie's fiancée, Emma, half-jogs, in gold stilettos through the mud, to where he stands ten feet away from me. Behind her, Kerry approaches almost shyly, hand in hand with my daughter. The two of them are wearing matching green jerseys – my heart swells at the sight.

Kerry pushes Millie in front of her, nudging her to run to me, which she does and I lift her up and swing her round the pitch with one arm, before beckoning Kerry over with the other. She steps towards us and I close the distance, pulling her into a triumphant one-armed hug. She's so tiny next to me. Before I can think about it, I sweep her into the air and drop a kiss onto her cheek, my two favourite women in my arms. A blush creeps up her neck. Her lips move but I can't hear a word she says over the chanting crowd. Cameras flash intrusively from every direction.

I need to update my tattoos – an intricate line for every point – but what I really want to mark, though I better not get it tattooed on me yet, is my growing feelings for Kerry. If I could freeze this moment forever, I wouldn't care if I never made captain. I think I have a new ambition.

CHAPTER FIFTEEN

KERRY

Once the men shower off the mud and glory from their bodies, they congregate with their families in the players' lounge. Millie sits at the bar with a packet of Tayto and a can of Coke. The grin on her face hints she's living the childhood dream. Half the Irish rugby team are fussing over her – she's learnt how to work the system already.

'Another drink, Kerry?' Emma calls to me across the bar. Her eyes are bright, her cheeks flushed with the look of a woman in love. Eddie rests a hand on her lower back, while he talks to Ollie, another player.

'No thanks, Em.' I look down at my almost empty glass.

I'd love another drink but I'm not a WAG like her, or the rest of them. I'm here to mind Millie and it's probably about time I brought her home. Some of the others are mumbling about heading into town and making a night of it. In other circumstances, I'd jump at the chance, and it's been ages since I had a good blow out. But I'm struggling to fit in here. I'm not Nathan's girlfriend, I'm his child's nanny and I'd do well to remember it because seeing his toned thighs and powerful shoulders tearing across the pitch did absolutely nothing to quench the unhealthy burst of longing surging through the pit of my stomach. It's far safer if I do what I'm being paid to do and take Millie home.

'Go give Daddy a kiss and tell him we're going home to watch *Frozen*.' It's the only bribe I know will get her out of there.

'Really?' Her little legs jump from the bar stool and she scurries across the room to Nathan, who is deep in conversation with the team coach. He scoops her up into his arms, where she high-fives him, and the coach, before whispering into his ear. His eyes light with surprise and scan the room, before landing on me. I watch as he excuses himself from the coach and crosses the room with five long strides. Thankfully, those thighs are now covered in a pair of jeans because I can't trust myself not to openly drool, his long, strong arms are more than enough to contend with.

'You're leaving?' Disappointment seeps into his tone. I thought he'd be happy I was talking Millie home. Or maybe that's why he's disappointed – she's been the star of the bar all afternoon.

'It's seven o'clock. She has school in the morning. Only three more days until the end of term.' When the hell did I get so responsible? This nannying craic is doing funny things to me.

'Will you come back out, after you put her to bed?' He takes another step towards me, leaning closer to be heard over the chatter of his friends, our friends.

'No, thank you though.' Apart from the fact it's really not appropriate, who would mind Millie?

'We could get a babysitter?' His hand rests on my upper arm, in an affectionate gesture. Emma shoots a look at me and winks. I pretend not to notice.

'I *am* the babysitter,' I remind him, even as the lines between us blur further.

He nods in silent acceptance. 'I'll get you a car.'

An hour and a half later, Millie's sound asleep in her bed, too tired to watch anything. In the kitchen, I kick off my pumps and pour myself a glass of red from Nathan's extensive stash. Like me, he's partial to a glass of wine. But where I'd pretty much drink anything, he has an appreciation of the good stuff and doesn't mind sharing.

'So, this is what Cinderella felt like, huh, Barbie?' I pat the top of the dog's head and pull out a chair at the kitchen table. The silence is deafening after all the shouting earlier. Sipping my drink, I mindlessly scroll through my Instagram feed. It's a bad habit because with all the gorgeous, cropped and filtered multicoloured images, I can't help the inadequate feeling that seeps into every bit of my bones. I'm thirty-one, with no permanent job, no house of my own, no children and a boyfriend who doesn't yet know I can't have them. A heavy sigh escapes my lips before I knock back the contents of the glass.

I have a reputation for being a party animal, a drinker, a good-time girl. The truth is, I drink to forget. When the alcohol and sugar crusade through my bloodstream, I feel invincible, temporarily at least. It's the only way I can escape my mind and my past.

Barbie rests her head on my lap and I pat it. She's great company. I'm contemplating pouring myself another glass from Nathan's stash, when a clicking noise from the hallway startles me. Barbie leaps to attention and runs out of the kitchen, a thunderous bark erupting from her. She's a better guard dog than I initially gave her credit for.

'Oh shut up, you dopey feckin' eejit.' The low drawl of a

woman echoes through to the kitchen, followed by the gentle thud of footsteps. Tiny hairs on the back of my neck raise in alarm. I run towards the knife block as a fifty-year-old woman enters the kitchen. Her bobbed hair is silvery blonde, her skin's too tanned to be natural and a cigarette hangs from the side of her heavily lined mouth.

'Who are you?' I lean against the counter, reaching my hand behind my back for a weapon, just in case. Looks can be deceiving and whoever she is, she's just walked straight into this house, uninvited.

'I'm your fairy feckin' godmother, love, who the fuck do you think I am?' She reaches into her handbag, produces a box of matches and proceeds to light her cigarette. I'm at a loss for words.

She takes a deep, throaty drag before exhaling three perfect rings of smoke. 'Cool hey? I learnt that at the bingo hall. Millie loves it when I do that, course Nathan goes off his bleedin' head if I smoke in front of her. So, it's our secret.' She coughs, slaps her chest and lets out a guffaw. I still can't manage to find anything suitable to say, but apparently it doesn't matter, because she continues anyway.

'Where is she, by the way?'

'In bed.' I put down my makeshift weapon.

'I can see why he likes you. You're pretty, in an under-stated way.' Appraising eyes run the length of me, barefoot, clad in skinny jeans and the Ireland jersey Nathan lent me.

'I...I...I.' I swallow the excessive saliva that's foaming in my mouth. Does she mean Nathan *likes* me? And how would she even know?

'Cat got your tongue? I'm Nuala, Nathan's mammy. He phoned and asked me to babysit. Get your glad rags on, Cinders. You're going to the ball.'

Nathan's mother? She looks more like a fifty-year-old version of Sandy from *Grease* after she went all hardcore with the cigarettes and the leather jacket. This woman couldn't be any more different to my own mother. I like her already.

'Seriously?' Heat creeps into my cheeks. Does Nathan actually want me to go out with them? Or is it just that he feels bad because everyone else is out and I'm stuck at home? I don't mind. I'm getting paid well to do it. Ok, I do mind, not because everyone else is out, but because he's out. I want to be with him. It's so wrong – I have a boyfriend, who I love. But he's away so much. It's so hard. Spending time with Nathan's becoming very dangerous, I can't deny it.

'Well, no, it's not an actual ball.' She rolls her eyes like I'm simple. 'He said they were heading to Flame, that restaurant in the city.' Nuala reaches up for a wine glass and helps herself to a glass from the open bottle. 'Go and get ready, love, I'll take care of things here.'

Flame is one of my favourite places to eat in the city and they have a lovely cocktail bar below the restaurant. It's been so long since I had a night out, the offer is too tempting to pass up. I vow not to drink too much, as Craig's familiar warning rings through my ears, 'Behave.'

Taking the stairs two at a time, I fling open my wardrobe door unsure what to wear. Flicking through the coat hangers, I select a black silk backless halterneck and a pair of black jeans. Business from the front – party at the back. The great thing about having small boobs is I can get away without wearing a bra. Backs can be just as sexy as boobs. Wait, who am I trying to impress? I'm treading dangerous territory and I know it.

My phone rings from where I'd thrown it on the bed. It's Craig. A ripple of guilt washes over me as I press the green button.

'Hey, you.' His handsome face stares at me from thousands of miles away. 'You look nice.' He eyes my top. Thankfully he's getting the 'business' side because he hates it when I show any skin.

'Thanks, I'm heading out. Millie's nan is here to take care of her.'

'Are you going somewhere nice?' A hint of jealousy creeps into his voice. I'm used to having to play things down, but this is on a whole new level. His jealousy is normally completely irrational, but tonight I wouldn't blame him. But I won't cross any boundaries. Hell, I don't even think Nathan wants me to. Either way, I'm not a cheat. Though, it's a good job he's relegated me to the friend zone because after seeing him in action on the pitch earlier, he's even more excruciatingly attractive than ever.

'I'm meeting Emma.' It isn't a lie but it isn't the truth. I'm getting ferociously frequent with my omissions.

'Will there be any guys there?' I hate it when he does this but know it must be hard for him to be away.

'It's a bar. I'm sure there will be plenty of guys there.' I stick my tongue out to lighten the mood.

'Hmm. The sooner I get out the better. You'll be switching those silky tops for maternity wear, if I get my way.' He sticks his tongue back out at me, as the blood drains from my face.

'I've got to go. Be good!' His tone is light on the surface but the undercurrent of warning is there. Usually his remarks are unfounded, but tonight they sear my soul.

CHAPTER SIXTEEN

NATHAN

I've checked the door five hundred times, and my phone, but nothing. Perhaps she sent Mam home? I can't imagine Nuala taking orders from Kerry, but I can't be sure. Both are pretty fierce, in their own way.

Eventually, she struts in, wearing six-inch heels and a pair of jeans that wrap indecently round her thighs. At least the top is high necked and fairly conservative, I need to rein myself in. She's the nanny, and she has a boyfriend. Though I'm seriously considering testing the strength of their relationship tonight. I already feel like I know her better in a few weeks than he does in eight years.

The table is set for eight, but only six of us sit around it: Marcus, Shelly, Eddie, Emma, Ollie and me. There's a seat free between Ollie and Emma, and one between me and Marcus. I'm curious to know which one she'll pick. If she takes the one beside Emma, I'll back off. If she takes the one beside me, I'll take comfort that the growing sizzling chemistry between us is not just in my head.

She greets everyone likes she's known them forever, but that week in Dubrovnik ensured none of us are strangers. Glancing between the two seats, she veers towards Emma's, then at the last second, she keeps walking and pulls out the chair next to me. My insides somersault victoriously. I bite back the grin that threatens to take over my face.

'You look fantastic.' I try not to watch as she slips out of her cropped leather jacket, revealing an almost completely naked back, bar the tiny bit of silk tied at the top and bottom. I imagine undoing that bow and watching it fall to my bedroom floor. It's almost too much.

'You don't scrub up too bad yourself.'

'Did Millie get her inhalers?' It's far safer to ask that, than to ask if she'd consider a repeat of Croatia, but I make a mental note to order some tequila slammers later. With the drink flowing, my resolve is waning.

'Yes. Then she conked out like a light.' Kerry takes a menu from the middle of the table, scanning it with her finger positioned thoughtfully over her bottom lip. Her subtle, feminine gestures are killing me. I deliberately look away. Emma's staring at me like she knows. She arches an eyebrow skywards in a silent challenge.

The wine flows throughout dinner, everyone glad to let their hair down after the pressure of the earlier match. When we finally finish dessert, the waitress asks if we'd like to move to a booth downstairs in the bar. Ollie stands to leave.

'I'm going to hit the hay. It was a big day.' It's no loss, he's spent most of the evening looking at his phone underneath the table. I'd almost swear he was texting a woman from the intermittent smirk that kept appearing on his face.

'Yeah right. Who is she?' I call him out on it and the tips of his ears turn red.

'Don't be daft. I'm going home...alone. See you during the

week.' He throws some cash on the table and strolls out of the restaurant.

'Who is she, do you think?' Emma asks.

'No idea, but there has to be someone. He's definitely sneaking around lately. Fuck knows why he won't introduce her to us,' Eddie says.

'Anyone would think he was embarrassed of us,' Marcus says, as though it's ridiculous, yet he's the man who streaks round the pitch naked given any opportunity. He's on his last warning from Coach after a holiday video of his hairy balls went viral.

'Ha. I wonder why that might be?' I stand, take Kerry's coat for her, and pull out her chair like the gentleman I'm pretending to be, while the barbarian inside reminds me about the tequila slammers.

A couple of hours later, the six of us sit in a row at the bar. Since Ollie left, Kerry and I have kind of coupled up, without the intimacy of course. She's on her third cocktail and her tongue is beginning to get a little looser.

'Thank you.' Kerry pats my leg and a surge of electricity shoots to my groin.

'What for?'

'For getting your mam in to babysit, for buying me dinner. I have a great job you know, I *can* buy my own dinner.' Her lips lift into a seductive smile, revealing naturally light, even teeth.

'It's me that should be thanking you – you've saved us.'

'Actually, I think it's you that saved me. Not only did I get the sack, but I got evicted too.' A sultry burst of laughter slips from her scarlet lips.

'You mentioned you were looking for a place to live, but you never divulged that information in your application. We'll have to review the situation, I'm not sure you're going to be a good influence on my household.' I squeeze her thigh playfully – an excuse to touch her, which I've been dying to do all night.

'I worry it's actually you, who might not be a good influence on me.' She runs a finger round the edge of her sugar-caked martini glass and licks it.

I straighten my back, dipping my face closer to her. With only a few inches between us, I can smell the sweetness from her breath. Locking into her glinting grey eyes, I admit the truth of it, unable to hold it in any longer. 'I'd like to not be a good influence on you.'

Her eyes don't leave mine and the air crackles between us with an intensity that's practically painful. She bites her lip and her head tilts to the side, not backwards or forwards, she tilts like we're in limbo, which is I suppose exactly where we are.

'If I thought you were serious, and I didn't have a boyfriend, I wouldn't hesitate.' The moment shatters at the mention of the B word and she turns her head away with a sorry little shake.

I beckon the barman over with two fingers. 'Six tequila slammers please.'

She slaps my arm, leaving her hand on my bicep a second longer than necessary, and laughs. 'That won't work for you this time.'

'Why not?' I'm pushing my luck. I hope I still have a nanny in the morning.

'Because last time, I didn't have a boyfriend. We were on a break.'

'Well, can't you take another?' The words are out of my mouth before I can stop them.

She swallows hard, gazing straight ahead, her glazed eyes hinting that whatever she's seeing, it's not in this room. I want to ask her about it, to know her more. I want to know if she loves him, if she imagines a future with him, and if she believes he'll want one when he finds out about her lie, or omission, whatever she calls it. Though it's pointless because even if she doesn't, I'm sure a few months with me and Millie would send her running for the hills.

'Things seem to have gotten serious all of a sudden,' she whispers, more to herself than me.

She's right. Things have got very serious all of a sudden. Because tonight I've realised, given half the chance, I could actually fall for her. Which would be stupid and pointless, but possibly inevitable. We knock back the tequila slammers and call for a private car. A hangover is no joke with a five year old asking a million questions. Especially when I have a million of my own.

CHAPTER SEVENTEEN

KERRY

Mags gazes round Nathan's kitchen, wide-eyed with envy. I try to remember how it felt the first time I came here, the sheer size of the place feels normal now. I shouldn't get used to it; I'm only here for another couple more months, then who knows where Craig and I will end up.

'Wow, you certainly landed on your feet.' She strolls through to the sitting area, eyes the enormous wall-mounted flat screen, then the sunroom opening up onto the well-maintained lawn, extending almost half an acre.

'Tell me about it. How's Arnie? I honestly don't miss the place.' Mags is supposed to be calling out to an au pair who's based fifteen minutes from here, but she phoned to ask if she could make a pitstop along the way.

It suited me perfectly. Today is my last free day. It's Millie's last day at school before the start of the nine week summer holidays, and Nathan's away at Carton House training. He's been gone two nights, the longest he's been away since I started. I hate to admit I miss him more than Millie does. She's happy enough, once I play tea parties with her and the lollipops keep coming.

I've been trying to convince myself it's just the adult company I miss, but it's a lie. Last night, Nuala called in for a couple of glasses of wine – she's an absolute hoot. It's like having a drink with a friend, rather than Nathan's mother. And though we shared a good few giggles, it did absolutely nothing to alleviate the growing pang of loneliness left by Nathan's absence. Worryingly, I miss his company more than I ever missed Craig's but then, with Craig, I've always known his place was in a regiment halfway across the world. Nathan's place is here with us.

'Arnie's still a pain in my ass.' Mags turns to grin at me, eyeing my less than casual attire: a pair of white skinny jeans, gold sandals and a turquoise off-the-shoulder top, which reveals a little more skin than might be appropriate for my day job. Nathan's due home today, and I'd be lying if I said I hadn't considered that when selecting my outfit this morning.

'We need to arrange a night out. It's like you disappeared off the face of the earth when you took this job.' Her pout could give Millie's a run for its money.

'We will.' God knows when though.

I make Mags a coffee, feeling a bit guilty as she noses round Nathan's belongings. At least the door to his personal man cave is locked. I double-checked it before she arrived, just in case. We haven't been in it since that first night. I've wanted to but he never asked, mind you, I did spend the first couple of weeks locked in my bedroom from eight o'clock each evening.

Picking up a framed photo from the sideboard, she asks, 'Is this the wife?'

I glance up to see which one she's referring to, though I

can already guess. It appears to have been taken in London. Millie's three-year-old face grins back from the glass frame, her parents either side of her. It's the only picture of the three of them in the entire house. Nathan's smiling, but it's a strained smile, which looks more like a grimace. Clodagh's eyes are a beautiful shade of blue, lighter than Nathan's and Millie's, but there's a dullness to them that nobody could miss.

I wonder for the hundredth time this week how she feels about me minding her daughter. I can't imagine how a mother could leave her child for months on end, but then I'm in no position to judge, nor ever will be. She calls regularly, always on the landline, never on a mobile.

'Yes. No. They weren't married.' I add a drop of milk and sugar, knowing exactly the way Mags likes it.

'She's an absolute fool. Imagine letting him go. If he were my fella, I'd hang on to him tightly with both arms and maybe even my thighs too, just to be sure.' She snorts, but I can't laugh with her. I've seen her in action too many times to think she's joking. When she sets her sights on a man, no wife, child or even an army could stop her. Funny how I never questioned it before, yet instinctively, I don't want her around Nathan.

She pulls out one of the heavy dining room chairs to sit, but I motion her out to the garden. The good weather's finally began to improve and I'm determined to make the most of it.

The garden's neat, but sparsely decorated. I make a mental note to buy some plant pots for it, maybe even a small water feature. Then I remember it's not mine to do that with. Being here feels so natural, sometimes I forget.

'So, what's he like?' Mags perches on one of the sun loungers I pulled out from the shed.

'What's who like?' I sip from my own cup, still more than a little disturbed about my newly awakening feelings about my boss, specifically his absence.

'Nathan, of course! Are you even listening to me? Were you drinking last night? Are you hungover? You don't seem to be operating on full capacity today.'

'I had two glasses of wine with Nathan's mother. She's an absolute character, you'd love her.'

'Hmm. I'm sure, but you still didn't answer the question.' She takes a sip of her coffee, her wide eyes staring over the top waiting for any juicy snippets. I suppose this is the most exciting thing that's ever happened to her, being in a famous athlete's house. Hell, it's the most exciting thing that ever happened to me too, though it has nothing to do with the house or his belongings. I pause, trying to think of the right words to do him justice.

'He's sweet and strong and kind. He's an excellent father to Millie. He's a good cook, though he tends to favour high protein healthy bullshit – you know I'd rather murder a burger and fries any day of the week. He's only twenty-six, yet somehow he has a maturity about him like he's been around a lot longer. He's oddly intuitive and really very caring.' I sip my coffee and pretend not to notice she's staring at me.

'What?' Eventually, I have to ask.

'You are in fucking love with him!' she practically shouts.

'I am not! Don't be ridiculous. I've only known the man a few weeks. And keep your voice down, we do have neighbours, you know.' I nod to the house next door, although there's about fifty feet between them and us. I'd hate for anyone to get the wrong idea.

'You are! It's written all over your face, it hangs from every word you just said.'

'I like him, that's all. I have a lot of respect for him. He's achieved so much, at such a young age. He knows where he's going in life, what he wants, and he's prepared to go the distance to make it happen.' Far more than I could have, or will ever do. If I had a fraction of his direction and determination, I'd be dangerous.

'Bullshit! I worked with you for almost three years – I used to spend more time with you than my own husband.'

'Probably why you're separated,' I remind her with a wry smile, anything to deflect the attention from me, because that niggling feeling in my gut warns me she's hit the nail on the head. Well, almost, I have a crush, that's all. It's not love, it's lust, and when my boyfriend comes back, I'll take my lustiness out on him and everything will be fine – I hope.

'Don't change the subject, Kerry, it's written all over your face. Think back to how you just described him to me.'

'I only told you the truth'

'That's my point. When I first met you, you'd been with Craig for what, five years? Do you remember me asking you back then what he was like?'

I honestly can't. My silence speaks volumes.

'I'll remind you, seeing as you seem to have forgotten. You said, "he's nice," and then we ordered another round of cocktails. It was the night we met those American tourists and ended up drinking in their hotel bar until five o'clock in the morning. We went straight from there into the office and slept at our desks until eight-thirty. When Arnie came in and smelt the drink off us, she sent us both home with a verbal warning.'

I smile at the memory. It was a great night, the unplanned ones always are. 'I knew from that night we were going to be great friends,' Mags says, which is a bit of a stretch. We were great drinking buddies, but now I've cut back I'm beginning to see things in a slightly different light.

'And as your great friend, I'm telling you to wake up and

smell the coffee. Unless Nathan feels the same way about you, you're setting yourself up for one almighty fall. And don't get me started on what Craig will do if he sees your mooning face, pining over another man. Craig's a good catch in his own right, you know you're lucky to have him.'

She has a point. Though, if Nathan was telling the truth the other night, he might have a tiny crush of his own, but neither of us had dared to bring it up since.

'Look, I know what I'm doing, ok.' My wavering tone isn't convincing either of us.

'What about the daughter, what's she like?' Mags changes the subject.

'She's a doll. A real little angel. I adore her. It's great to have an excuse to traipse around the children's wear, we even buy matching outfits sometimes.'

'Don't get too attached, Kerry. You know all this,' she gestures at the huge house and garden, 'will come to an end at some point. A man like Nathan isn't for keeps, especially not for the nanny.'

She drains her coffee and stands to leave. 'He's in a different league. He probably earns more in a day than we do in a year. He mixes with celebrities. You are the hired help. I mean it in the nicest possible way. I'm telling you as your friend.'

Her comment strikes a nerve deep within me. I often describe my mother as my father's hired help. When I was about twelve, she suggested going back to work as a legal secretary in the firm she worked in when they got married. I'll never forget the bellowing laugh he offered right into her face, before reminding her a woman's place was in the home.

I follow her back through the house and show her to the front door. Barbie lets out a growl as Mags passes by.

'Let's get a drink soon, yeah? I miss you.' She air kisses my cheek before leaving.

I close the front door and slide to the floor behind it. She's right. Even if I didn't have a boyfriend, which I clearly do, Nathan is way too good for me. Even if his celebrity friends are actually some of my own friends. I need to stop lusting after my boss, and using Millie to fill a void in my own life. But mothering her is the closest I'll ever get to being a mother – is it so wrong to enjoy that time? They really are the perfect package; they'll make some lucky woman really happy one day. I'm sorry it won't be me.

Pulling my phone from my pocket, I try to ring Craig and remind myself where my head is meant to be at. He doesn't answer. The sound of the letterbox above my head startles me and I glance up to see a tiny white envelope gliding over my head onto the floor in front of me. It's sealed, but there's no name on the front of it.

Opening it with a sigh, I figure it's probably some charity looking for a donation, which I should definitely give, now I'm in a better position to do so. I slide out one single folded sheet of A5 paper. It's covered with letters which look like they've been cut out from a newspaper. There's only one line.

You think you're so special. I'm going to show you you're not.

A shudder ripples across my spine and the hairs jolt up at the base of my neck. I don't think I'm special, in fact, I literally came to the conclusion that I'm not, thirty seconds earlier. Someone went to a lot of trouble to cut those letters out, stick them down and to drop it here. I jump up with a start, realising it was hand delivered only moments earlier. I don't dare open the front door, instead I run up the stairs to Millie's bedroom, which overlooks the street below. There is literally no one to be seen, not a single soul. A shiver runs over me again and my pulse quickens.

It was probably some stupid kids. I stuff the letter in a kitchen drawer, to show Nathan when he gets home. It's probably nothing, but I double-check all the doors and windows are locked before I leave to collect Millie from school.

CHAPTER EIGHTEEN

NATHAN

I could easily have driven up and down from Carton House, but I thought it better to put some space between Kerry and me. However, I can't avoid her forever. My feelings for her are escalating inappropriately – there's no denying it. Apart from her fantastic ass and unrestrained sense of humour, the way she seems to love my daughter pulls at my heart in ways I couldn't have predicted. I shouldn't have said what I did the other night. She made the situation crystal clear from day one; she's taken.

I need a distraction, preferably a beautiful one. Driving through the lush, manicured gardens of Carton House, I scroll through the contacts on my phone for Serena. We didn't exactly part on bad terms, it was more like after that night with Millie she lost interest.

My fingers thrum against the steering wheel as I pull out onto the main road, wondering if Serena will pick up the phone. Just as I'm about to hang up, she answers.

'Nathan?' Her questioning tone suggests she didn't expect to hear from me again. I didn't expect to be calling her either.

'Serena, how are things? I wondered if you'd be free to go out for dinner, Friday night? I feel like I need to make it up to you, you know for the intrusion the last time…'

'It certainly put a bit of a dampener on the evening, didn't it?' Her Polish accent coos through the sound system. It might have put a dampener on her evening, but seeing my daughter's smiling face could never put a dampener on mine. Which was exactly why I hadn't bothered to call her afterwards.

I brush off her remark, refusing to let it irritate me. I'm not looking for marriage, just a night out and some female company to take my mind off the forbidden female currently residing under my roof.

'How about it? I could pick you up at eight.' My fingers roam my stubble, as I wonder if I've lost the plot entirely.

'I can't do this Friday, I'm going to Paris for a shoot. I have a busy couple of weeks but I could be persuaded to go out Friday the 7th July, as long as you promise it's just you and me? No kids?'

If it were Kerry and me going for dinner, Kerry would likely insist Millie came with us.

That's because Kerry is Millie's nanny and not your date.

'Just us.'

'Great, because you know what they say, two's company, three's a crowd. See you in three weeks.' Her high-pitched laugh screeches round the car before she hangs up. What the fuck have I done?

The phone rings again before I can overthink it. It's Mandy from the team's PR department.

'Nathan Kennedy, I have got some exciting news for you!' Mandy shrieks in her distinct Cork accent.

'Good, because life is not quite exciting enough at the

minute.' My eyes roll to the sky, as I contemplate what the fuck I'm playing at getting back into bed with 'Serena The Child-hater'.

'*Men's Health* magazine saw the photo taken after Sunday's test match of you, your girlfriend and your daughter in the paper today. They want to offer you a four-page spread on "life as a young father in the fast lane"– that's a direct quote. I'd say an individual spread in a magazine like that could open up some sponsorship deals.' Her voice practically singsongs the words at me.

'What photo?' I've spent the last two days running round the pitch, and the last two nights having a few cheeky midweek snifters with the boys. Carton House provides its own little bubble to us; I barely hear what's occurring in the real world.

'It's Wednesday,' she reminds me.

On Wednesdays *The Irish Sports News* goes to press, it's a national weekly paper. We've been known to disappear on a Wednesday for a long weekend, following a really embarrassing loss, just to avoid the backlash from the press.

'I haven't seen it yet, but that's great news, I guess.' Apart from the fact that the woman in the picture isn't my girlfriend, she's my child's nanny.

'I'll email you the details and you can get in touch directly with them if you agree to their terms and the price.'

'Great, thanks a million.' I hang up, before glancing at the clock. Even if I stop to pick up the paper, I should be home in thirty minutes. A ripple of excitement courses through me. I tell myself it's all for Millie, but I know the truth of it. Turns out, absence really does make the heart grow fonder.

The house is eerily quiet as I enter the front door. Silence is suspicious with young children, and my heart sinks a little as

I realise they must have gone out somewhere. Stupidly, I kind of assumed they'd be here waiting for me, why, I don't know.

Barbie pads through from the kitchen to greet me in the hall, her bushy wagging tail throws hundreds of blonde hairs cascading to the floor. The sound of laughter floats through to the kitchen. I glance up to see the back door is open and Millie and Kerry are sprawled out on two sun loungers, wearing matching polka-dot bikinis and denim shorts. Holy fuck, this woman might be the death of me. I'm not sure what's worse, the fact she's half-naked in the garden and I can't touch her, or that she's twinning outfits with my daughter. Both affect me, but in very different ways.

Strolling out to greet them, Millie leaps up, races towards me and jumps into my arms.

'Daddy, we missed you!' Well she did, at least. Kerry, I'm not so sure about. I inhale the familiar scent of her strawberry shampoo and relish the feeling of her tiny arms around my neck. The overwhelming urge to protect her swells within my chest.

'Hey, I hope you don't mind me pulling the garden furniture out of the shed.' Kerry sits up, grabs a turquoise top from the grass beside her and pulls it over her head. I look away, but the memory of her exposed skin sears into my mind.

'It's great to see it getting a bit of use.' It's barely been sat on in the three years I've owned it.

'Are you hungry? I made fajitas. I made the salsa myself, so you don't need to worry about hidden sugars!' She smirks at me, but it amazes me how well she knows me already. I check every label in the supermarket before it goes into the trolley.

'Thanks. Maybe we can enjoy the sun for a bit first?' I peer up at the blue, cloudless sky in awe. It's so rare, it'd be a shame not to make the most of it. 'I'll grab a drink and be straight back out. Here.' I throw the rolled up newspaper I bought to her. She catches it with one hand.

'What's this?' She unrolls it and places it on the checked mattress between her thighs.

'You're famous. Have a look. Although, I'm not sure where they got the idea you're my girlfriend.'

I head into the house and return with three cans of Diet Coke. The colour's drained from Kerry's face. Most people aren't used to seeing themselves on the news, or in the paper. I forget what it's like.

'So, I was thinking...I've got two weeks off at the end of August, how would you guys like to go to Euro Disney?'

'For real?' Millie squeals with excitement, jumping onto my lap, nearly knocking the Coke all over me.

'Yes. Would you like that?' I'd promised I'd bring her once she turned five. Her birthday was in April, but this is the first chance I've got. Plus, I'd love to have Kerry with us. Not only is it so much easier to manage a five year old with another adult around, but she's great company. Just because I can't have her, doesn't mean we can't be friends. In fact, we seem to be great friends. She's the one woman I'm completely myself around – secret irrational fears of hidden sugars included.

Kerry's oddly silent, still staring at the half-page photo of the three of us from Sunday, but Millie more than makes up for it, wondering aloud if she'll get to meet the real Elsa and Anna.

'Is everything ok, Kerry?' I nod at the picture. 'I'm sorry if it offended you that the media got our situation confused.' Looking at the picture, I can clearly see why anyone might get confused. The camera caught the euphoric moment I swept both Millie and Kerry into my arms. We're all absolutely beaming and my lips are millimetres from Kerry's cheek, caught the split second before I kissed it. It's a fabulous shot.

'It's not me that's going to be offended.' As her voice trembles, realisation sinks in. The boyfriend.

At that second, the shrill ring of her mobile pierces the air. She snatches it up from the grass with a shaky hand and stalks towards the house. From twenty-five metres away, I'm able to hear the aggressive shouting from a male. Instinctively, I march in the back door to her defence. It's a misunderstanding; I can appreciate it looks bad, but there's absolutely no need to swear at her like that.

As I approach, she shakes her head and silvery wet eyes silently plead with me not to interfere. She runs upstairs. I hear the door slam and the abuse continues. It takes every bit of willpower I own not to barge in and give him a piece of my mind. Real men don't speak to ladies like that.

'Dad?' Millie calls from outside, and reluctantly, I leave Kerry to face the only object between us.

CHAPTER NINETEEN

KERRY

The abusive video call continues for forty-five minutes straight – *liar, cheat, homewrecker*. He's right. Well, I did lie, but the only home I've wrecked is my own, the one I'm supposed to be setting up with him.

'How long have you been sleeping with him, Kerry?' His face contorts into ugly lines of anger. In this second, I have never been gladder of the distance between us because from the irate way he's screaming at me, I'd be terrified to be in the same room as him.

'I told you, I'm not sleeping with him, Craig. I swear.'

'You're lying.' His venomous tone spits thousands of miles, flooding the pink walls of my bedroom. Anxiety rips through my veins, and I close the window, hoping Millie doesn't hear any of it from the garden.

'I'm not lying.' I'd be lying if I said I hadn't been imagining it, but I never crossed the boundaries. I wouldn't. I'm not a cheat.

'Kerry, you completely neglected to mention that you've

moved in with the youngest member of the Irish rugby team, who you met at your friend's wedding last year, and who just so happens to be newly single. It's too much of a coincidence. I can't believe a word that falls from your lying lips. We're already over.' As the anger subsides from his tone, huge salty tears roll from both my eyes. Eight years together and he doesn't trust me. I'm only just beginning to realise he never did.

'I swear to you, Craig, I never slept with him. I'm sorry I didn't tell you who I was working for. You can be a little paranoid sometimes, and I knew you wouldn't like it, but I swear nothing's going on.'

'Paranoid? Me? What the fuck? You've been caught on camera, in the act. Any suspicions I've had over the years have probably been well founded. How many others have there been?'

'None, Craig, I swear.'

'We're never going to come back from this, so please just put me out of my misery.' He runs a hand through his military crew cut, the fight seems to have drained from him.

I open my mouth to say I never even kissed him, but the words catch in the back of my throat. Because they are a lie. I have kissed Nathan but not behind Craig's back.

'You never even what, Kerry? For once, just tell me the truth!'

'Ok, ok. I'll tell you. Please don't be mad, it's not what you think.' I perch on the edge of my powder pink quilt and swallow the bile forming in my throat. I hate confrontation, and this is the worst I've ever experienced. The fact it's with someone I've spent eight years loving is crippling.

'Last year in Dubrovnik, I was single—'

'Barely!' he interrupts before I can explain. 'Fucking hell, Kerry! We split up for ten days! Who jumps into bed with someone else straight after they break up with their boyfriend of seven years? Someone who never cared in the first place, that's who...' The anger returns to his voice, and through the screen of my phone I glimpse his fist bust through a plasterboard wall next to him.

'It was one drunken kiss, Craig. That's all. And it's never been repeated.'

'Whatever. Have a nice life with Nathan-cock-sucking-Kennedy. I hope you both rot in hell.' He disconnects the call.

I flop back onto the bed and cry until there are no more tears left. Eight years of my life, ruined by one stupid lie. The worst thing is, his suspicions, though unfounded, were right at the forefront of my mind. I've been so stupid, fantasising over a man I could never have, while the one I should have been concentrating on was doing his best to make sure we could eventually be together, build a life together. What a stupid useless fool I am.

I can't bring myself to go back down for the rest of the evening.

CHAPTER TWENTY

NATHAN

The frosted door to the travel agents opens automatically. The walls are lined with posters of exotic destinations, promising cloudless skies, white sandy beaches and turquoise tropical oceans.

It's Thursday, two weeks have passed since the abusive video call in the garden, and Kerry's a shadow of her former self. She's barely eating, the whites of her eyes are permanently tinged red and she's physically distant. She won't eat with me, she started going straight to her room again when Millie goes to bed, and any trace of the humour that attracted me to her in the first place is well and truly absent, though I haven't forgotten it.

It's over with her boyfriend and while I once might have been secretly ecstatic with this information, seeing her miserable is unbearable.

I take a seat in front of the first available assistant, a middle-aged woman with red hair and freckles. She offers me a curt nod and a pinched smile. Her cool blue eyes show no indication she recognises me, but then again, she doesn't look like the stereotypical rugby fan.

'I'd like to book Euro Disney for myself and my daughter, and another adult please.' My fingers drum on the desk between us. There's a possibility the other adult won't be availing of her ticket, but I want her to have a choice when the time comes. When will she break free from the cloud that hovers over her? I can't even persuade her to come for another driving lesson and I was certain the prospect of feeling in control would entice her.

'Certainly, sir.' Long slim fingers tap the keyboard in front of her. After a few seconds she turns her computer screen towards me, so I can see the options available. 'What type of accommodation are you looking for?'

'The best. Whatever you have. No expense spared.' A couple of grey hairs blend into the amber eyebrows, noticeable only as they raise a fraction. Her eyes run over my casual jogging bottoms and rugby jersey. I'd come directly from Carton House, but she clearly has no idea of that.

'Okay, this is the best we've got.' She points to the screen and flicks through a gallery of photos boasting marble hallways, a fifty-metre indoor pool, a luxury spa and tiny portions of food that I could devour in one bite.

'It's a five minute walk from Disney. It's the most luxurious accommodation available, but a room here costs five hundred euro per night.' Her tone rings heavy with an underlying apology, as though she's already decided I can't afford it. I get it a lot; I'm young, I dress in a tracksuit instead of a suit, but please, why does everybody judge a book by the cover?

'Is there a suite available? Preferably one with three bedrooms. If it has a view that would be even better.' I slide my black AmEx across the table.

'I'll have a look for you now, sir.' I bite back the smile. I don't want to be anyone's sir, I just want to be treated the same as everyone else in this city. You don't need to wear a suit to be successful. Just like you don't have to be a dick because you're successful.

'I'm probably really pushing my luck now, but is there anything carrying the Disney theme through it? You know, like luxury for the adults, combined with a little Disney magic for the kids?'

'I'm not sure, but I know the manager. I'll email the hotel directly for you and ask them to decorate one of the bedrooms with a Disney theme if you like? Any preference on which characters they use?'

'*Frozen*. My daughter just can't let it go...'

She laughs and lifts my credit card from the table. I tell her to add five per cent commission on for herself.

When I get home, Kerry's sitting at the kitchen table colouring with Millie, the sweet smell of home baking lingers in the air. Glancing round, I locate the source of evil – a two-tier chocolate fudge cake sits cooling on the stand, chocolate sauce next to it ready to be poured for the final touch. It calls to me, with all its sugary evil – between the sight of it and the scent of it, the temptation is too much.

'Don't even think about it, Daddy.' Millie fires one of my own favourite lines back at me.

'Is it my birthday?' I ruffle her hair, then kiss the top of her head, inhaling her familiar strawberry scent.

'No, it's not for you.'

'Well, who's it for then?'

'We're a having a party, Dad.' She rolls her eyes like a teenager, oh how I'm dreading those teenage years already. 'Kerry's friends are coming over.'

'Really? It's not even the weekend yet, check us out having a spontaneous Thursday night party.' My eyes turn towards

Kerry, who's wearing a cute denim shirt dress and that crimson lipstick again, dare I hope she's beginning to feel a tiny bit better?

'Is that ok?' As a flicker of light sparks in her silver irises, flickering sparks within me at the prospect of getting my friend back. How I've missed her infectious laugh and inappropriate remarks. I hated thinking I'd inadvertently caused her pain, even though the picture was innocent, and she's far better off without Craig judging by the way he treated her.

'Of course. This is your home, for as long as you want it to be.' I won't yet ask her outright to stay on, but I'm hoping with the change of circumstances she might not disappear at the end of August as planned.

'Well, technically they're your friends too...' The smile playing at the corner of her lips, tugs at my insides. Seeing her coming back to life stirs something protective deep within me. Given half the chance, I won't let anyone put her down ever again.

'Eddie and Emma?' I stroll over to the cake, unable to resist a second longer, plus it'll piss Eddie off if I tell him I licked it before he got here.

'And Abby and Callum. Abby's parents are over from Carrick so they're babysitting.'

Realising what I'm about to do, Kerry leaps up from the table and swipes my hand away with a swift stoke of hers. The chemistry that pulses from her fingers to mine is electrical. The skin-to-skin contact sparks a fire in my belly that spreads to my loins. Her hand darts away as though she's been burnt.

'For a man who has OCD about hidden sugars, you certainly don't mind the obvious ones – the real deal.'

'I'm all about the real deal when I've chosen to put it in my mouth. A treat should be a treat. It should be fabulous, and not for everyday indulgences.'

'There's one hell of an inuendo, one that could come back to bite you on the ass some day.' She slaps my arm playfully.

'Here's hoping.' My eyes lock into hers and she looks to the floor, but when she doesn't immediately let go of my arm, I grab her hand and pull her into me for a hug. It feels like the most natural thing to do.

'Welcome back.' I have to stoop two feet to whisper into her ear. I inhale her shampoo, it smells like a fresh mango smoothie. Her tense body relaxes into mine and her hands tighten around my waist.

'Sorry I've been such hard work.' Her voice is low enough that Millie can't hear.

'You haven't. I just felt so terrible, it was all my fault and I didn't mean for that photo to come back on you, or to cause problems.'

'It was all *my* fault. I didn't take his feelings into consideration. I've been really selfish and I've paid the ultimate price for it.' She steps back from my embrace and glances up at me.

I hate that she's hurt, but I love that she's single. I want nothing more than to shelter her, but if I want to avoid terrifying her, I'm going to have to give her time, maybe even wait for her to instigate the first move, because I'm one hundred per cent certain there's going to be one. I want her more than I've wanted anybody. I've never met anyone else like her, and I'm not likely to again. Apart from her being sexy as hell, it dawned on me yesterday, if the way she minds Millie is anything to go by, she might be the one woman in the world who isn't terrified by my single-father status. It's killing me, but I'm just going to have to practice a little patience.

Kerry sashays over to the fridge, returning with fresh olives, feta cheese, diced, spiced lamb and a variety of other tapas inspired treats.

'What are you making?' I watch her begin chopping intently.

'Joe Wick's *Lean in 15* spicy lamb.'

'Want me to help?'

'You can peel the potatoes. Cube them, we'll sauté them.' She pours olive oil into a frying pan and adds the onion and garlic to serve with the lamb. We work side by side, like it's the most natural thing in the world, while Millie colours in her books behind us.

At eight-thirty the doorbell sounds. I greet Callum with a high five and kiss Abby on the cheek. Before I can close the door, Eddie's fist jams into the space.

'Wait for us, I heard there was a party in here tonight, apparently, your nanny is newly single... I bet you're gonna break out the Bollinger.' He winks at me, and I give him a light thump on the arm.

I make sure the girls are out of earshot before I bluff, 'What makes you think I care?'

'Oh, I know you care, my friend.' His dark brown eyes glint knowingly at me, and his lips curl into the smooth cool grin he sports when gets a whiff of trouble.

'Whatever.' I don't bother denying it further.

The Bollinger's not a bad idea, although I prefer the effect tequila has on that particular nanny.

CHAPTER TWENTY-ONE

KERRY

Nathan beckons everyone through to the sitting room, veering right, towards the man cave door. 'I'll get you a little aperitif. Kerry's been cooking up a storm, hope you're hungry.'

As he stretches up to reach the key from above the door-way, his Ralph Lauren polo shirt rides up, revealing low hanging jeans and a light, fine happy trail. I tear my eyes from his taut midriff. I'm only human. Even though I'm single, Craig's disgust still haunts me. It bothers me more than him actually breaking up with me.

Abby and Emma flock to the hot tub overlooking the garden, and Callum and Eddie follow Nathan to the sliding doors. They've clearly been here before. At the bar, Nathan adopts the role of barman, while the other two each take a stool. He organises the drinks while I open up the patio doors. A slow electronic dance music fills the air, before the popping of a cork.

'I hope you brought your swimsuits,' Nathan calls across

the room as Abby and Emma pull back the cover of the tub. I'm surprised to see it's already on, crystal clear bubbling liquid pops in front of my eyes. What kind of night does Nathan think this is going to turn into?

'I don't need one.' Eddie wiggles his eyebrows again and Emma shoots him a look which begs to differ.

Nathan brings over three glasses of champagne on a tray, he's really taking barman duty seriously.

'Get in if you want, ladies. There are towels and robes by the sauna.' He points to a cupboard against the far wall.

Abby glances down at her dress. I can't imagine she's embarrassed about her post-birth body. She looks amazing. 'Maybe after dinner.'

The boys begin talking shop at the bar – rugby, rugby, rugby. They seem to live, breathe and sleep it when they're together. Abby tells us how wonderful it is to escape for the night, and I sip my drink, hovering by the open patio doors.

It's only a matter of time before they ask about the break-up. I'd put one message on the WhatsApp group to let them know. I also said I didn't want to talk about it. I'm still annoyed with myself at my own stupidity. What was I thinking, lying to Craig? He deserves so much better. I might not have cheated on him, but he was bang on in some respects.

There's no denying the attraction with Nathan. Though I wouldn't have acted on it, and for all Nathan's drunken flirting, I doubt he would have either. Sure, our alcohol-fuelled chat in Flame cut close to the boundary, but for once in my life, I had it under control.

Although, I might as well have shagged his brains out because Craig refused to believe I didn't.

I've spent the last few weeks worrying about what it might be like when he comes home, what it would be like to be part of a proper couple, not one who only see each other a handful of times in the year. Just as I was beginning to get my head round the idea, to accept it might be time for me to pack my party pants away and grow up a little bit, the prospect was ripped from underneath my feet.

'Earth to Kerry? Are you ok, love?' Emma snaps her fingers in front of my face, jolting me into the moment.

'Sorry, I was just thinking. I'm going to check on Millie and the food. I'll be right back.'

'We'll come and help.' Abby nudges Emma. I'm clearly not getting off that easily. Nathan shoots a wink at me, which Emma clocks, glancing between the two of us as if she's bouncing a tennis ball back and forth with her eyes.

The second we reach the quiet of the kitchen she pounces. I invited them all over together, thinking the presence of the boys would dilute the situation and hinder any plans for an interrogation, but the questions begin immediately, just not the ones I'm expecting.

'What's going on with you and Nathan?' She towers in front of me, hand resting on her hip.

'Nathan? Nothing. God, not you as well?' A groan rumbles from my throat, but it's not in any way a surprise.

Abby steps forward, the good cop, bad cop routine in full swing. 'What do you mean?'

'Craig said the same thing. He saw the picture in the paper and went mental. That's why he ended things.' A lump forms in my throat as I utter the words. I take another sip from the champagne flute gripped in my right hand.

'I thought maybe he'd had a change of heart about getting out?' Abby's doe-like eyes flood with sympathy.

'No, as far as I know he's still leaving, but I haven't talked to him since he ended it. He was adamant it's over. I did lie to him, so I can't blame him.'

'Oh, sweetie, I'm so sorry.' Abby clucks over me like a mother hen, while Emma scrutinises my face for any hidden truths.

'It's ok.' And I mean it. Yes, it hurts. I miss talking to Craig. I miss having someone to call just to say hi, but I'm beginning to see that things weren't perfect between us anyway. I've spent the last two weeks overanalysing – tonight I'm ready to get drunk with my friends. If only they'd stop asking questions and let me do exactly that.

'The day that you and Nathan called out to see us, I got the impression you weren't sure about Craig coming home.' It's not a question, but her tone ensures it is.

'It was just such a shock. We hadn't even discussed the possibility, then all of a sudden it was happening and he was talking about houses in Scotland and babies...'

'Scotland?' Emma shrieks.

'Yes, it was never going to happen. I'd hoped to persuade him to travel for a year, then maybe settle here, but he had other ideas.'

'Sweetie, he's been travelling for years, he's bound to want to lay roots when he gets out.' Abby places a gentle hand on my arm.

'I guess, but like I said, it wasn't something we'd discussed. Anyway, I'd just started getting my head around the idea, when he saw the paper and decided that Nathan and I are having some sort of illicit affair.'

'And are you?' Emma shoots straight from the hip; she always has.

'No! Of course not. I wouldn't do that.'

Emma pauses for a split second, glancing at Abby. 'I saw you.'

'You saw me what?' If she's referring to the photo being taken on the pitch, she'd know it was completely innocent because she was standing right next to us.

'In Dubrovnik. I saw you and Nathan kissing in the bar.'

'What the hell, Kerry? Why didn't you tell us?' Abby's elbow connects with my arm in a conspiring nudge.

Heat floods my cheeks and I raise my hands in defeat. 'Girls, it was one drunken kiss. Nothing's ever happened since. I'm not a cheat. I didn't want to put a downer on your wedding, Abby, but Craig had broken up with me. He said the distance was too much. Then when I got home, he was all apologetic and bombarded me with flowers, and it was like it never happened. I never told him, or anyone. There was nothing really to tell. It was one drunken kiss.'

'Well, from where I was standing, it looked like the best kiss of your life.' Emma's perfectly shaped eyebrows arch, challenging me to deny it.

'Look, Nathan's gorgeous, anyone can see that. I won't even try to deny I find him attractive. But he's in another league. He's a professional athlete. He probably has loads of women wanting a piece of him.'

'And?' they both say in unison, Emma crosses her arms over her pristine and no doubt expensive outfit.

'Well, it's ok for you two, you look like a couple of super-models! Me, I'm like Tweedle-fucking-Dum. I could never keep a man like Nathan, besides, there was no need to try, I had one of my own.'

'Had being the key word in that sentence,' Emma states bluntly.

'Ouch. Don't hold back, hey?'

'Look, Kerry, I'm sorry if you're still upset about Craig, but can I tell you something honestly?' Emma's free hand rests on her hip, in a pose that reminds me of a school teacher. Actually, scratch that, we went to a convent school and there's nothing nun-like about Emma Harvey, with her seductive slim-fitting clothes and immaculate make-up.

Abby shakes her head, warning Emma not to say whatever it is she's about to.

'Why hold back now?' I down my champagne in three mouthfuls, preparing myself for the worst.

'We never liked him.' Emma's face scrunches up like she swallowed a wasp.

'Emma. That's not fair.' Abby places a hand on Emma's arm, a silent warning to watch her mouth.

'What? I'm only telling her the truth.' She shrugs.

'What about you, Abby?' I don't know why I care, but it feels important.

Abby pauses, clearly considering her words more carefully than Emma. 'It wasn't that I didn't like him, but I didn't like the way he treated you.'

'Really?' I eye my empty glass, longing for another drop to get me through the next round of the interrogation. 'He was always so good to me. Every bit of free time he had, he wanted to spend with me. If I couldn't afford the holidays, he'd pay for me because he wanted me to be there with him. Anytime we were together he treated me like a princess.'

'He treated you like a prisoner more like!' Emma blurts. 'If you didn't pick up his call on the first ring, he'd phone you repeatedly until you did. Once, he called you fourteen times in two hours – I counted. That's not normal.'

'He's in the military, he has to make calls when he can, sometimes they go to places with no signal for days at a time.'

'And the way he used to say "behave" or "be good" at the end of every conversation, like you needed some sort of warning. It was almost like a threat.' Emma counts Craig's failings on her outstretched fingers. She has a point with the last one, it used to bug the life out of me.

'And the way he'd say he wouldn't be able to make a weekend that you'd planned, but then he'd turn up to "surprise you". Did it never occur to you he was checking up on you?' She thrusts a third finger under my nose.

'And what about that guy he punched in Majorca?' Abby interjects, an apologetic wince crinkling at the corners of her eyes. Emma's fourth finger raises with the others.

'Ok, Craig's always been a little on the jealous side but at least he cares. Cared, I should say.'

'That's not caring, sweetheart, that's controlling,' Emma voices a niggling suspicion I'd been harbouring. When I finally accepted the phone wasn't going to ring, I felt a tiny surprising sliver of relief, freedom almost. After my experience with Married Martin at twenty-one, I vowed the next person I dated would answer my calls, would call me, would want to know how I was and where I was. But, I'm beginning to realise, that mightn't be as healthy as I'd hoped either.

'Look, even if there's a bit of truth in what you're saying, I can't just switch off the last eight years. There's a void in my life which he used to fill. We were a couple for eight years, even if he was out the country for most of that time. I'm not sure if we would have survived as long if we actually lived together, since he said he was getting out it's kind of come to light that he wants kids...I can't...'

I swallow down the words I have never admitted to my friends, unable to bear the thought of their pity, or worse, for them to think I am less of a woman because I can't bear children. I rack my brains for a suitable explanation of how I feel, without revealing all.

'I can't imagine that life with him, but still, I need to lick my wounds.'

'I'm pretty sure I know a man who will lick them for you!' Emma blurts, with a smirk. 'I'm telling you, Nathan Kennedy is a ride and, from what Eddie says, he's mad about you. You could do a lot worse, love.' She almost chokes on her own saliva as the man himself struts into the kitchen.

'Everything ok in here?' Nathan saves me from any more home truths, truths I'm not sure I'm ready to face.

'Yes, I'm just going to check on Millie, will you turn down the oven?'

I run out to the hallway, not before Emma can say, 'Look at you guys, all domesticated and everything.'

My eyes roll into my head at her less than subtle hint. It would suit them perfectly if Nathan and I got together. We'd be together all the time and I'd finally be properly back in the gang, all WAGs together.

The trouble is, though they're my best friends, I'm not the same as them. They're high-flying, ambitious, classy ladies. I'm the stumpy friend, who shops in the kids department of Debenhams, drinks until she drops and never knows when it's time to go home. I'm the resident family black sheep and overall disappointment.

Every point the girls voiced about Craig, deep down, I already knew. I'm beginning to realise, the only person I've ever truly been lying to, is myself.

Living with Nathan and Millie the past few weeks has made me realise what I want. I like having someone to talk to over breakfast, to laugh at the day's trivial details with over dinner. I've been living alone for a long time, but only when I moved in with Nathan and Millie, did I realise I was actually lonely.

But if, and I mean *if*, Nathan and I were ever to get together, it would be short lived. He'd get bored. I'm not sexy or exciting, hell, I can't even drive. I only have a job because he gave me one. And he knows my deepest darkest secret. He knows I'm broken and, if the way he dotes on Millie is anything to go by, he's bound to want more kids, something I'll never be able to give him.

Tiptoeing through the darkness, I place a hand lightly on Millie's forehead. She's out for the count, her breath falling evenly from her open mouth as she snuggles her beloved *Octonauts* teddy. Stroking the stray strands of hair from her eyes, I press a kiss on her forehead, wondering, not for the first time this week, if Nathan will ask me again to stay on now I have nowhere else to be at the end of the summer, no one coming to claim me.

If he does, I'm unsure what I'll say. As ever, I'm unsure about everything, and now with Craig out of my life, I have no excuse not to take the reins myself. It's an unnerving thought, but it's also an opportunity to do what I want with my life, instead of fitting in around anyone else's plans. The only trouble is, I don't know what I want – I'm still completely lacking in direction, as ever.

CHAPTER TWENTY-TWO

NATHAN

Last night ended tamely, the gang left around midnight and much to my dismay, no one made use of the jacuzzi. I was dying to get Kerry into it, relishing the thought of her semi-clothed and confined in a small space. However, she's asked for a second driving lesson this week to make up for lost time, and it's an opportunity to spend some alone time with her, even if it means endangering my life in the process.

'Millie, get your shoes on, Nanny Nuala will be here any minute,' I call up the stairs for the twentieth time.

'Daddy, I can't find my new Elsa t-shirt with the sequins on it!'

I mount the stairs to look for it. It turns out even tiny women have to change outfits five times before they head out the door.

Kerry sticks her head out into the hallway. 'It's here, Millie. I washed it yesterday. You can't wear the same shirt all week, honey.'

'Why not? Daddy does.' Millie appears shirtless on the

landing with Minnie Mouse ears stuck on top of her head and a purple tutu round her waist.

'I have ten of the same t-shirts. It's not the actual same shirt.'

'Well, can you buy me ten of those Elsa ones? Please, Daddy.' I bite back my laughter – at the age of five, my daughter knows how to work the system.

Kerry throws the shirt up the stairs, then heads back to the kitchen. As I battle to pull it over Millie's bobbing head, the front door opens.

'Is everyone decent in here?' My mother's familiar hoarse voice echoes through the hallway.

'We're up here, and I never claimed to be decent in my life.'

My mother is a subtle as a brick. Since the night I called to ask her to babysit, so I could bring the babysitter out, I haven't heard the end of it.

Mam was young when she had me. She's only fifty now, and consequently, she treats me more like a friend than her son. Some of the stuff she deems appropriate to talk to me about is frankly horrifying. I do not need to know who she had sex with when she was twenty-two, or how bad the change of life is. She has no filter, a bit like another woman I know.

Footsteps approach the bottom of the stairs and she peers up at us. 'Hi, Millie, how are you, sweetheart?' She doesn't wait for an answer before her nose gets the better of her. 'So, Nathan have you sealed the deal with Kerry yet?'

My eyes roll in my head, seriously, sometimes I feel like I have to parent her. 'Mam, please, not in front of Millie.'

'Sealed what deal?' Millie glances from Mam, to me, then back again.

Explosive snorting erupts from the kitchen below and Kerry enters the hall again, with a tea towel slung over her shoulder and a grin that extends all the way to her eyes. 'No, Nuala, he hasn't, I'm clearly out of his league.' Kerry rolls her eyes to the heavens and laughs. Her sarcasm demonstrates she has no idea of her own appeal, or what she does to me. Being around her and not being able to touch her is almost unbearable. This week, as the temperatures have soared in the city, so has my blood pressure.

'Let's see how funny you are when you're in the hot seat in a minute.' That driver's seat has become ridiculously hot since she started parking her backside in it, in a pair of tiny denim shorts.

I was certain that dickhead would realise what he'd thrown away and come crawling back. If I'd found any flower deliveries, I was planning on dumping them, well, I'd contemplated it at least. But there'd been nothing. Which leaves her very much single and available – when she's ready. I'm just not sure she is yet, but one thing I have is time. I'm going absolutely nowhere.

A thud from the hall catches my attention as I lead Millie by the hand down the stairs. A heap of post lands through the letterbox. It looks like a pile of catalogues. Kerry must be planning on spending some of her new salary. Millie runs to my mam, pleading to go to the park. I stop to pick up the post. It's addressed to Kerry, but the plastic wrapping is clear. It's a brochure for Trailblazers, a company specialising in those one-way round the world tickets. She can't seriously be thinking about travelling the world alone? A rush of nausea runs through my gut.

I'm such a fucking fool, just because I have time, it doesn't mean she's going to spend it with me. I assumed she'd stay on, now Craig isn't an issue. With only weeks left of the summer holidays, I need to make a move, before it's too late. I can't lose her, before I've ever really had her. She leaves me no choice but to up my game.

Barbie nudges my leg and I pat her on the head. 'It's too hot, Barbs. We'll bring you out later. I promise.'

In the kitchen, I hand Kerry her post. She squints at it over her coffee, then snatches it almost guiltily, realisation glinting in her eyes. I force the frown from my face as she looks away and shoves the brochure in the kitchen drawer.

'Are we ready?' She drains her coffee cup and slips it into the dishwasher. I try not to stare as she bends over in front of me, rearranging cups and plates into a position that satisfies her. Oh my god, how I would love to satisfy her. It must be written all over my face because my mother slaps my arm and says, 'Put your tongue away, son, I didn't raise you to be slobbering over women, like that useless feckin' dog of yours.'

I don't slobber over women. I slobber over one woman. Having her here under my roof, living with me, is almost too much, yet the thought of her not being here is way worse.

'Yes, clearly a vertically challenged older woman is bound to set one of Ireland's most eligible men salivating. Control yourself, Nathan, will you.' She slips a tea towel off the counter and whizzes it round in circles until it forms a rope like appearance. With one rapid flick of her wrist, she cracks it across my backside with an ear-splitting whip.

'Ouch.' I attempt to grab the tea towel off her, but she flings it in the utility room and struts to the hallway, presumably to escape the house before I can get her back.

Mam bites back her smirk. 'That, my boy, is the equivalent of pulling pigtails in the playground. She likes you, trust me.'

'Of course she likes you, Daddy,' Millie interjects from where she's sitting at the table colouring in a rainbow. Wide eyes gaze up at me filled with innocence. 'She's always looking at your photo when you're not here.' She points to a picture on the wall of Callum, Eddie, Marcus, Ollie and me, taken the day we won the Six Nations three years earlier.

'Is that right?' Perhaps there's hope yet. I ruffle Millie's hair and kiss her forehead. 'You be good for Nanny, won't you?' She nods in response.

To my mother I plead, 'No bingo halls, no betting shops and no pubs, please.'

'Huh! Spoilsport!' I only hope she's joking.

I pull my wallet out of my back pocket and slip my mother five hundred euro. 'Go shopping, go for lunch. Have a lovely day out.'

'Thanks, son.' She slips the money into her worn looking leather purse. 'Take your time now, have a day out for yourselves. Bring Kerry somewhere memorable.' She wiggles her eyes suggestively. Ha, if only. I'd bring her somewhere very memorable if she'd let me, without even leaving the house.

I slip out the front door and into the garage where Kerry waits in the driver's seat of the X5. I hop in next to her. Her familiar perfume lingers in the air between us. It's my favourite smell.

'Ready?' Her left index finger hovers over the start button, and she flips her sunglasses from her head down over her eyes.

I pull my own sunglasses on from the centre console and clear my throat, masking my apprehension at what I'm about to say. 'Yeah. I was thinking we could go for a longer drive, maybe get some lunch out somewhere?'

We eat together every day, usually twice, so I shouldn't feel weird asking her to eat with me, but I do because it's the closest I can get to asking her on a date, without actually asking her on a date. I have less time than I thought and I have every intention of using it wisely.

She bites back a smirk and presses the start button. 'Sure. Where do you want to go?'

'Skerries.' I'm hoping it might provide a romantic setting.

We take the long route to the seaside, reaching Skerries

an hour later. It's full of gorgeous little restaurants over-looking the Irish Sea and predominantly populated with the up and coming or the celebs of Dublin. I couldn't care about that bullshit, I brought Kerry here because of the view and the food, not because of who we might bump into.

'There's a parking space five metres ahead. They're few and far between round here. Do you think you can reverse in? If not, I'll do it for you.'

'No, it's fine. I've got to practice, right?' Tiny dewy beads of sweat appear on her brow and she bites her lower lip in concentration, a gesture that drives me wild.

How hard can parking be with BMW parking sensors to help you? Still, I can barely look as she narrowly misses the Merc in the space next to us, then switches the engine off, sighing with what I can only assume is relief.

'Err, Kerry, it might be ok for someone with your tiny frame, but there's no fucking way I can get out of this car, parked here.' Two inches sit between my wing mirror and the Merc.

'Alright, you big show off, with your big muscles and hunky shoulders.' Kerry uses her forearm to wipe her brow, then restarts the car. I can't process the compliment because a crowd of men in their fifties pause in front of the car, nudging each other. I can only assume the Merc belongs to one of them. No pressure or anything.

'Take your time, Kerry. Don't be put off by anyone looking.'

'Ha! I thought you'd know me better than that by now.' She lets the window down and gleefully shouts, 'Honk if your horny!' Sticking her head out of the window, she presses the palm of her hand on the horn. The men stare open mouthed. A burst of laughter explodes from my chest. Four attempts later, she manages to park the car in a position where we can both get out.

'I need a drink,' she announces, hopping out of the car and handing over the keys.

'I take it I'm driving home?'

'If you're not, then we're spending the night.'

Now there's a thought, especially with the horny remark, but a thought is all it can be. Last night's sporadic evening aside, I can't do spontaneity, I have a daughter to get home to and a dog that needs walking. No wonder Kerry's considering swanning off around the world. As fortunate as I am, a life with me can offer no such excitement. It's what I've known all along but for some reason today, with her potential departure on the cards, it cuts through me like a freshly sliced wound.

CHAPTER TWENTY-THREE

KERRY

Sweet relief pumps through my bloodstream to my jelly-like legs. How can I seriously be considering travelling the world alone, when the thought of reverse parking reduces me to a trembling wreck, no matter how well I hide it? I'm a fucking joke. A thirty-one-year-old joke. The only thing I wasn't joking about, was needing a drink.

Whenever I'm stressed, or anxious, it's my go to. Far from being the fun party animal friend, I'm the unstable friend who drinks to avoid reality. Although, since I've been living with Nathan and Millie, I haven't gotten out of hand once. They're clearly a good influence. Let's hope today is not the day I start. Mags is still relentlessly bombarding me with texts, pleading for a night out. The truth is, I'd rather sit in and have a glass of wine with Mr-Fucking-Eligible-Himself than get shit-faced in Temple Bar.

Nathan fetches a parking ticket and we stroll companionably through the little sunny streets. It's been years since I was here. My parents brought me for a weekend when I was a teenager. They're a couple of sticklers for routine. I'm not sure how they managed to produce such an unstable daughter, with their combined love of tedious, predictable schedules.

Mam has the dinner on the table at six o'clock sharp. On Fridays she serves fish, Saturday's it's beef, Sunday is lamb, Monday is stir-fry, Tuesday is roast chicken, Wednesday is curry, Thursday is pasta, and Friday the whole thing starts again. He then 'retires to the study' while she cleans the kitchen. Remembering it, I realise today's the day they will ring. It's always the same, every second Friday at five o'clock.

No doubt it will be the same questions over and over. When am I coming to visit? When is Craig getting out? When am I going to get a proper job? And my all-time favourite: When am I going to go back to college and finish my Master's? As their only child, and a long awaited for one at that, I'm under no illusion how frequently I disappoint them.

Is it any wonder I dread visiting? Craig only came with me once in eight years. I thought it might take the edge off the interrogation, but instead, we both got one. I took comfort in the fact he didn't have a long-term plan either, until he did, of course.

'What are you thinking?' Nathan's deep masculine voice is like music to my ears. He's so easy to be around, apart from the fact that he's ridiculously hot, and now I'm single I have to constantly remind myself not to throw myself at him. He's my boss. And if he wanted me, he would have made a move by now.

It was safe to flirt that night in Flame because he knew I was unavailable, nothing could or would come out of it. It was a bit of harmless drunken fun. Now I actually *am* available, he hasn't come near me, hasn't made a single move. Mind you, what do I have to offer a man like him? We get on brilliantly because I'm not one of those daft women that's silly enough to throw themselves at him. We've come to be friends. I wouldn't be stupid enough to mess with that, but it doesn't stop the explicit fantasies every time I close my eyes.

'About my parents. They're always getting on at me to do something with my life.'

'And aren't you? You have a great job...' He runs a hand over his stubbly jaw, before correcting himself. 'Sorry, I'm not saying it's great working for me, what I meant is, you have a job where you are valued, and I hope one that gives you satisfaction.'

'Are you kidding? I love working for you. I adore Millie. And you pay pretty well too.' I give him a jab in the ribs to show I'm joking.

'If you love working for me, why are you ordering travel brochures?' He catches me by the hand, slowing to an almost standstill in the busy street. Electricity pulses between our fingertips.

'All good things must come to an end.' I shrug, faking nonchalance. Terrified of being trapped into a mundane life like my mother, travelling might be the only sure way to avoid it.

I'm not stupid enough to think this is a long-term position. I know that's what he mentioned initially, but at some point he's going to get a girlfriend who will take care of him and Millie, and do it for free. As if to prove my point, three blonde women, who could pass for sisters, stop in their tracks and stare at Nathan open mouthed. One physically pushes me aside to touch his arm.

'Oh my god! Are you Nathan Kennedy? Can I please get a photo with you?' Her friend is snapping away on an iPhone before he can grant or deny permission. Reluctantly, his mouth twists into a fake smile for the camera, he then immediately steps away.

'Hey, I don't suppose we can buy you a drink?' The tallest one pouts her lips out at him, puckering up like blowfish.

Nathan looks at me, then back at the three women.

'Oh wait, is she your girlfriend?'

He opens his mouth, then closes it again.

'Of course she's not,' the second one says, thrusting her large bust under Nathan's nose. 'She couldn't be.' Her eyes roam distastefully over my white vest top and denim shorts. I will the ground to open up and swallow me. I know I'm not good enough to be his girlfriend, I really don't need her pointing it out to me.

Nathan watches the exchange, pulling his sunglasses on top of his head to get a better look. He grabs my hand and pulls me into him, places my cheek against the thin cotton covering his strong muscular pecs. His toned, tattooed arm drapes around my shoulder protectively and his lips press against my head in a tender gesture.

'This is Kerry. She might not be my girlfriend yet, but I'm working on it.' He winks at me, deliberately saucily. A look which is full of promise but surely can't be real?

'Now, if you'll excuse us, I'm going to take her somewhere fancy for lunch and hope she drinks enough wine that she might consider having sex with me, preferably straight after, in the backseat of my car, because I have been thinking about it since the second she sat in it.'

The three women stand, wide-eyed and lost for words. Chuckling, he pulls me away, his arm still draped protectively round my shoulders. I remind myself he did that because he's my friend, not because it's the truth, but that doesn't stop the hum of longing spreading down my arms, across my chest and right into the very core of me.

His head tilts down towards mine. 'Women like that are everywhere. I hope they didn't upset you.'

'Not at all. I can see why they wouldn't put the two of us

together. Thank you, but you didn't have to defend my street cred, to be honest, I don't have any to start with and I couldn't give a shit about it anyway.'

'You wouldn't put us together?' His arm remains around me and his fingers run the length of my bare forearm, tracing the skin up and down, raising every hair on my body despite the summer sun. My fingers itch to trace his, to trace the lines of his tattoos, to ask what they represent to him, to know him more and to feel him. But I can't, this can't be real.

I swallow my urges, struggling to meet his eyes knowing lust is probably lighting my face. 'I said I can see why *they* wouldn't put us together.'

'I think we might just be the perfect fit.' He flexes the arm he still has wrapped around me; I fit in the space below his armpit like I was made for it, and I can't help wondering where else he might fit perfectly. Saliva pools in my mouth, as I force out an image of him between my thighs in the backseat of the Jeep.

Our stroll slows to a stop outside a line of beach-facing restaurants. 'What are you thinking?'

As tactfully as ever, I blurt, 'I was thinking about the backseat of your car.'

'Seriously?' A devilish glint creeps into his cobalt eyes and he uses one finger to tilt my chin up when I try to look away. His arm drops to my waist, then his fingers trace a tiny patch of exposed flesh where my top has ridden up over my shorts.

'I am only human, and according to *Tatler*, you're one of Ireland's sexiest bachelors.' His finger continues to stroke my flesh and the intensity of his stare has me almost breathless. I feel like Julia Roberts in *Pretty Woman*. He's out of my league, yet the way he's looking at me this second, the way his eyes bore into mine, I could almost swear—

'Nathan?' A red-haired woman, dressed in a slim-cut mini-dress grips his bicep in a way that's too familiar for my liking.

His arm drops from my waist as he turns to see who called him.

'Serena? How are you?' He shuffles from one foot to the other and pulls his sunglasses back down over his eyes.

'Great. Fancy seeing you here.' She touches his arm again. Millie was right, she is pretty, if you're into five-foot-eleven twigs, with chiselled porcelain cheekbones.

'I know it's crazy, right? I was actually going to call you...' Nathan scratches his stubble, pausing while he finds the words he's looking for.

'To confirm tonight? It's the 7th? I've been looking forward to it since you called. Eight o'clock, right?' She licks her lips in a cat-like gesture and my heart plummets to my size four Nike pumps. To think I almost thought he was interested? My cheeks flood with heat and I only pray he'll believe I was joking when I mentioned the backseat of his car. In fairness, it's the sort of stupid thing I'd come out with anyway.

He continues running his fingers over that dirty blond stubble. Only then does Serena notice me. She offers her immaculately French manicured hand to me, as a quizzical look forms on her neat even features. 'I'm Serena, and you are...?'

'I'm Kerry, Millie's nanny.' My clammy hand clasps her soft one and shakes it vigorously. She doesn't try to hide the way she wipes it on her dress the second she lets go, but her face relaxes into a smile.

'Ah, wonderful, you're the reason this handsome man is able to take me out tonight. Do you do overnights?' She eyes Nathan's torso suggestively and bile forms in my throat at the prospect of him going to bed with her tonight, when not thirty seconds earlier, I was foolish enough to think I might be.

'I do, actually, every night's an overnight.' A small ripple a satisfaction washes over me. 'I live with them.'

Nathan coughs, a distraction technique if ever I saw one. Oh my god, I can't believe I was so stupid. What on earth possessed me to think he was still interested in me, when he could have someone like her? I'm delusional now, as well as unbalanced and lacking direction.

Nathan gathers himself, standing a little bit straighter, appearing to have recovered from his shock. He meets my eye for the first time since Serena joined us and shoots an apologetic look. Oh god, the last thing I want is his pity.

Serena looks at him, then at me, then back to him. 'Wonderful.' Her clipped tone doesn't match her words. 'Perhaps with you living with Millie, I'll get to see a bit more of this handsome man?' Her eyes train intently on his face and his Adam's apple bobs as he swallows.

'Actually, I meant to ring you, Serena. I'm so sorry. I completely forgot about tonight. It was weeks ago when we arranged it. It went straight out of my head. I meant to cancel.'

Relief engulfs me like a river, as he takes a tiny step in my direction. His movement is discreet, but it's not unnoticed, by any of us. Serena's cheeks blush a deep crimson – Nathan's gesture isn't subtle.

'Oh, I see. Well, have a nice day with Nanny McPhee.' She turns on her heels and struts off into the throng of people lining the streets.

'I'm so sorry.' Nathan takes both my hands, tugging them towards him.

'What are you apologising to me for? I'm not your keeper.'

'I arranged to go out with her before—'

The restaurant manager steps out from the Italian we are

standing in front of and interrupts, before Nathan can continue. His blazer must be stifling under the summer sun, but not nearly as hot as I am with the events of the last few minutes.

'Table for two?' He brandishes menus almost as big as his offensively charming smile. 'Somewhere discreet, perhaps?' Clearly he's another person that recognises my companion. I don't think I'll ever get used to it, another reason we'd never truly work in the real world, despite my increasing longing. Still, the challenges of the real world might not be enough to stop me from spreading my legs in the back of the BMW, given half the chance.

'Is this ok for you?' Nathan ignores the manager and glances at me earnestly. I love Italian food, a fact he knows well at this stage after living together for almost seven weeks. Or does he mean the whole thing? This weird awkward situation we've stumbled into. And I thought I needed a drink before.

'Yes. Let's go in.'

As we're led across the restaurant, a loud guffaw sounds from the right side of the room.

'Well, well, well...look what the cat dragged in!' Marcus Williams bellows across the room and I sigh internally. If Nathan might have been about to say something meaningful, he didn't get the chance. Lunch at home would have been so much easier.

'Marcus, Shelly, how are you both?' Nathan crosses the room to greet them and I follow helplessly behind.

'We've just got here. Will you join us? Shelly's mam has the kids at the aquarium for the day, so we said we'd come out for some grown-up time. Sit, please.'

Shelly smiles and pulls out the chair next to her, her hands enthusiastically gesture for me to sit. Any other time I'd have been delighted; out of all the WAGs I'd recently been introduced to, I really warmed to Shelly. She's so down to earth, completely unpretentious, and she even seems to have the same inability to think before opening her mouth as me. I sit down, parking my backside in the seat, along with any secret hope of a bit of alone time with Nathan. At least he's not going out with Serena tonight.

I order a gin and tonic and settle in for the afternoon, wondering if Nathan and I have just dodged a bullet. Though the growing chemistry is palpable, he's my boss, and I'm leaving soon. It might be best left well alone, for both of our sakes. Because I can't imagine it ending well. After all, we live in different worlds.

CHAPTER TWENTY-FOUR

NATHAN

Three weeks have passed since I overheard Emma Harvey telling Kerry to give me a shot, and despite coming close two weeks earlier in Skerries, I still haven't actually taken one. Though, the growing pull of Kerry Walsh has me sitting in hours of traffic each day, up and down the motorway to Carton House. I'm unable to spend a night away from her. It's worth the dreaded commute when I arrive home to both the fabulous ladies in my life.

Since that in day Skerries, she doesn't disappear upstairs in the evenings anymore, which is both a blessing and a curse. There's only so much *Too Hot to Handle* a man can suffer on Netflix, with a woman who could pass for a poster pin-up of the understated-but-oozing-sex-appeal, girl-next-door, two feet away. My couch has never seemed so stupidly huge. Next time, I'll buy a smaller one.

She's taken to wearing the tiniest shorts and skimpy vest pyjama set. Ok, it's the end of July, summer is at its peak, but doesn't she realise she's killing me? Sometimes I wonder if it's deliberate, if she's trying to provoke a reaction from me after our near miss that day. Something almost happened between us, but with Marcus and Shelly crashing our casual date, the opportunity passed by and with Millie between us every day, there hasn't been another like it since.

I've taken to showering twice a day because after an evening admiring her smooth thighs and tiny waist, I am unbelievably hot. Getting into bed, knowing she's on the next floor up, single and alone, is almost too much to bear.

Now she doesn't spend her evenings FaceTiming a guy who never deserved her, we've slipped into a new routine. We eat, then take Barbie for a walk in the nearby park. Thankfully, having a woman and child with me makes calling the dog's name in public slightly less ridiculous, but only slightly. We've started bathing Millie together, before putting her to bed. Millie loves the attention both of us shower upon her. I try not to overthink what will happen if Kerry does actually leave at the end of the summer – it will likely break both of our hearts. The more time I spend with her, the more I appreciate her. I even love how she utters the most inappropriate things without thinking. Yesterday, when we were getting into the car for a driving lesson, I commented on how dirty it was. She blurted she 'liked it dirty' before licking her lips and exploding with laughter. If the blood wasn't rushing somewhere else, I might have even blushed. On second thoughts, I wouldn't, though I'd love to make her blush.

I'd usually assume that kind of behaviour is an attempt at flirting, but with Kerry's accompanying cackle, it was apparently intended as a joke. That didn't stop me spending the entire night fantasising about how dirty she might actually like it.

It's been on the tip of my tongue so many times to pick up the conversation we started in Skerries, but truthfully, I've been summoning the balls. Kerry is one of the bluntest women I've ever met in my life. If she wanted me, wouldn't she have said? I blatantly dumped Serena for her, in front of her, yet she's never mentioned it since.

And despite the electricity crackling between us, hanging out together in the friend zone is so much safer, with no danger of short circuiting, or someone blowing a fuse. I made my feelings crystal clear that night in Flame. I'm not averse to telling her again, and perhaps showing her, if she'll let me. Enough time has passed. My patience has evaporated, along with every other reason I shouldn't touch her.

In the sitting room, Kerry sits cross-legged on the couch with Millie. The two of them are playing snap with a pack of cards. Her denim skirt reveals those tanned thighs again and a flimsy strappy top captures her perfectly angled collarbones. Who even knew collarbones could be sexier than cleavage?

As Millie shouts, 'snap,' Kerry sticks her tongue out and starts to sing a Hot Chocolate song, 'You Win Again'. Her voice is low but even at that volume I can appreciate its rich warmth, like thick, sweet honey. Leaning on the wall behind them, I pause to watch and listen. I could watch Kerry all day.

Some women try to be sexy and no amount of hair flicking or winking helps. Every movement Kerry makes is deliberate, she seems completely comfortable in her own skin, and she doesn't pretend to be something she's not. She really has absolutely no idea of her own appeal. To me, it's the sexiest thing on the planet.

She finishes singing the chorus, and I clear my throat to announce my presence.

'Daddy! Did you know Kerry's an awesome singer?'

A giggle slips from Kerry's mouth. 'I won't show you the dance moves that go with it. I usually reserve them for after midnight.'

'I'm not tired,' Millie claims, but the yawn that slips out says otherwise.

'Neither am I,' I say, imagining the swaying of hips that happens after twelve. Kerry stands, throws a cushion at my head and laughs.

'I think it's bedtime for a little lady.'

'Aww, five more minutes?' Millie uses her best puppy eyes at Kerry.

'If we go up now, I'll read you two stories instead of one. How about it?' She knows exactly how to manage my daughter.

Millie scrambles to her feet. 'Ok, but I get to pick them. You always pick *Red Riding Hood*.'

'That's because she's the only one not waiting for some daft prince to rescue her.' Kerry lifts Millie up into her arms and carries her through the living area out to the hall.

'Yes, her daddy saves her instead. Do you have a daddy, Kerry?' I follow behind them, pausing to get a glass of water to leave on Millie's bedside locker.

'I do, but I don't see that much of him.' Kerry's feet gently pad on the stairs.

'Don't worry, my dad can save both of us if the wolf comes knocking.'

It's almost like she's saying the words I can't say myself.

Twenty minutes and two stories later, Millie's gently snoring.

'She's lucky to have you.' I hover a couple of feet behind her, gazing at my sleeping daughter from over her shoulder. 'Clodagh's absence would have been a lot harder without you.'

'I'm the lucky one. Thanks for trusting me to mind her, when I can barely mind myself.'

'You don't give yourself enough credit. You're a natural.'

'A natural accident just waiting to happen.' I think she means it as a joke, though she doesn't smile.

We creep out of Millie's room, pulling the door half-closed. Kerry glances at my bedroom door, I deliberately leave it wide open these days. I couldn't make the unspoken invitation more obvious if I tried. Her eyes dart over my bed, but she turns away the second she catches me watching her.

'Want to be a hero and rescue some wine trapped in a bottle?' She continues down the final flight of stairs. 'I feel like a change from the usual Friday night gin.'

'Sounds like a plan. I have to get my heroic kicks somewhere, I can't see the big bad wolf calling here tonight. But just in case, I've got you covered...' It's on the tip of my tongue to ask her if she wants to go into the bar with me, into the man cave, preferably the jacuzzi, but the words won't come.

'Red, or white for a change?' I reach up to the wine rack over the porcelain sink. Her eyes run over my stomach and I flatten down my t-shirt with my left hand, skimming the bottles with my right. She looks away, but not before I've clocked it.

A half-smile curls at her lips. 'Red. I love white wine but it sends me looney.'

I pull down a bottle of red and a bottle of white, and put the white in the fridge for another day. 'What kind of looney?'

'I wasn't joking about Hot Chocolate dance moves. Just ask Emma, or Abby for that matter.'

'That's no fun, I'd prefer to see them first-hand.'

'Be very careful what you wish for... Let's just say it's a good job you keep that door locked.' She points to the man cave. 'I'm dangerous when I get going.'

'I do have a vague recollection...' I chance meeting her eyes as I uncork the bottle of merlot, a glimmer of remembrance flickers in her graphite eyes, her finger traces her lower lip. Her gestures are like her mouth, blunt. And it speaks directly to my dick, but I can't be sure she's ready or willing to do something about it, something that risks rocking our carefully constructed domestic boat.

'It's my way of letting off steam, though I'm like a pressure cooker with the lid stuck firmly down at the minute.' She accepts the glass I hand her with a smile of thanks. 'I'm frightened the next time I let loose, I might actually explode.'

Now that's a prospect I'd love to experience, preferably all over my lower half. It's right there, dangling unspoken in the air between us. It's now or never. Coach always says, the only shots you miss, are the ones you're too afraid to take. Fuck it.

'And is there anything I can do to help you with that?' I'm talking in code, but behind the smoky innuendos a raw truth remains – the offer is genuine, she can take it anyway she likes.

She arches a single eyebrow and takes a sip of her drink before answering. 'You want to help me let off some steam?'

'Sure. Whatever you need.' My casual shrug is fooling no one, least of all me. 'Want to have a blow out in the man cave?'

'Now there's an offer I can't refuse, but better not give me any tequila! You know I can't be trusted with it.' Her fingers touch her lips again. I'm desperate to touch them myself. The air is charged with something promising. Enough time has passed, we've been dancing around each other for weeks, and I want her. I'm ninety per cent sure she feels the same, but I get the distinct feeling I'm about to find out for certain.

I take her hand – the buzzing static between us travels straight up my arm, straight to my core – and lead her to the door. She doesn't drop it, and this time when I catch her looking at my exposed middle again, she doesn't look away.

CHAPTER TWENTY-FIVE

KERRY

Nathan pulls out a bar stool for me. 'Sit up here, if we're getting drunk, we're going to do it right.' I've got a feeling I'm getting more than a drink, at least I hope I'm not reading him wrong. Over the past couple of weeks, his proximity is killing me. He's always by my side, yet that little bit out of reach. After that day outside the Italian, I thought, if he wanted me, he'd have made a play by now. Instead, he's tiptoed around me like I'm a wounded animal since Craig broke up with me. I'm an animal alright, but wounded isn't the word I'd use to describe myself.

I can't work him out. He talks the talk, with his flirtatious remarks and lingering stares, yet he hasn't once acted on it. For the previous two weeks, I've been deliberately sitting next to him on the couch every evening, half-naked, yet he hasn't once made a play. Short of offering myself on a plate, I'm not sure how to move things along.

'It won't be pretty.' I know exactly what I'm like when I get going, and after our near miss in Skerries, I can't trust myself not to get spectacularly hammered and throw myself at him.

'That's where you're wrong.' His voice has taken on a new husky tone, a far cry from the dad voice he used only twenty minutes earlier. If only he'd fucking act on it!

Perching on the stool next to me, Nathan's legs rest slightly apart, hips pointing straight at me. He sets his glass on the bar, before his eyes roam across what little cleavage I own.

Is it a full moon? Because the atmosphere's charged tonight, like if it was ever going to happen, it might just be the night. If it is, I won't discourage him; I wasn't joking about the steam. I've come to the conclusion everyone thinks I'm shagging him anyway, so given half the chance, I just might. It's only fair I warn him.

'If I start slurring or stripping, I'm probably two drinks away from vomiting or passing out.'

'If you start stripping, you definitely won't be getting another drink.' His cobalt eyes glint with lust fuelled promise. I'm tempted to down my wine and strip off this second because this is the closest he's got to coming on to me since that day in Skerries, and I'm reluctant to let the moment pass.

'You don't serve naked women in the man cave?' I take a sip of my wine, eyeing him over the crystal glass.

'Oh, I serve them alright' – his Adam's apple bobs and he runs a tongue over his upper lip in a way that sends my insides soaring – 'just not alcohol.'

Holy fucking shit, we've gone from nought to ninety, in under ten seconds. A deep rooted lust presses in my chest, in the pit of my stomach and surges down between my thighs. I wanted this man physically, long before I was allowed. Now I am allowed, the feelings have only multiplied.

'Well that sounds pretty interesting, from where I'm

sitting.' The words come out low, husky, unrecognisable to myself.

'Oh, you wouldn't be sitting there, sweetheart.' He drags out every syllable deliberately slowly, emphasising them with shakes of his head.

Hot, raging fire spreads wildly inside, rippling through my core to the very depth of me. 'Really? Where exactly would I be sitting, should I happen to be naked?' I silently congratulate myself for not throwing myself at him immediately. The words even come out a lot more composed than the crap I normally spout.

He swivels forty-five degrees on his stool to face the bar and moves his wine glass out of the way. Positioning both hands a foot apart on the polished bar, his upturned palms open as if he's primed to hold on to something. His muscled biceps curl as he holds the pose and his head cocks to the side, displaying an intoxicating intensity burning in his pupils. 'If you took your clothes off in my bar, you'd be sitting right here.' He cups his hands, flexing long, strong fingers. My thighs press together to stop me from openly wriggling at the thought.

He's killing me, but apparently he's not finished yet. 'And my head,' he dips his face, lowering it towards his hands, 'would be right about here.'

The room spins before me in a lust driven dizziness I've never previously experienced. Holy fuck. I might be blunt, but he is suddenly brazen. Clearly, I'm not the only one struggling to deal with the accumulating build-up of chemistry between us. It's the single hottest thing anyone has ever said to me. The fire inside smoulders and grows, flames licking every cell and nerve ending within. He swivels back towards me. A tightness in his jaw and the thrumming of a vein in his ripped arms suggests he's as hot for the prospect as I am.

'What can I say? You're killing me, Kerry. There's a line, and it's yours to cross.' He raises his arms and shrugs, before picking up his glass and taking a sip. I watch as he savours the liquid in his mouth. When he swallows, it does nothing to alleviate the thirst in his eyes.

My body aches for his touch, more than I've ever ached for anyone. But this is a dangerous situation. I know what he needs to quench that burning thirst haunting him – it's the same as what I want – but where does that leave us afterwards?

I swallow the excessive saliva pooling in my mouth. 'What are we doing?'

'I'm trying to persuade you to have sex with me, without actually laying a finger on you.' His smirk is strained, at least we both seem to appreciate how much we have to lose if this ends badly, not least the easy friendship we've built.

'And why is that exactly?' I cross my legs and pray my lady parts don't combust.

'We came close before, but now you're Millie's nanny. I need you, in more ways than one. And...' He takes in a deep breath and exhales slowly before uttering, 'I like you.' His emphasis on the word like is heavy. Though his mother told me the same thing weeks earlier, I still can't get my head around it, why would a man like Nathan be interested in someone like me? He seems to sense my uncertainty.

'You're the sexiest woman I've ever met. You are also one of the funniest, kindest people on the face of this earth.'

My finger traces the stem of his wine glass. 'Is that your first drink tonight? Or have you been secretly swigging in the kitchen all evening? Because tonight, you're different. I was beginning to think I'd been permanently relegated to the friend zone, though I'm not entirely averse to being a friend with benefits...'

'Is that what you want?' He straightens in his stool, as lust-filled eyes scrutinise my face.

For once I'm not awkward. My inability to keep my mouth closed is either going to get me sacked or laid. The tension is volcanic, something's going to blow one way or another. I'd rather it was me.

'What I want is for my ass to be on that bar, gripped by your hands, and your face to be somewhere round here.' My fingers trace my breast, travelling downwards over my stomach, before stopping at the waistband of my denim skirt.

His lips purse together in a thoughtful gesture, like he's imagining the scene unfolding. Time stops as my heart pounds erratically in my chest.

'Well, we've been dancing round the issue long enough, what are you waiting for?' His eyes flick hungrily over my body, and flat palms pat the solid wooden bar in front of him.

I've thought about this moment in my head a million times over the past few weeks, but in my wildest fantasies, I didn't expect him to be so unashamedly forward. Longing burns in his darkening pupils, eradicating any previous doubt that he might want me. It's reinforced by the intensity of his stare, and by the bulge in his trousers.

Slowly, deliberately teasing, I lift my top up, inching it high enough to reveal my lack of bra. I barely need one, and I've noticed him stealing glances at my chest lately. Greedy eyes drink in my flesh, and a low hiss escapes his lips as I lift the material higher revealing the underside of my breasts.

He tears my top off completely, tutting in what looks like appreciation. 'Fucking hell, Kerry.' The flick of his tongue over his lips has me salivating.

Slipping down from the stool, I deliberately brush my chest against his legs as I wiggle out of my skirt. As it falls to the floor, I rise to stand before him, wearing only a triangle of red lace, having been subconsciously preparing for this moment for weeks. Though nothing prepares me for the level of longing crusading through my blood.

A low whistle hums from his open mouth, then before I can stop to question myself, he lifts me effortlessly onto the bar in front of him, my bare cheeks cupped in each of his hands as promised.

'Oh, Kerry, you have no idea how many times I've imagined you up here.' His tongue traces his lips again promisingly. Lowering his head, he encapsulates my nipple in his mouth in a quick, feral gesture. His tongue rolls, licking, sucking, humming. Goosebumps rip across my bare skin, despite the heat. Moving across to my other nipple, he works my flesh as though it's the most delicious treat he's ever sampled. My back arches, pushing my pelvis forwards in a pleading gesture that I can't bring myself to be ashamed of. My lust is almost unbearable – the intensity of my longing has been multiplying for weeks. The way his tongue caresses my skin is doing nothing to relieve it.

'You like that?' The cool confidence in his tone assures me he already knows the answer. He's completely in control of my pleasure, and I don't doubt his ability to release some of that aforementioned pressure.

'You know I do.' My head lolls backwards, pushing my chest towards his full lips again, but instead of taking me in his mouth, he offers teasing little circular licks. It's nowhere near enough, the groan that slips out of me expresses it clearly enough to make him chuckle.

'I've wanted to touch you, to taste you, since that first night in Dubrovnik.' His moist heavy breath blows out across my chest, then his tongue rolls downwards over my naval, before returning to my breasts. 'You made me wait a long time. I think it's only fair you experience some of that torture, don't you?'

'Nathan, please...' My words are slurred, but not by alcohol for once.

'Please what, Kerry? Tell me, what is it that you want? I need to hear it from those seductive little lips that so often give me cheek.' His tongue rolls downwards again, this time he lets it reach as far as the red waistband, dipping a centimetre inside, before rolling upwards again.

I'm so ready, he'd barely have to touch me there. He wants me to say it, to ask him to please me. I'll fucking beg if he doesn't give it to me soon. If I had any dignity, I left it on the floor with my skirt.

'You promised to help me let off some steam, yet here I am, trapped at your mercy with the heat cranked up. I'm about to blow.'

His busy mouth works over the lace that stands in the way of my pleasure, his breath seeping through the flimsy material. 'So, you want a release?'

'Uh huh.' Watching his face right there is nearly enough on its own. The image sears deep into my brain, I'll never be able to unsee it, and I never want to.

'Like this?' His hot, wet tongue runs across the centre of me, but the material remains blocking the way. His teasing is pure torture, yet I don't want it to stop.

'Uh huh.' I'm unable to form actual words, let alone a coherent sentence, dizzy with lust. My fingers grip the bar beneath me, as his tongue continues to torment me, so close, but still so far. Strong hands grip my backside, even as a gentle thumb strokes my flesh. Even the way he teases me is compassionate.

I want that lace gone, and I'm happy to remove it myself. As I struggle upwards, his eyes dance with mischievous delight.

'Going somewhere, Kerry?'

I slip my hand between his mouth and the material and

pull it to the side, moving the lace out of our way, pinning it to the side with my finger.

'You're so beautiful when you're teetering on the edge.' The wicked glint in his eyes tells me exactly how much he is enjoying this. 'Tell me what you want, Kerry.'

'I want your mouth on my flesh. I want to run my fingers through your hair as you taste me.' I can't bring myself to look away as his tongue dips to the most intimate parts of me, but the relief is short lived as he continues to torture me with long, slow strokes, that don't quite reach my centre.

'Like this?' His tongue strokes, then pauses.

'You might be the death of me.' I still can't take my eyes off him, fascinated with the erotic scene in front of me. I have never been so turned on.

'We can't have that now, can we? Perhaps I've teased you enough, for now?' His mouth works me, kissing, licking, stroking – he doesn't hold back this time. Within seconds I blow spectacularly. My release pulses through me and a million stars explode behind my eyelids. I grip his hair between my fingers, as I gently come back down to earth with a sigh. His tongue traces the inside of my thigh, as his fingers gently caress my breasts.

'You are some woman,' he murmurs into my leg. I pull his hands out from their position securing my bum and slip off the bar into his lap, a leg either side of his waist.

'You're not bad yourself, you know.' It's the understatement of the year. He's the most gorgeous thing I've ever seen.

Shimmying back onto his long thighs, I scoot far enough to undo the button at his waist and free him. A low moan escapes his lips. Payback's a bitch. I pull his t-shirt over his head and examine the lines of his symmetrical pecs and perfectly proportioned six pack. The tattoos alone are enough to make me wet, but the whole package has me drowning. My tongue traces the lines of the intricate inkwork decorating his body.

'Tell me what you want.' I mock him with his own words.

'You are a cruel woman, you know that, Kerry?' His head falls back as I take him in my hands.

'Oh, I'm just getting started.' I wink at him. 'Tell me you're prepared?' I'm not on the pill; I've never needed to worry about getting pregnant.

'Behind the bar.' He leans forward and fumbles across the bar, while I perch on his knees, watching his face as I work him with my hands. He locates a shiny foil square and goes to unwrap it.

'Oh, no, not yet you don't.' A teasing laugh falls from my lips.

'I'm not ashamed to beg, Kerry. I've waited over a year for this, please, put me out of my misery.' Smouldering eyes burn into mine. I can't deny him, and I can't deny myself any longer. I want him.

'Ok, just this once, but next time I'm going to make you suffer.'

'Next time? I like the sound of that.' His words almost catch in his throat as I slip the rubber onto him. Glossy, glazed eyes roll back in his head as I inch onto him, taking in the length of him, allowing him to fill me. He was right, we fit perfectly, like he was made for me.

'With your earlier performance, you made sure I'll be back for more, let's not even pretend.' My hands clasp the back of his neck and my thighs wrap tightly round his waist as I slide up and down his flesh. Only then do his lips actually meet mine. It's the first time in a year, yet it's familiar because he's the sweetest thing I've ever tasted.

I continue my rhythm, slow and steady, and his tongue dances with mine, licking, savouring, until he pulls his mouth from mine. 'Kerry, I...fucking hell, you feel so good.'

His face tightens with pleasure, as he squeezes my back-side. His eyes bore heavily into mine in a moment of sublime intimacy as he gives me everything he's got.

My lips fall to his neck while our heart rates battle to regulate into some sort of normal rhythm. 'Now, about that drink...'

CHAPTER TWENTY-SIX

NATHAN

Whatever fantasies I'd concocted about Kerry, were absolutely nothing compared to the real thing. I lift her back up onto the bar and go in search of towels from beside the sauna. She reaches out for her discarded top, but I hold a finger up to stop her.

'You won't be needing that.' I have nowhere near finished with her and the smile tugging at her lips hints she's happy to hear it. As I pass the jacuzzi, I flick it on and lift the lid.

'I know your game,' she calls across the room. I have never seen anything more beautiful than her sitting topless on that smooth mahogany. She lifts her glass and raises it in a silent toast, before taking a sip.

'Pour that muck away. It's definitely a night for the Bolly.' I return to her with two towels, passing round the back of the bar to the fridge. The familiar popping of the cork resounds round the room and I pause for a second before pouring the fizzing liquid into two crystal flutes, listening in case the noise had woken up my daughter. After ten seconds silence,

I'm happy she's still asleep. Even though I'm fairly sure Kerry wouldn't do a Serena over it, it would definitely kill the mood somewhat.

I hand over her new drink and we clink crystal, with a gentle chime. 'Cheers.'

She takes a sip, then licks her lips in apparent apprecia-tion. 'Wow. I'm rarely lost for words, but fucking hell, Kennedy, you knocked me for six there. I didn't see that coming.'

'You've got to be joking? The second you became single, it was inevitable.' I resume my position on the bar stool, resting my free hand on her bare thigh.

'Inevitable? Jees, you are sure of yourself.' She places her hand on mine and squeezes it, to show she's joking. 'I wish I had a fraction of your confidence.'

'What I'm sure of are my feelings for you. I didn't do this lightly.'

She gazes down at me and drags her fingers lazily through my hair. 'That must have been why it took you so long!' Her silver specked irises sparkle. I'm ecstatic to be the one to put the brightness back in to them. 'You're awful soppy for a big fella, you know.'

'The second you turned up at my door, I wanted you. Hell, even before that, but I had no way to get close to you. When you turned up in my hour of need, it felt like fate.'

She takes another sip of her drink before pausing thoughtfully. 'I must admit, I'm surprised. Like, you're this super-hot rugby star and I'm just the vertically challenged nanny.' Curiosity crinkles at the corner of her eyes; she might be comfortable in her own skin, but she genuinely has no idea how gorgeous that skin is. I don't know if it was Craig that knocked it out of her, or her experience before, but I'm determined to instil a bit of it back into her.

I lean back and allow my eyes to roam over her almost

naked body. The red lace is back in place, no longer pushed to the side. I should have taken it off when I had the chance.

'Kerry, you are so fucking hot, it's been killing knowing you were the floor above me for the last couple of months. So many times I wanted to knock on your door, but I couldn't. The only person that doesn't see your worth is you. I should have told Marcus we wouldn't be joining them for lunch because I was so close to telling you then how I felt.'

She remains slightly puzzled looking but shrugs. I plant a kiss on the taut skin of her smooth stomach and she wraps a hand round the back of my head, pulling me in for a cuddle. Rome wasn't built in a day, but I'm going to build her up, show her her own worth. Because she's the only one that doesn't see it.

My tongue finds her skin again; I could spend all day licking every inch of her.

'Easy tiger, or you'll start something you might not have the energy to finish.' Her index finger finds my chin and tilts my head up to meet her glinting amorous eyes.

'You needn't worry about that, Mrs Robinson... do I need to remind you you're sleeping with a younger man now?' Her nipple hardens and I take it in my mouth.

'Mrs Robinson...huh! I'll show you.' Her nails run the length of my spine, electrifying every single hair on my body to attention. And that's not the only thing.

'Jacuzzi, now. I'll bring the bottle. Loose the panties; they're cute, but I prefer what's underneath.'

'Yes, sir.' She hops off the bar, drops her underwear, then her hips sway across the room to the swirling, foaming bubbles. I think I might have died and gone to heaven. Picking up the bottle, I'm on her heels, pausing only to remove my shorts.

'I'll open the doors. It's going to get steamy in here.'

'Promises, promises.' Her tongue roams her lips as she

slips under the water, hiding everything below those fabulous collarbones. Slipping in next to her, I take her hand. She turns to me, tilting her head to rest it against my shoulder.

'Things won't be weird now, will they?' Concern mists her bright eyes when she glances up at me.

I kiss her forehead gently. 'No, sweetheart, things won't be weird, but we'll need to be careful around Millie. I don't want to get her hopes up too soon.'

Kerry takes a large mouthful of champagne, then another and another. She thrusts her empty glass forward for a refill.

I hope I haven't upset her. I want to tell Millie, but I need to make sure Kerry's planning on sticking around first, especially after seeing the travel brochure. But that conversation is too serious for tonight, I have no intention of terrifying her this early on in our relationship. If that's what this even is. Her friends with benefits remark sticks in the back of my throat – I won't swallow that one easily, but it at least opened the door for me.

'Is that ok?' I lift her onto my lap and she wraps her legs around my waist again. It's where they belong, where she belongs – with me. I knew it from day one. Ironic that Clodagh was the one who delivered her to me, in a round-about way, by leaving.

'Of course, the last thing I want is to confuse Millie.'

'Let's just enjoy tonight.' My lips find hers and push them apart. Her tongue rushes to meet mine, twisting, tasting and exploring. She grinds herself against me in a manner that's only going to end one way.

The following morning, the detangling of our various limbs rouses me from the deep dreamless sleep I'd fallen into. Fighting the heaviness from my eyes, I blink them open, dazzled by the early morning rays streaming in. Kerry slips from between the satin sheets of my bed into a upright perched position on the edge. Though my body silently screams in protest, I don't stop her, unsure if despite our promises things might be a little weird between us.

I needn't have worried. She glances backwards over her shoulder, a grin beaming from ear to ear, with her finger pressed against her parted lips in a shh motion.

'What time is it?' I catch her arm, reluctant to let her slip out of the bed it took me so long to get her in to.

'It's six-thirty and I promised a little princess she could have pancakes for breakfast this morning.' She pulls her hand back and reaches for the t-shirt I had on last night, which I discarded on top of my laundry basket when we came up.

'Have a sleep in, I'll take care of things.' She presses a tender kiss on my cheek.

'You really are my dream woman, you know that right?' I pull her in for one more kiss, this time on her full mouth, hoping my morning breath isn't enough to put her off forever.

She stands with a smile. 'It's my job.'

'Ok, but tomorrow, I want you to have a lie-in. You don't work Sundays, but if you choose to spend the day with us, I'll make it worth your while.'

'Promises, promises.'

I roll on to the pillow she slept on and inhale the material, searching for the scent of her perfume. It's faint but it's there. Fucking hell, if the lads could see me now I'd never live this down. Mind you, if they could have seen her eight hours earlier, they'd understand.

From the floor below I hear the sound of the electronic whisk rotating. No matter how tightly I close my eyes, sleep will not return. The churning excitement in my stomach makes sure of it.

CHAPTER TWENTY-SEVEN

KERRY

In the kitchen, I flick on the radio and do a ridiculous girly jig around the table before hugging myself. Mind-blowing sex with Nathan certainly provided the release I was looking for, but the trouble is, it's like the warnings we're given about taking drugs – one hit is never going to be enough. I've only just crept out of his bed and I'm already wondering when I'll be able to get back into it.

I whisk the batter for the pancakes I'd promised Millie and try unsuccessfully to wipe the smile from my face. Footsteps approach from behind. Instead of being startled, I'm thrilled. Familiar, muscular arms slide either side of my waist as I work. Nathan's mouth nuzzles the back of my neck, his bare chest rests against my back, his chin on my shoulder and his morning glory, barely concealed in tight black boxers, presses into my back.

'Just can't stay away, can you?' My hands are occupied with the task in hand, but I grind my bum against him to show the feeling's mutual.

'Did I mention I've waited a year to get my hands on you? That's a lot of fantasies I've accumulated and need to act out. Come back to bed. She won't be awake for another hour at least.' His mouth gently tugs at the sensitive skin on my earlobe. Lust sears through me as his hands slip under my t-shirt – his t-shirt – to caress the tingling skin of my breasts.

I place the whisk on the counter and spin around. 'Do all of these fantasies revolve around the bedroom?' A meaningful glance at the kitchen table sets his eyes darkening lustily.

'Oh, Kerry, I knew you were going to be trouble.' He scoops me into his arms, as if I weigh nothing, and my legs automatically wrap around his waist. He kicks the kitchen door closed, before placing me on my back, spreadeagled on the cold wood.

'Do you know how crazy I've been going? Sitting next to you on the couch with these legs begging me to spread them?' His hands grip the insides of my thighs, spreading them while his hungry eyes roam over me like I'm a long-awaited Christmas present.

I gaze up at him as his enormous frame towers over me. Despite the sheer size of him, there's a gentleness in his eyes, a tenderness in his stare. 'About as crazy as I've been going, when you walk around shirtless with that ripped body on display, begging to be touched.'

A noise on the stairs has me leaping up from the table, as Nathan drops onto the nearest seat.

'Morning, Kerry. Morning, Daddy.' Millie flies through the door wearing her favourite *Frozen* nighty, with Captain Barnacles shoved under her arm. She runs to the counter where I'm clutching the whisk again. I hug her into me and for the first time in my life I glimpse what it might be like to truly be a mother. It doesn't matter what I want, or how badly I want it. This little girl comes first, always.

'Good morning, honey. Did you sleep well? How's Captain Barnacles this morning?'

'He heard the whisk and begged me to get up.'

Nathan lets out a tut from his position at the table. 'We'll have to start making the batter in the evenings. Can't have Captain Barnacles waking up so early again, can we?'

He mouths 'sorry' across the room. He has no need to apologise for the fact he has a gorgeous daughter who happens to be excited about chocolate pancakes on a Saturday morning. I hope my expression relays this.

'How about another driving lesson today, Kerry? Will I ring Nanny Nuala and see if she can pop over for a while?'

'Yeah!' Sheer joy glistens in Millie's eyes at the prospect. 'Nanny always lets me eat three lollipops, as long as I promise not to tell you we stopped in the betting shop.' Millie's hands fly over her mouth as she realises she let the cat out of the bag.

'What?' An unfamiliar sternness infiltrates Nathan's voice.

'I'm not actually allowed in, but I wait in the doorway with the treats.'

Nathan's eyes lock with mine, a frown flickering across his face. 'If she's going to continue placing bets, I'm going to have to at least teach her how to do it online.' His head shakes, irritation flaring along with his nostrils.

'Perhaps we shouldn't ring Nanny Nuala today? We could just hang out here, or maybe go to the park or something?' I'm in no rush for the driving lessons really. As much as I'd like to pass my test, my favourite part about the lessons is being locked in a confined space with Nathan, and somehow, I don't think that's going to be limited to the car now.

And I don't want Millie being somewhere she shouldn't be.

'Awwwww, please, Daddy? I didn't see her since last week. Please?' Millie's pleading eyes meet mine, silently looking for support. I won't go against Nathan, she's his daughter, I just work here. Although the situation's quickly becoming as entangled as Nathan's recently vacated bedsheets.

He runs a hand over his dirty blond stubble thoughtfully. 'I'll call her and invite her over for breakfast. By the look of it, I'm going to have to have a word with her anyway.'

Two hours later, Nuala walks in the front door, letting herself in as usual. I make a mental note to take that into consideration as well, next time I'm contemplating having kitchen sex with her son, my boss. She's very easy going, but it might be a bit much, even for her.

The faint smell of smoke surrounds her platinum bob, as she leans in to greet me. Nuala's heavily made-up eyes take in my summery shift dress and red pumps. A grin pulls at the sides of her weathered lips. 'You've gone and done it, haven't you, girl?'

Heat floods my neck, crawling into my cheeks. I'm quickly saved by Nathan entering the room, dressed in shorts and a tight white t-shirt, sunglasses tucked into the front of his collar.

'Morning, Ma. Give poor Kerry a rest, will you?' He crosses the room and kisses her on the cheek.

'I'll have to.' Nuala shoots a conspiratorial wink at me. 'It looks like she didn't get much last night.'

I hold my hands up, admitting defeat. My own grin is as wide as Nuala's. I'm not sure why she's so excited about the idea of her son and I getting it on, but who am I to comment?

'Well thank god for that, I thought you two would never get your act together! You're far nicer than those giraffe-like models he used to strut around with, all legs and no feckin' personality. The only craic you'd see with them is their arse crack in one of those daft miniskirts.' Her nose scrunches distastefully. 'Then, they'd have the cheek to look down their noses at me!'

'Mam, you only met Serena once, and she—' Nathan's cut off by Nuala's raspy smoker voice.

'Once was enough. This one here is much more down to earth. Literally.' Her head jerks in my direction and I don't even mind the short girl reference.

'It's early days.' I shrug in fake nonchalance, barely daring to meet Nathan's eye.

Millie trundles down the stairs just as Nuala says, 'Welcome to the family, pet.' She pats my arm in an affectionate gesture as Nathan visibly cringes across the room. Is he cringing at his mam embarrassing him? Or at the idea of me potentially getting big ideas about being part of his family. He said he wanted me, but he gave no indication of it being more than sexual.

'Is Kerry in our family now?' Millie's innocent eyes dart between Nathan and me, hope dancing before her button nose.

We are all saved by the ringing of the house phone. It'll be Clodagh. She rings every Saturday morning without fail, regaling Millie with all the glamourous places she's been and all the fabulous people she's met along the way. I don't know why she never FaceTimes, maybe she doesn't want to see us all here in the background playing happy families while she's away pursuing her dreams.

'Mammy!' Millie yanks the cordless phone from the receiver and heads to the sitting room to chat to her mother.

'Mam, never mind about Kerry and me, Millie says you've been in the bookies again.' Nathan crosses his arms over his broad chest and glowers.

'Pah! What's wrong with a little flutter now and again? It's only a couple of quid here and there. It's not like we can't afford it.' She straightens her back defensively.

'That's not the point. It's a bad habit and you shouldn't be bringing Millie. Jesus, Mam, can you imagine if the press got a picture of my daughter hanging around outside a betting shop – alone – while her nanny has "a little flutter" inside? No amount of lollipops could sugarcoat that story. And don't even get me started on the clientele.'

She has the grace to look at the floor.

'It's only a bit of craic. It's ok for you, with your rugby and your teammates and your new girlfriend.' She jerks her head at me again. 'Did you ever stop to think about me? I'm lonely. I'm grateful I don't have to work anymore, don't have to scrape together enough money to get by. But with that gone, I've lost me purpose, son. I don't exactly fit in with the ladies who lunch type, do I? The pub or the bookies are the only two places I feel comfortable. I've known those people, "the clientele", for my entire life. They're decent, grounded people. They don't judge me. And they don't hound me about my superstar son. They just accept me, like they have done for the last twenty years.'

I glance from her to Nathan, rapidly getting the feeling this is a private conversation, one that I shouldn't be witnessing.

'Look, Mam, I get that, I do. But you can't put Millie at risk like that.'

'She's not at risk, sure you were raised the same way and you turned out fine.'

Nathan sighs, he seems to be getting nowhere fast. 'Mam, I'm going to ask you one more time, please do not take my daughter to another beer garden, or another bookies. If you don't want to take her for an afternoon, I'll get a babysitter.'

I cough and look at the floor, technically, that's what he's paying me for.

'You're missing me point, son. I don't take her because I can't stay away from these places for a day or two; I take her because my friends like to see her.' Nuala lets out a long sigh and scrambles in her handbag for something.

'Don't even think about lighting up a cigarette in here.' Nathan's eyes roll to the ceiling.

'Jees, you're an awful dry shite, son.' Nuala winks at me as she passes through the kitchen to the back door.

'No more pubs and no more bookies! And don't smoke around her, it's not good for her asthma,' Nathan reinforces.

'Fine.' Nuala doesn't glance back, only stopping to kiss Millie's head, where she sits on the couch talking to her mother.

'We don't have to go anywhere.' I cross the kitchen and stroke his hand.

'She needs to spend time with her nan. She's already missing her mother, I can't take her granny as well.'

CHAPTER TWENTY-EIGHT

NATHAN

Half an hour and another stern warning to my mam later, we're in the car again. Kerry's driving has improved dramatically since the first time I took her out. Still, I don't chance distracting her, even though my hand itches to rest on her thigh. The silence between us is deafening. There are so many questions I want to ask her, like if it was as good as she'd expected, if we're a thing now and most importantly, if she's dismissed her ideas about travelling.

'So...' Kerry chances a sidewards glance at me.

'Eyes on the road, lady. At least this way I can ogle you for hours.' It's on the tip of my tongue to suggest we book her driving test, though that means our lessons will be over, although if last night was anything to go by, there's a lot of other things we could teach each other.

She snorts. 'There's not much to look at, it should only take you a few seconds.'

'Why do you always put yourself down? How many times

will I have to tell you you're gorgeous before you'll actually believe it?'

'Hello, have you met my friends? They're like a couple of Alice in Wonderlands and I'm like Tweedle-fucking-Dum.' She snorts again and shrugs.

'Alice always was a bit too obvious, with her long hair and hallucinations. I like that you are very much what you see is what you get. No airs or graces, no bullshit.'

'Are you trying to say my friends have personality disorders?' Kerry's laughter erupts around the car.

'No, but Emma certainly has Eddie by the balls. You wouldn't expect that type of strength from a cosmetic queen.' It's on the tip of my tongue to ask if she'll tell them about us. 'We should invite them over again, they never did get into the jacuzzi that time.' I'm deliberately dangling the carrot to see if she'll take it, testing the water to see if we are going to be an ongoing item – the friends with benefits remark still haunting me from the night before. I don't want to be her friend with benefits. I want to be her fucking everything.

'I think we should leave it a few weeks.' Kerry's eyes dart to me again and she licks her lips, her subliminal body language screaming to me.

'Oh really? Why's that?'

'That tub is going to be occupied every night for the next few weeks at least. And I'm all for a bit of kinky sex, but being watched by your teammates and my friends does not fall into that category.'

'Well, I can't wait to see what does.'

We drive to Dundrum shopping centre. Kerry manages to park the car into a pretty tight spot. It's no joke, even I struggle with these tiny multistorey parking spaces in the Jeep.

'Do you think Millie's ok?' she asks, switching off the

engine. My heart floods with warmth at her concern for my daughter.

'Yes. I don't honestly think my mam would let anything happen to her, but still, I don't want her in those type of places.'

'Do you want my opinion?' Kerry turns in her seat to face me.

'Go on.'

'I think your mam is bored. She's got too much time on her hands by the sounds of it. She needs a hobby, something productive. What does she like doing?'

'She likes drinking, smoking and gambling. As you can tell, she's not your average granny.'

'We need to find a way to utilise that. Like, how about you ask her to organise a charity casino night or something? Or a day at the races? Let your mam organise it and run the show? She'd be well able and it would put her unusual talents to good use.'

Leaning across the centre console, I tilt Kerry's chin up towards mine to meet her silvery eyes. 'You, Kerry Walsh, may just be a keeper.' A blush flushes across her neck and I battle not to stare.

'If you keep looking at me like that we're going to end up steaming up the windows with some filthy car sex. It might not be entirely appropriate in the middle of Dundrum parking facility.'

'The way I want you, I'd nearly do it anyway.'

'Tonight. All good things come to those who wait.' She winks at me.

We spend a couple of hours trudging round the shops, Kerry is easily pleased, so different to the high maintenance girls I'd dated since Clodagh and I split. She seems happier with H&M and Zara, than Harvey Nichols.

'You do realise we're in the kids department?' I ask, when she picks up a black sequinned dress for a thirteen year old.

'Hello?' She flicks a hand over the front of the dress she's wearing. 'I'd drown in actual grown-up clothes. Besides, this way, I can get myself and Mills matching outfits.' Her grin extends all the way to the crinkles of her eyes.

I love the way she loves my daughter. I love the way she abbreviates her name with affection. I love how she didn't bat an eyelid when we were interrupted this morning, even though her body was blatantly screaming for me only seconds earlier. If that had been Serena, I'd say she'd have left in a huff in search of a vibrator. Fuck it, there's only so long I can deny it to myself, I love everything about her. I'm falling in love with the nanny, there's nothing surer.

Watching her exit the dressing room and twirling round in a variety of different outfits, not only sends blood rushing below, but that warm fuzzy feeling floods through my insides. I never had this with Clodagh. Or anyone else for that matter. Kerry's so fucking refreshing, and we fit together like we were meant to be together. I've got it bad.

Later in the evening, we sit in the hot tub, Kerry's legs wrapped deliciously round my waist as she rocks back and forth on top of me. I silently thank my lucky stars it was her agency I rang two months ago. I can't get rid of the feeling she was meant to be here. Suddenly, and inappropriately, her earlier remark flashes through my mind, the comment about the hot tub *we should leave it a few weeks.*

Surely she can't still be thinking of leaving at the end of the three months? I can only assume she's staying, especially when she's grinding herself against me and murmuring she could do this forever.

CHAPTER TWENTY-NINE

KERRY

For two blissful weeks now, I've been having filthy, rampant sex with one of Ireland's most eligible men. What he doesn't do to me… And my friends want all the details, my real friends that is, not my drinking buddies. Mags' texts have stopped. She's given up trying to drag me out to get rip-roaring drunk and frankly it's a relief.

'Girls, please, I'm not going to divulge details about Nathan's private anatomy.' I roll my eyes and take a sip from the mojito in front of me. We're out for dinner at TGI Friday's in the city, a long overdue girls night out. 'Suffice to say, that not only is it impressive,' I wrap two hands round my cocktail glass and grip it suggestively, 'but what he knows how to do with it is even more impressive.'

Karen snorts doubtfully and nudges Fran. My lesbian friends stick their tongues out at me in unison and Abby and Emma convulse with laughter. 'Oh, girls, you have no idea what you're missing out on.' We had to stop calling Karen,

Ellen, her nickname, once she came out because of the actual Ellen scandal.

When the laughter dies down, Emma leans across the table. 'So, are you two like official, or what?'

That's the weird thing. We haven't talked about it. And he's still paying me to mind his daughter, something I'd happily do for free, especially if I'm his girlfriend. But a niggle deep down taunts me, whispering he's still paying me because it's easier to keep me round as an employee, than commit to being a couple. Normally, I'd vomit it straight out but for some reason, I can't just spit this one out, secretly, I think I'm terrified of the answer.

'Ah, we're just keeping it casual, for now.' My hand swats the air in front of me, dismissing the question that's been internally bugging me.

My original due date to finish in a few weeks and he hasn't brought up me staying on again. It's a conversation we're going to have to have, at some point. Each night I get into his bed. Each night we make love, like it's actually love. He caresses me with a tenderness I've never experienced before. The next morning, we go back to being normal, slightly distant even, so as not to confuse Millie. Yet, the person who's most confused is me.

'Anyway, did you get your invitations to Nuala's charity horse racing event? It's going to be epic, like bringing the Galway races to Dublin. Better get digging out your frocks and fascinators, ladies.' I take another sip of my drink, washing away the niggling trace of worry that's threatening to ruin my evening.

'Yes, it looks class. Such a good idea!' Abby says, flicking her glossy blonde hair from her face. I glance between her and Emma, taking in their composure, confidence and natural allure. Is it any wonder Nathan hasn't asked me to be official with him?

I don't fit in the players' lounge with these two successful beauties, even if they have been my friends for years. Apart from my obvious plainness, I'm basically a well-paid au pair, still completely lacking in any direction, a fact my father reminded me of again earlier on the phone. I didn't think to tell them I'd been too busy shagging my boss to contemplate my future.

Yet again, I'm stuck in a rut waiting for a man to decide the fate of my life, to decide if I'm staying or going. I've accidentally given Nathan all the control, instead of voicing what I want, because yet again, I still don't know exactly what that is. Ok, I want him, but I can't be his nanny forever. It was supposed to be a stopgap, until Craig came home, yet, I've pushed all thought of the future out of my head and replaced it with blind lust, living only in the here and now.

Am I any better off than I was at twenty-one – a bit on the side, someone to sleep with but not to openly commit to? Hell, when I think about it, even Craig kept me at arm's length, in his little box which he used to open and play with whenever he felt like. Kerry The Good-Time Girl, that's all I've ever been good for.

No. I force the dark thoughts away, Nathan is nothing like Married Martin, or Craig for that matter. He's not stringing me along, he's just not outwardly labelling us. I order another drink, then another, determined to obliterate the worries invading my gut.

'Easy, tiger.' Abby places a hand on my arm and eyes the mojito. 'Everything ok? Her voice is low enough not to be heard by the others, who are debating which bar to go to next.

'Everything is fucking dandy.' The alcohol is raging through my blood and I can't hide the bitterness in my tone.

'Let's get some air.' Abby pulls me up from the table and I pretend not to see the six fingers she holds up to Emma, behind my back. They tease me relentlessly about The Kerry Scale, and believe me, I know I'm teetering on the edge. But tonight, I need a release and not one delivered by my boss-cum-lover.

'What's up, sweetie?' Abby stands in the courtyard with me, her doe eyes examining my face for any tell-tale clues.

'It's Nathan. I think I might be in love with him.' Drunk Kerry is in full swing. What little filter I own, I swallowed with my third cocktail.

'And? That's great, isn't it?' Abby rubs my arm in a supportive gesture.

'It would be, if he felt the same. I'm supposed to be finishing up nannying for Millie in a couple of weeks, the summer's drawing to an end and he hasn't asked me to stay, or even mentioned it. Now we're having sex, I feel really weird about taking his money, but I don't want to tell him I won't take it, in case he thinks I'm getting ahead of myself, making assumptions about a permanent role in his life and forcing my way in.'

I don't voice my biggest worry, no matter how drunk I get, I know I'll never say this one out loud. Nathan's the only person I've ever said it to, and even then I assumed he was a complete stranger I was never likely to meet in person.

I'm worried that he won't want me long term because he knows I'm broken. He knows I can't have children. And he is the most amazing father ever, so he's bound to want more. Which leaves me utterly useless to him, and utterly helpless about the fact I'm falling in love with him.

'Seriously, Kerry? The man is mad about you. Those lads don't let just anyone into the players' lounge. Jesus, he trusts you with his daughter, his pride and joy, and he drools watching you mother her.' I visibly flinch at that remark.

'Then why hasn't he asked me to stay?' I wipe a stray tear

away from my cheek, telling myself it's the drink that has me upset, not my escalating feelings for my boss.

'Talk to him, Kerry, you're normally an open book. Just tell him what's on your mind.'

She passes me a tissue from her back pocket and I dab my eyes, trying not to smudge my make-up. 'Ok. Let's go.' I tug her hand back into the restaurant, so I can grab my bag and flag a taxi. Abby's right. No time like the present.

Abby's pink lips form a perfect little o. 'You're leaving now?'

'Yes, didn't you tell me to sort it out? That's what I'm going to do.'

Karen and Fran wave goodbye. I hear Emma ask Abby if I'm ok as I strut away. I need to do this now, while I'm feeling brave enough.

CHAPTER THIRTY

NATHAN

The couch seems ridiculously big without Kerry here to share it with. She's on a well-deserved night out with the girls. It doesn't stop me pining for her like a love-sick puppy, wondering who she's talking to, or what time she's coming home – shit – what if she doesn't come home? Technically, we aren't official, I haven't been able to officially ask if I'm her boyfriend, it sounds so childish and despite her tiny size, she is all woman.

And after enduring eight years of suffering under Craig's tight control, I don't want to pressure her into the commitment of being my girlfriend, even though that's exactly what I'm dying to do. And being the way that she is, if she wanted it, surely she'd just come out and say it. But what do I expect? I'm tied here and my life revolves around Millie. I've always known it would be a hard sell for any woman, but for Kerry, who seems mad set on travelling and partying, it's barely even worth asking.

The crystal tumbler in my hand contains a large measure

of Jameson, but the whiskey burn doesn't come close to the fire Kerry's ignited in me. I'm clock-watching and scrolling through my phone, waiting for Kerry to come home.

Just before midnight, the sound of an engine slows outside the front door. Damn, I told Kerry I'd get a car for her. She doesn't need to rely on taxis when I have access to a private chauffeur twenty-four seven. I hold my breath, kicking my feet up on the sofa in a relaxed pose, waiting for the sound of the key in the door, but it doesn't come. She's probably tipsy and struggling to find it in her bag.

My bare feet pad across the thick carpet, out into the hall. Barbie's snoring outside Millie's door. Some guard dog she is. I peer out the peep hole, laughing to myself as I realise Kerry would be below the eye line of it anyway. Opening the door, the sound of distant crickets pierce the night air. Kerry perches on the bottom step with her back to the front door. Her head angles upwards, gazing at the bright crescent moon and a hundred tiny stars blotting against the midnight sky.

'Aren't you coming in?' I announce my presence so as not to startle her, put the door on the lock and perch next to her.

Her face tilts towards me and she squints, slightly worse for wear, but a small smile curls at the corners of her lips. 'Just thinking.'

'About what?'

'You. Us. Everything.' She shimmies closer towards me on the concrete and I drop an arm over her shoulder. 'We need to talk.' And there it is, like a bullet between the eyes, the girl I'm used to, the one that says exactly what's on her mind, no matter how inappropriate.

I cough to mask my nerves. 'Should I be worried?'

'I don't know. I guess it depends what you want.'

My hand automatically goes to her thigh, fingers squeezing her bare flesh gently. 'What I want is you. Anyway I can have you.' I hope my eyes convey I'm not just talking about the physical. She has to know that I'm in love with her, even if I haven't said it outright. I can't bear the thought of her leaving in a couple of weeks. It's only my terror at terrifying her that prevents me from shouting it from the rooftops.

'Are we talking about in or out of the bedroom?'

'Both. You were the one who mentioned friends with benefits.'

'I was, wasn't I?' The top she wears has no straps and the moonlight reflects off the sharp contours of her bare shoulders, deliciously illuminating her skin. Every inch of her begs to be kissed. I'm tempted to start now and not give her the chance to say what she has to say because I'm terrified it won't be what I want to hear. Either way, I need to hear it and hopefully she'll let me kiss her anyway. I swallow back my desire long enough to tell her how I feel.

'You're just out of a long-term relationship. The last thing I want to do is put pressure on you, but seriously, Kerry, I think if we gave it a proper go, became a proper couple, we'd be unstoppable.'

She bites her lower lip and swallows hard. 'I'd like that. A lot.'

Her hand finds mine and rests over it, on top of her leg. Earnest eyes gaze up at me intently. 'You don't mind that I'm...'

'What?'

'Broken?' The word comes out as a whisper, and I pull her into a tight hug.

'Sweetheart, we are all broken. That's how the light gets in.' I'd heard that particular saying a long time ago and it resonated with me ever since.

She sniffs the front of my white shirt, inhaling the material. 'You're not broken.'

'Don't believe it for a second, we all are. Everyone has a

story in this life, no one makes it this far without accumulating a few scars. And you, Kerry Walsh, are no more broken
than anyone else.'

'But I can't have children.' She pulls back and wipes a
stray tear from her eye with the back of her hand.

'You might not be able to bear children of your own, but
you can still have them. Look at the way you mother Millie.
And I'm not sure if I ever told you this, but I'm happy with
the one I have. Parenting is hard work. I wouldn't be without
Millie, but with the hours I'm away training and on tours, it
wouldn't be fair to have any more.'

'Seriously? You don't want more children?' She sits up a
little straighter and blinks back the tears.

My lips find her forehead to press a reassuring kiss
against. 'It's a decision I made long before I met you.'

She releases a pent up sigh. 'Sometimes I feel so fucked up
on the inside. That's why I used to get so obliterated with
drink. It was my way of escaping. Since I've met you, I've
barely felt the need. You do something to me.'

'I can assure you, the feeling's mutual. You've fitted into
this house and made it a home with your cooking and baking
and singing. The thought of you leaving at the end of the
summer is unbearable – I want you to stay. But I don't want
to terrify you either. You've spent the last eight years living in
Craig's shadow, even when he's been a million miles away. And
you've been carrying a huge secret round with you for years,
carrying the weight of what that married man did to you, like
you deserved it. Kerry, you are the most amazing woman I've
ever met, the only person that doesn't see it, is you.'

'Do you really think so?'

'I know so.' I plant a kiss on her forehead. 'Will you think
about staying?'

'I don't need to think about it. I'm in, but we need to
negotiate the pay.'

'Sweetheart, you can have a raise, you can have a uniform, you can have whatever you like, just don't go.'

'I don't want a raise, you eejit!' She smacks my arms and scoffs. 'If I'm your girlfriend, I'm not taking money to mind your daughter. I can't. It's not right, and besides, I enjoy being with her too much to call it work.'

'It's ok to enjoy your job. I enjoy mine.' I shoot her a sideways glance, barely able to keep the grin from my face. 'Besides, if you don't fulfil the nanny role, I'll have to get another one and then she might start giving me eyes across the kitchen, or rubbing her breasts in front of me, hell, she might even brush them against me in the corridor.'

'Huh. Ok, I'll keep the job, but please, a fraction of the money would be more than enough. You give me so much, just by being you. The girls are great, but you're the closest thing I have to a best friend.'

'Don't think you can start holding out on me now that we're official though. I might be your best friend, but I'm going to do things to you that any other friend can only dream of. And I haven't ruled out the uniform idea either.'

Though she's sitting right next to me, she's still too far away. I sweep her up into my arms and carry her across the threshold. 'Welcome home, sweetheart.'

I kick the front door closed with my foot and take Kerry's clothes off in the hall.

CHAPTER THIRTY-ONE

KERRY

The following morning when Millie wakes, I'm still entangled in Nathan's bedsheets. It's the first time she's seeing us together as a couple and to me, it feels massively significant. Though, apparently Millie doesn't feel the same way. She lurks in the doorway I had every intention of sneaking out of, but I overslept. Nathan had me up late. A smile twitches on my lips at the memory.

'Are you guys in love now, or what?' Captain Barnacles is stuffed under one arm and her other arm rests on her hip in a very grown-up gesture.

'Hmm?' Nathan stirs, turns over and blinks his eyes open. As he rubs the sleep from them, his biceps flex and those tattoos curl. How can this man officially be mine? Still, Millie's question is one that's not a million miles from my mind.

'Are you guys getting married?' Millie runs across the room and hops under the covers in between us, as if she's done it a hundred times before. Thankfully, I had the foresight to put one of Nathan's t-shirts on before falling asleep.

'No, sweetheart, not right now.' Nathan winks at me and shrugs. 'Would you mind if we did though?'

Her tiny features glance between us as she contemplates the notion. 'Would I still be your princess?'

'You'll always be my princess, even when your thirty.' He reaches up to ruffle her hair, before flopping back down on the pillow.

'Thirty's ancient,' Millie says.

'Thanks, Millie!' I nudge her in mock indignation, but she does have a point. I am six years older than her daddy. It's a thought that used to bother me, but since he's so much bigger than me and mentally more mature, it's no longer an issue – not for me anyway.

'Mrs Robinson,' Nathan teases.

Millie picks up Captain Barnacles and leaps from the bed again. 'Can we have pancakes for breakfast?'

'Sure.' And that's the end of the conversation about Nathan and me. Millie simply accepts it, the way that children do. Though that doesn't stop her from telling her mother when she calls a couple of hours later.

The outrage is audible through the phone, twenty feet across the room, where Millie has Clodagh on speaker.

'He's what? Put your daddy on the phone, right now.' Millie winces as she crosses the kitchen and hands the phone over to Nathan who rolls his eyes. There are no secrets where children are concerned.

'Clodagh?' He runs his fingers through his messy, bed hair.

'I can't believe you're shagging the fucking nanny, Nathan! Fucking hell, what kind of an example does that set to our daughter?' Her rage exceeds anything I'd anticipated – they've been split for almost two years, and it's not like she doesn't know he dates occasionally.

'Relax, Clodagh. Everything is fine. Millie's happy, we're happy, everything is fine.'

'Everything is not fine! You've shacked up with some floozy, in MY house, with MY daughter and you're seriously telling me everything is fine.' Her anger ripples in thunderous waves between us.

Nathan mouths 'sorry' at me, as I stand rooted to the spot, unable to simply walk away, like I know I probably should. The depth of her anger surprises me. As far as I'm aware, he ended it, but she left willingly.

'How old is she anyway? I hope she's legal, Nathan.'

I snort; that's one thing she doesn't need to worry about, anyway.

'Might I remind you, my love life is none of your concern.'

'So you love her?' Clodagh's voice cracks with a deep heartfelt emotion, and for a split second I almost feel sorry for her. Imagine having a man like Nathan, then losing him. A shudder ripples through my spine at the sheer thought.

Silence hangs heavily in the air. I wait for his answer with bated breath. I love him, of that I'm sure. But is the feeling mutual?

'Look, Clodagh, it's early days. Please give me a break. You're doing what you always wanted to do. Now go and enjoy yourself. Millie is happy, she's well cared for, and we'll see you the second you're back on dry land.'

Apparently Nathan knows how to placate his ex because her voice lowers significantly enough for me not to be able to hear it after that. Other than the odd, 'uh huh' and 'of course' from Nathan, I don't get any more of the conversation.

I head upstairs to get ready and to clear my head, unsure why I suddenly feel pissed off with Nathan. What did I expect? Him to declare his love for me to his ex? Still, it burned when he didn't. Especially when it was the second time this morning he was asked and both times he refused to confirm his feelings.

Pulling on a white shirt and denim skirt, I send up a silent prayer that I'm not setting myself up for a major fall here. The worrying thing is, I've already fallen...

CHAPTER THIRTY-TWO

NATHAN

The end of the summer holidays is looming; it's time we got Millie's school books and her new uniform. Thankfully Kerry's agreed to go shopping with us because personally, I find traipsing round the kids department alone torturous. Kerry and Millie walk ahead of me, holding hands, discussing the merits of having fire or ice as a superpower. The *Frozen* obsession has continued longer than any other Disney obsession. I can't wait to see Millie's face when I tell Euro Disney is booked for two weeks time. Or Kerry's for that matter.

Now that Kerry and I are official, she no longer sleeps on the top floor, the only place she sleeps is on top of my chest. She's slipped into every part of my life so effortlessly, like she was always meant to be here. It's almost too good to be true. Each morning, Millie creeps into bed with us – we've come a long way from that awkward hug on the first morning.

Kerry glances backwards over her shoulder and winks at me, sending a rush of love through my previously hollow chest. Oh I love her, there's no doubt about it. Though I still haven't said those words yet, they radiate from every part of me each time I'm inside her, which is daily at the moment.

My stomach growls, reminding me it's way past lunchtime. 'Are you ladies hungry?' Their pace slows to a crawl and I catch up to them with two long strides.

'Can we please go to Nando's?' Kerry asks Millie, as though it's naturally her choice.

'Sure. Do you think they do lollipops?' Hope lights in her sparkling eyes.

'Maybe if you eat your dinner you can have an ice cream.' I ruffle her hair, take her free hand and she swings between myself and Kerry, happier than a kid in a toy shop.

Nando's is busy, it always is. We find a free table and I go up to order the food and a Tiger beer for Kerry and me. When I return, the table next to us is being vacated. I slide Kerry's drink over to her and give Millie her glass to fill from the machine a few metres away.

'She's a great kid,' Kerry says, before taking a sip of her beer.

'She adores you.' I take Kerry's hand across the table.

'The feeling is mutual. I never thought I'd get to take a little girl shopping, spoil her and do all the girly things we get to do.' Kerry's eyes mist wistfully, she blinks twice and turns her attention to me.

Picking up the beer mat from the table, I tap it on the wood, mimicking the sound of a drum roll, as Millie returns, clutching her fizzy orange in two hands.

'So I've got a surprise for you, girls.'

'A surprise?' Millie shrieks. 'I love surprises!'

Kerry groans. 'I hate surprises. Tell us, please. Put me out of my misery.'

A low chuckle falls from my lips. 'You'll like this one, trust me.'

She rolls her eyes. 'The suspense is killing me.'

'I booked Euro Disney for the end of the month.' I say the words slowly, deliberately drawing them out for effect.

'Shut the front door!' Kerry shrieks and Millie leaps from the table excitedly, almost knocking orange everywhere.

'Serious, Dad? Am I big enough for the rides now?' She squashes onto my knee and throws her little arms round my neck.

'Oh oh.' Kerry shakes her head. 'Am I big enough for the rides?' She slaps the table hard, laughing at herself.

'You'll both be able to go on the same ones, at least.' Millie leaps off my lap and sits between us again. Millie chats excitedly about all the characters she'd like to meet. A warm glow inches into Kerry's cheeks, as she answers Millie, but continues to glance up at me with an almost coy smile.

'What on earth did I do to deserve you?' she murmurs over Millie's head.

'It might not be the travel arrangements you were planning, but I'll help you tick off a few from your bucket list, a week or two at a time.'

'It's better than my lonely plans, trust me. And would you believe I don't have a bucket list?'

'What? You've got to be joking me? We'll write one tonight when we get the little lady to bed.'

'Well what's on yours?'

'Oh just the usual.' I shrug to show I'm joking before adding, 'World domination. I want to make team captain one day, a multimillion euro sponsorship deal with Calvin Klein and I'd like to marry a woman that makes me laugh every day of my life.'

'You're so funny.' I don't tell her I'm not joking. I've always quietly striven for my dreams, only shouting about them after I've achieved them. No point talking the talk, if you can't walk the walk.

Kerry's face inches upwards towards mine and I lean in to brush my lips against hers. The sensation sends electricity shooting through my nerve endings. 'Roll on eight o'clock,' I whisper, but Kerry's staring straight past me, white faced and wide-eyed, like she's seen a ghost or something.

I glance over my shoulder in the direction of her gaze. All I can see is a blonde woman, sitting with a burly looking man with a crew cut. His back is to me, so I can't see his face, but his frame is broad and the shirt he wears clings to the muscles of his back. His military grade boots tap against the floor impatiently, as he leans closer to hear what his companion is saying. She has short bobbed blonde hair and an obscene amount of eye make-up on.

'Mags,' Kerry's voice is loaded with surprise, it comes out almost strangled.

'Your friend from work?' Kerry's mentioned her a couple of times.

'Yes, she's there with...'

Before Kerry can finish, Mags' male friend turns to look at us. An expression of surprise freezes into the weathered lines of his tanned face, his lips purse together in a frown and he shakes his head in a gesture of disgust.

Instinctively, I reach for Kerry's hand, but she's already taken Millie in her arms, who sits on her lap now, happily oblivious to whatever the fuck is going on.

My head swings back to the guy, he's vaguely familiar, though I can't quite place him. He rises from his seat and strides over to our table. I stand protectively in front of my girls, if his stance is anything to go by, he means trouble. He's a big man, but not quite as big as me. I weigh him up, certain I could take him, should it get that far.

'Well, this is fucking cosy, isn't it?' he practically spits.

Millie looks to me and shrinks further into Kerry's arms.

Before I can open my mouth, Kerry speaks in a low tone.

'Hi, Craig, this is Nathan. And this is Millie, his daughter.'

'I fucking knew it.' He visibly seethes, fists clenching and shaking with a rage that threatens to erupt before us.

'Language in front of my daughter please.' I battle the adrenaline pumping through my veins in an effort to remain calm.

'It's not what you think.' Kerry sighs, stroking Millie's hair. She glances round to see if the other diners have noticed, but it's so noisy and the table next to us is still vacant. Why would she try to deny we are a thing now? She should have told him straight.

'Do you know what? You're welcome to her. Cheats never prosper.' He turns on his heels and exits the restaurant, not bothering to say goodbye to his date.

Kerry slumps back in the chair and exhales.

'That was the man that lives in your phone,' Millie states.

'He doesn't live in my phone anymore. He lives in my past. And so does she.' Kerry shoots daggers at the blonde, who shrugs, mouths 'waste not, want not' and walks out of the restaurant.

'Apparently he lives in my friend's phone.' A look of puzzlement knits Kerry's brows together. 'I can't actually believe it.'

'You're better off without both of them.' I inch closer to plant a kiss on her soft lips, but they're firmly planted on my daughter's head, who has apparently forgotten all about the drama and is busy colouring her menu pink with the new colouring pens Kerry bought her for school.

I'm happy Millie is unaffected by the brief but intense scene, but I'd be happier if it was me Kerry was clinging to for support, instead of my daughter. Sometimes I wonder if she'd be as keen on me if I didn't have Millie, but I push that stupid thought away immediately. No one would willingly take on someone else's child if they weren't seriously into them. Even a person that couldn't biologically have their own.

We eat our chicken, slightly subdued, and I pray Craig's return won't have an impact on our new relationship. I've only just got her, I'm not prepared to lose her already.

CHAPTER THIRTY-THREE

KERRY

The following week is Nuala's big charity horse racing night. She's spent weeks organising it, and if it hasn't kept her out of the bookies and the pub, it's at least stopped her bringing Millie with her.

I try not to feel weird when the babysitter arrives. She introduces herself as Josie and is about twenty-four, with long legs captured in tight leggings and an Abercrombie hoody. Millie shows her her dolls, and introduces Captain Barnacles, before asking the girl if she wants to have a tea party.

I watch on, as if seeing myself in the girl's position the first time I came into this house. Nostalgia floods me, engulfing me in emotion as I remember experiencing it all first-hand.

'Will you be ok?' I check with Josie for the fifth time before we leave.

'We'll be fine. Enjoy yourself and don't worry about a thing.' Her tone is confident and very reassuring.

'Ok.' I gather my keys and purse. Nathan waits by the front door where a car awaits us.

'Give your mam a kiss now, Millie.' Josie nudges Millie forward and both of us laugh, but neither of us correct her.

'We'll check on you the second we get home. Have fun with Josie. And stay away from the lollipops, it's too close to bedtime.

'You will remember to brush her teeth?' I've turned into one of those fussy mothers, and Millie isn't even mine.

'Of course. Go, enjoy yourselves.'

I slide into the leather car seat next to Nathan, who eyes my backless dress appreciatively. 'You look stunning.'

'Ha! I'm trussed up like a bag of sprouts. Give me my denim shorts any day.'

We arrive at the event twenty minutes later, on the outskirts of the city, at a track that doesn't get much use anymore. Nuala somehow managed to persuade the latest Irish popstar to sing a few songs before the racing begins. Tickets cost two hundred and fifty euro a pop, and the charity selected is one for struggling single parents. I imagine it's one she might have turned to herself, once a upon a time.

The men congregate around the bar and the women have taken residence on the balcony, swooning over the up-and-coming twenty-three-year-old crooning about the power someone has over him.

Nuala's in her element, in a black long-sleeved cocktail dress, flitting from group to group, welcoming and thanking each and every person that arrives. The rugby team has a huge collective reach between its players and their partners. Abby for one provided massive marketing for this event on her radio show, giving away two tickets every day last week. Actresses I've only ever seen on television swan around the place like they own it.

Abby hangs off Callum's arm, wearing a baby-blue full-length dress, Emma's opted for a red knee-length sweetheart dress which nips in at all the right places. I mingle with the people I know and spend forty minutes giggling with Marcus's wife, Shelly, before settling in for a cocktail with Emma and Abby.

'Oh, girls, this is so perfect.' Emma fans herself with her hand. 'Who would have thought we three would have ended up bagging ourselves three rugby players?'

'Speak for yourself.' I nod at the enormous rock on the fourth finger of her left hand. 'It's early days for me yet.'

'Trust me, you guys are made for each other. Tell me, is it hard?' Emma's tone piques with curiosity.

'Well not right now, I hope.' I glance over to Nathan where he's talking to a gang of men in their sixties, clad in identical pinstriped suits.

Emma smacks my hand lightly and chuckles. 'Not that, I mean is it hard with Millie? Does she mind you guys being a couple? Does she worry you're trying to be her mam?'

I can't expect them to understand our situation – it's unique – they could never comprehend the void that Millie and I fill in each other's lives. Speaking of which, I better phone and check on her. A sense of guilt attacks me, I'm supposed to be her minder, not Josie.

'No. It's not hard at all. It's honestly a blessing I never thought I'd experience.'

Emma's perfectly pencilled eyebrows lift in surprise.

'I'm so happy it's all working out for you. I never had you pegged as the maternal sort.'

Huh, she got that right, just it was a decision that was taken from me, rather than one I consciously made.

'I'll be back in a few, just got to make a quick phone call.' I push through the crowd and make my way to the toilets to make the call. The phone rings continuously for four solid minutes, with no answer. It's odd, to say the least. I swallow down the anxiety that threatens to engulf me. My instincts are running high that something isn't right. I dial the number again, still no reply.

Glancing round, I search the place for Nathan, with no luck. A famous golfer stops to ask me where the toilets are, confirming what I already know – I look like the hired help. I glance down at my silver silk backless dress, it's beautiful, but I can't say it suits me. I want to go home.

Eventually I find Nathan, wedged between the same throng of men, not far from Abby and Callum. From memory of the last time I was here, I think they're on the board of directors.

'Nathan.' I touch his elbow and he pulls me into his chest.

'Guys, this is my girlfriend Kerry.' Pride taints his tone, and a swell of love rises in my chest, but it's not enough to ease the niggle within.

'She's a beauty.' A man with grey hair and oval glasses stoops to kiss my hand, his eyes lingering on my body a little longer than appropriate. 'Such a beautiful figure. She's like your very own life-size doll, Nathan.' A sexist chuckle rolls from his dirty mouth.

I snatch my hand back and Nathan drops an arm protectively over me.

'At least this one has the option of keeping her figure.' The man nudges Nathan. 'You've already provided a child for her to rear as her own. You and Millie are like the perfect microwave meal – pre-cooked and perfectly packaged.'

Red rage seethes beneath my eyelids and I turn on my heels, marching away before I say something I can't take back. Patronising bastard.

'Wait.' Nathan's straight on my heels, I barely reach the door before he catches me.

'I came to tell you the babysitter's not answering the

house phone. I'm going home to check on Millie, but after that, I'm not coming back.'

'Ah, Kerry, Millie probably pulled the phone out the wall playing hide and seek, you know what she's like. Don't let that silly old fool put you off. He's been involved in the club since the dark ages, and his views are plucked directly from there. Stay, Millie will be fine. The agency comes highly recommended, the girls are all Garda vetted. Millie will be snoring, safely in her bed. Let's just enjoy being out together with other adults for once.'

'I'm going, Nathan. Can you please get me a car?'

Disappointment darkens his cobalt eyes. He nods towards his mother, who stands with a microphone, ready to make her speech. 'You're overreacting. Millie will be fine. Relax, have a drink with your friends.' He nods towards Abby and Emma.

'I said I'm going, Nathan, I've got a bad feeling about this.'

'Are you sure it's not just an excuse, Kerry? Because you feel like you don't fit in here? I know you have this mad notion you're not as polished as some of the others and it's ridiculous.'

He's hit the nail on the head, I'm not comfortable here, not in the slightest, but my concern for Millie is genuine.

'I'll go check on her.'

Frustration ignites in Nathan's tone. 'For goodness sake, Kerry, she's fine, relax, will you.' He lets out a long, low sigh, before muttering, 'She's not even your kid.'

A hot stabbing pain pierces my gut. He only spoke the truth, yet those few words rip me apart. Foolishly, I'd allowed myself to fulfil the maternal duties, cooking, cleaning, raising a child, temporarily forgetting that whichever way you look at it, I'm still the hired help. I'm no better off than my mother, except I'm not even a mother. I turn on my heels and slink out the door before anyone else can notice I'm gone.

CHAPTER THIRTY-FOUR

NATHAN

It's three in the morning before I get home. The night was a massive success – over three hundred thousand euro was raised for Mam's charity and she had a blast in the process. If only I could keep all the women in my life happy at the same time.

The hall light is on, but the house is quiet as I open the door. The gentle welcoming thud of Barbie's tail bouncing off the hall carpet breaks the silence. Creeping up the stairs, I peek in on Millie. She's fast asleep with Captain Barnacles tucked under her left arm and her silky hair scattered over the pillow. Across the hallway, I notice my own bedroom door open, the sheets still tucked immaculately in place. Kerry must be pissed off with my parting remark. I hadn't meant to upset her, the words were out of my mouth before I could overthink them. Her openness seems to be rubbing off on me, and not necessarily in a good way.

I creep up the last flight of stairs, to the bedroom Kerry

hasn't slept in for weeks and nudge open the door. The pink bed is also still made. A nervous energy thrums through my body as I remember Kerry's remark about the phone and a flashback of that poison note I received a few months ago. A variety of scenarios flit through my mind, alcohol only fuelling the monstrous thoughts. Jogging down the stairs, I check the landline, lifting the old-fashioned receiver to my ear. There's no dial tone.

I pull back the sideboard it sits on and kneel on the floor to see if it's been unplugged. Barbie's squeaky bone is wedged next to the wires, as I pull it out, the claw marks where she tried to dislodge it become apparent. Sinking back onto the heels of my feet, relief floods through me, though there's still no sign of Kerry.

She has to be here somewhere, there's no way she'd leave Millie alone. I search the house, starting with the sofa, with no luck. I open the door to the man cave, even though I know it's pointless because she won't be in there if it's locked. The room remains in darkness, I don't even bother to go in. Locking it again, I notice the patio doors aren't closed properly. Adrenaline spikes again, crusading through my veins as I dart across the room and out into the garden.

There Kerry sits at the outdoor table, with the bottle of Jameson in front of her and a tiny tumbler. If she's hitting the hard stuff, she must be in worse shape than I thought.

'Jesus, Kerry, you scared the shit out of me.'

She barely glances round as I sit at the table next to her. The temperature's dropped dramatically this hour of the day, so I reach for her empty glass and pour myself a good measure of whiskey. It's only as I lean across the table I notice the book in front of her. The thick glossy pages of the Trailblazers brochure opened to boast pages of mile-long white stretches of beach and promises of self-discovery and adventure. Kerry's bolting at the first hurdle.

'You're leaving?' My hand shoots out towards the brochure.

'I'm thinking about it. You were right, Millie's not my daughter. The longer I stay here, the more attached I become. It's not right. It's too hard. I don't want to turn into my mother, stuck at home wondering if there's anything else out there for me.'

Realisation strikes harder than the toughest tackle. The knowledge is more shocking than her impending departure, although why, I'm not sure. I always knew no one would take Millie and I on full-time. It's too much to ask anyone. Let alone a woman who can't have children and will never have to be tied down because of them. Kerry's like a little bird with huge wings, she just needed confidence to use them. A part of me is elated, even as I'm devastated, that somehow I've been the one to enable her to do so. To think I was stupid enough to think having Millie might be an attraction for Kerry. I've been such a fool.

'About earlier...' I swallow down the emotion that's threatening to choke me.

'Forget it.' She dismisses it with a casual wave of the hand, but her hard, set jaw tells a different story.

'I shouldn't have said it. I just didn't want you to think you're the only one who cares about Millie. I'm her father, I won't let anything happen to her. There's CCTV in the house. I didn't want to alarm you by thinking it's necessary, but after I received the unusual notes I upped the security round here. The cameras are linked to my phone. I can check on Millie anytime of the day.'

Kerry's grey eyes cloud like thunder. 'Have you been checking on me too?'

'No. The cameras are by the front door and one in Millie's bedroom. I'd never violate your privacy like that, Kerry. But

Millie's safety comes first, what kind of a father would I be if it didn't?'

'Message received, loud and clear: you're her father. I know nothing. I'm sorry if you think I overreacted. I know I'm not her mother and never could be, but you made it my business to care when you employed me to mind her. I never should have come tonight.'

'Kerry, you deserve a night off, you deserve to have some fun with your friends, and I want you at these things with me, as my girlfriend.'

Kerry blows out the breath she'd been holding and the thunder is chased from her eyes by huge overflowing rain clouds that spill directly onto her cheek.

'Come here.' I pull her into my arms but she shrugs out of them, refusing the comfort.

'I can't stay here, Nathan. I'm sorry. I'm of no worth to you until I find my own worth inside myself. I'm not girl-friend material, not for a man like you. It was supposed to be fun, effortless and now I've ruined it all.'

'You haven't ruined anything. Maybe we could get you set up with a counsellor? I think a lot of your self-esteem issues come from what happened when you were twenty-one.'

'You sound like Abby! I don't want to spend hour upon hour dissecting the past. It won't change it. What I want to do is focus on the future.' She glances down at the photos of the exotic locations and smiling faces, promising adventure and friendships to be had along the way.

How can I compete with that?

'Sleep on it at least, Kerry. We've both been drinking. I said some stupid stuff. Please, don't do anything rash. Let's go to bed.' I take her by the hand and although she eyes me warily, she follows me inside.

We undress and brush our teeth side by side in my en

suite. It's the first night in weeks we don't make love. Even as she lies beside me, my chest pressed against her back, I get the impression she's already a million miles away. And there's nothing I can do to fix it.

CHAPTER THIRTY-FIVE

KERRY

Two days have passed, and neither of us have addressed the elephant in the room: my potential departure. Nathan is distant, understandably. The atmosphere's heavy, like a damp fog from the sea, hanging between us, preventing both of us from seeing straight. Millie's the only reason I haven't packed my bags and left already.

The weight of the situation, the past few months, hell, the last eight years, maybe even before, bears down heavily on my shoulders. The urge to escape is magnifying by the second. The thought of leaving Nathan and Millie is crippling, but they aren't mine to keep. They're their own family. He said it himself, I'm not her mother. Foolishly, it's a role I allowed myself to believe for a while, especially when I fell in love with her father. At least my own mother, trapped as she may be, had her own child to raise.

The stuffy old guy in a suit was right in some respects, they are the perfect microwave meal. Actually, they're both perfect, full stop. It's me that's broken.

The landline rings. I glance at the clock, knowing Millie's actual mother always phones on a Saturday morning.

I'm closest, so I answer it.

'Hello?'

'I'd like to speak to my daughter please.' Clodagh's never rude to me, but the few times I've gotten her on the phone she's not exactly warm either. You'd think woman to woman we could get on, seeing as we both have her daughter's interests at heart, but she can't even give me the time of day.

I carry the cordless phone out to the garden and hand it to Millie, who's currently searching the plant pots I bought for a sign of any fairies.

'Mammy?' She squeals down the phone, as I backtrack through the garden. I don't mean to eavesdrop, but Millie's high-pitched tone is carried by the southerly breeze.

'You're coming home? Seriously? When?'

I close the patio door, not even bothering to meet Nathan's eye. If I was in any doubt of what I was going to do, Clodagh's return has swung it for me. I'm no longer needed.

Sitting at the kitchen table, I flip the phone in my hand over twice, while I find the nerve to do what I need to do. The number emblazoned boldly on the page in front of me, taunts me. I punch it into the handset, before I can talk myself out of it.

A woman answers on the first ring. 'Trailblazers, Suzie speaking, how may I help you?'

'Hi, Suzie, I'd like to book one of those one-way round the world tickets you have advertised.'

'Ok, that's fantastic. I'll take some details from you now. Just to make you aware, you can only go one way around the world. The ticket doesn't allow you to double back on yourself, so plan each stage of your trip carefully. You have a full year to use the ticket, starting from the day of your first flight.'

'That's fine. I don't even have a real plan; I'd like to take in a few exotic locations, but I'm not fussy which.'

'When are you thinking of leaving?'

It's a question I haven't dared to ask myself yet, but this is the new decisive me, the one that doesn't rely on what any man thinks I should do. Still, Nathan's been really good to me, I don't want to drop him in it. But then again, with Clodagh's return, he really doesn't need me.

Will they have a happy family reunion? Will they go back to the shared care? Or will distance have made Clodagh have a change of heart? Will they patch things up? I remind myself it's not my business.

I clear my throat, buying time before I give Suzie my answer. 'Maybe a week, but that could change.'

'Do you live locally? Perhaps you'd like to call in and we can make a plan for you together?'

'That sounds brilliant, thank you, Suzie. I'll drop in this afternoon.'

The gentle thudding of footsteps alerts me to Nathan's approach as I disconnect the call.

'Who was that?' The frown on his face tells me he already knows.

'Travel agent. I'm going to do it.' My voice oozes way more confidence than I feel. Truthfully, the thought of going to a different country scares the shit out of me, but I need distance, space and I need to find myself. I can't do that here.

'Is it because Clodagh's coming home? Nothing's changed on that front, we broke up long before you came on the scene.' Nathan's beautiful blue eyes swim with suppressed frustration.

'It's not that. Though, I guess if Clodagh's coming back you won't have to worry so much about a nanny.'

He drops into the seat next to me, taking my hand. 'What is

it, Kerry? I thought things were going well between us. I thought you were happy to stay. I know it's a big ask, to take on a guy with a child, believe me, I know, but I thought we were different.'

'It's not a big ask, truly, but it's too hard, too complicated. Millie's your daughter, your responsibility, you told me yourself. We'd agreed that you'd stop paying me and I'd mind her because I love her as much as I love...' I swallow the words before they can hang awkwardly in the air between us. 'But when it came to it, the other night when I expressed my concern, you immediately defaulted back to the fact I'm not her mother.'

'It was a fucking stupid thing to say, Kerry. So fucking insensitive. You've been more of a mother the past few months than Clodagh's ever been.' He runs his hand through his hair, a frown creasing his brow.

'It was only the truth. I seem to have accidentally morphed into my own mother, with the cooking and the baking, and living in your shadow. I need to spread my wings, see a bit of the world, figure out what I want to do with my life. I can't do that if I have to answer to you. It's been over eight years since I only had to answer to myself and not anyone else. I need to figure out what makes me happy. I'm sorry.'

He bites his lip, as if to hold back whatever he's thinking of saying, then offers one curt nod of acceptance. 'When are you leaving?'

'I don't have a date yet. I'm going to go into town this afternoon and sort out the details.'

I barely recognise the man that stands in front of me. 'Just go, if you're going. Don't prolong the agony. It'll be easier on all of us.' He glances out towards where Millie sits in the garden, chatting to her mother.

'Do you want me to wait until Clodagh returns?' I can't

bring myself to say 'gets home' because the thought of her here shacking up with him, rips me apart.

'No, just go.' He stuffs his clenched fists into his pockets and turns on his heels.

My aching heart constricts with agonising pain as I go upstairs and pack my few measly belongings.

CHAPTER THIRTY-SIX

NATHAN

As Kerry hugs Millie goodbye, I look away. The crying is too much for me to bear, from both of them. Millie clutches Captain Barnacles under her arm, gripping him round his neck as though he might leave too. She's wheezing so badly, I have to run to get her inhalers. Millie's taking Kerry leaving worse than she took her own mother leaving. The guilt is ripping me apart, guilt and sorrow. I wish we could be enough for Kerry. Even Barbie whines by the front door, head hanging low.

'I didn't mean you had to go today.' Hot shame fills my cheeks. I'd acted rashly because I was hurt, am hurt. I hate the thought of her leaving, so I pushed her away first.

'It's for the best. I better spend some time with Mam and Dad before I jet off.'

The car I'd insisted calling for her pulls up. She never did sit her driving test. I failed to even do that properly for her.

'There are some boxes in the room still, I'll have a courier collect them during the week.'

'There's no rush.' I'm backtracking now, but it's too late. If she doesn't want to stay, I won't beg her to.

'Send me a postcard from everywhere you go,' Millie pleads. 'Call me too.'

'Of course I will, sweetheart.' Kerry pulls Millie in for one last hug, squeezes her towards her and drops a kiss on her fair head.

'Thanks for everything.' I can only hope my voice conveys my sincerity, despite my irrational behaviour.

'Thanks yourself. This was the best summer job ever.' Her steely grey eyes soften for a fraction of a second and I can only assume her memory is taunting her with the same flash-backs as mine. For a while, I truly believed we could be it.

And just like that, she steps down the pathway, where the driver loads her bags into the boot.

CHAPTER THIRTY-SEVEN

KERRY

Leaving Nathan and Millie was the hardest thing I've ever done in my life, which reinforces it's the right thing to do because if this went on into the autumn, it'd be even harder when it eventually drew to an end.

I'd told Suzie I needed a ticket asap, knowing that a week living with my parents would be six days too long. I know I'm a disappointment, I don't need them to tell me. We barely get through dinner the first night, when the questions start.

'So, Kerry, you finished up nannying for that rugby fella?' Dad's voice has always had a talented way of expressing disapproval with every syllable.

'Yes.' I chew my asparagus for way longer than necessary, just to buy myself a little time.

'And, what are you going to do now?' He breathes in the scent of his half-empty glass of vintage wine, before taking a tentative sip. At least I'm not the only thing he's judgemental about. The half-full glass is supposed to be sophisticated, but

I'd rather mine was filled to the brim, I've a feeling I'm going to need it.

He takes another sip and nods his approval at Mam across the table. Her shoulders visibly relax. However hard he is as father, I can only imagine he's harder as a husband. His beady eyes return to me again, his only daughter and heir.

'I'm going travelling.' I deliberately pop a large chunk of slow-cooked tender meat into my mouth, so I can't say another word.

'Travelling?' Instead of shouting, his voice gets lower, a sure sign of never-ending disapproval. 'Where are you going travelling? Didn't you and that army chap do enough sunshine holidays? It's about time you settled down. You're not as young as you once were, madam.'

Mam coughs and busies herself rearranging her flower napkin over her lap.

'I need to get away, find myself.' The words fall flat on his open mouth.

'You're a thirty-one-year-old woman, almost thirty-two, not one of these eighteen year olds taking a year out to indulge in illegal substances and promiscuity on their way round Australia. You should be thinking about settling down, starting a family. We aren't getting any younger. Your mother would love grandchildren.'

I flinch at the mention of grandchildren, but he's too busy waving his hand wildly across the table at my mother to notice. She doesn't look up, still pretending she's engrossed in smoothing out her napkin. It wouldn't surprise me if she actually ironed the damn things.

I've never told them I can't have children. I never wanted them to disappoint them that way, in addition to dropping out of my Master's. Why I'm protecting their feelings is beyond me, because they certainly don't spare mine. Well he doesn't at least.

I take a large glug of his vintage wine, barely bothering to taste it, merely looking for the effects.

'Too fond of that stuff, you are.' He nods at the wine glass, as I set it back on the table. 'Probably couldn't abstain for nine months, hey? Is that what it is?' It's like after years of biting his tongue, he's just letting the tear out now. Probably because he knows if I get on that plane, the chance of me coming home is slim to none.

Mam finds her voice at last. 'Thirty-one's not old these day, love.' She speaks to my father in a gentle, encouraging tone, as if he's a king to be pandered to. It's one of the first times I've witnessed her almost stand up to him.

'It's not, if you were guaranteed the lord would bless you with a child the first time you tried. But you know yourself how long it took for this "blessing" to arrive.' He snorts and takes another sip of his wine.

For the first time in my life, I realise where my insecurity and low self-esteem arises from. It's from the very man who fathered me. After spending the summer watching Nathan dote on Millie, I can see clearly how fucked up this situation is.

I'm his only daughter, you'd think he'd be proud of me, whatever I did in life. All Nathan wants for his daughter is for her to be happy. And the same with his mother, all Nuala wanted was Nathan to be happy, whether he was sleeping with a million dollar model, or the nanny.

I push my chair back from the table and throw my napkin straight onto my plate, where it soaks and ruins in the gravy. My mother gasps.

'Sit down. We haven't finished talking.' My father's voice is dangerously low, as though he's speaking to a disobedient child.

After everything I've been through, losing Nathan and Millie, suffering under Craig's control and being used at the hands of Married Martin, I've had enough. I sit, but not because I'm ready to take another load of abuse, but because I'm ready to deliver a few home truths of my own.

'You need to make a plan, Kerry, to do something with your life. Everything you've ever started, you've left, dropped out or given up on.'

'You have no idea.' It's barely a mutter that leaves my lips, but it's the most insolent thing I've ever said to my father.

'I beg your pardon, young lady?' He rises from the table, but even at full height, he's only three inches taller than me. No wonder he has little man syndrome.

'A minute ago I was an old spinster, now I'm "young lady".' I help myself to the bottle of wine on the table and pour myself a proper glass.

'How dare you answer me back.' He bangs his fist off the table and Mam jumps.

'I came here to visit you before I go off travelling, I might be gone for a year, I don't know. I wanted to leave on a good note, but you're not making it easy for me.'

'Get this travelling idea out of your head, girl. Find yourself a man and start a family, lay some roots, find a decent job, at the very least finish your Master's!'

The wine's coursing through my blood, providing that false sense of empowerment that I love. 'You never did ask why I didn't go back.'

'I know why you didn't go back. Because you can't commit to anything you do in this life.'

I drain the remaining wine in the glass, as my father glares at me in open disgust. 'I didn't go back because I got pregnant, by a man I didn't know was married.' Another gasp bursts from my mother's lips, she clamps her fingers over them in shock.

The colour drains from my father's face. He sits back

down in his chair and takes a sip from his own glass. Minutes pass with a shocked silence. I pour myself another drink.

He eventually asks, 'And what of the child?'

'There was no child. It was an ectopic pregnancy. As you know, I had the childhood cyst. So this ruptured the only chance I had of having children. There will be no grandchildren, ever.'

Mam sobs into her napkin. I wonder for a second if I should comfort her, then decide it's not my place to parent my parents.

'Perhaps it was for the best, after all,' Dad says, swirling his wine around the glass.

'And why is that exactly?'

My father clasps his hands together, in a lord-like manner, as if he's speaking down to one of his lowly subjects. 'Being a parent is hard work. It's not for everyone.'

'Well I'm sure I could have done a better job than you.' I go straight to my room, the bedroom I had as a child. Peach wallpaper covers the walls, matching frilly curtains frame the windows and the matching bedspread is ironed to within an inch of its life. This bedroom reminds me of everything I don't want in my life: predictability, strict structure, boredom and confinement to what is deemed polite, appropriate and socially acceptable. I want a life that's real, colourful and meaningful. Fuck what's appropriate or socially acceptable.

My mind wanders to Nathan, Millie and Nuala. They're real, their souls are so vibrant their personalities emit from them in multicoloured projected lights. Even though he's tied to his role as father, he makes it fun and entertaining. Millie won't grow up lost like me. For the millionth time, I wish things could have been different, but I couldn't spend my life as the hired help, no better off than my mother.

CHAPTER THIRTY-EIGHT

NATHAN

We are due to go to Disney the day after tomorrow, then when we get home, Clodagh should be back in the country. Hopefully that will cheer Millie up. It's bad enough wallowing in my depression, I can't bear the crippling weight of Millie's sorrow on top of my own. I even offered to have a tea party with the dolls but she just looked at me, rolled her eyes and closed her bedroom door. She blames me for letting Kerry leave, and she's right. The house is desolate without her bouncing around it, singing and laughing, and making inappropriate remarks.

Last night, I drank half a bottle of Jameson and tried to call Kerry fourteen times, before concluding I'm no better than her ex bombarding her. Each time, it went to voicemail. I've checked my phone a hundred times and there's been not a single hint that she feels the way I do, and I'm terrified she's left the country already.

The sound of metal against metal alerts me to the sound of the post arriving. Dragging myself from my position hunched at the kitchen table, I head to the hallway to check what arrived.

Another thick, glossy brochure sits on top of the door-mat. It must be for Kerry. Picking it up, I'm surprised to see it's for Trinity College. It's a postgraduate course guide, holy shit, Kerry must have been weighing up all of her options, not just the travelling one.

A flicker of hope ignites, sparks, then dies inside. If only this had arrived a few days earlier, I would have known she was considering all options, not just the one that involved fleeing the country. A weighted sigh heaves from my thorax. It's too late, she's probably a million miles away by now, some-where exotic, hot and child free. I swallow down the lump in my throat. I'll never make captain if I cry like a girl. Oddly enough, it's not even a priority anymore. Some things are more precious than a title. The greatest honour comes from allowing another person in, and being allowed in. I fucked up. It's clearer than the light of day.

A smaller envelope lies on the floor where I lifted the brochure from, someone must have hand-delivered it without my noticing because there's no postmark or address. The envelope is blank, small and white. The same as the one that arrived at Carton House and the one I found stuffed in a kitchen drawer, which Kerry must have borne the brunt of. The poor woman probably thought it was intended for her. The hair stands attentively on my neck, pricked and ready for confrontation.

Could it be Craig? He seemed aggressive enough that I can't rule it out. Although the first one arrived before I even hired Kerry, so truthfully it couldn't be him. I rack my brains trying to think who could hate me enough to spend a painstaking amount of time cutting out letters from a news-paper to abuse me.

It was one thing having mail delivered to the club, but

coming to my front door is on a whole new level. I grip it at it's very edges, trying not to spoil it for fingerprints. At the table, I use a knife to slit it open. One small square of paper tumbles out on to the desk, with similar letters cut from a newspaper. This one reads:

You almost had it all, but eventually you got what you deserved.

My blood runs cold in my veins and my heart palpitates rapidly in my ribcage, but it's not fear that has me this way, it's anger. Not only has someone got the cheek to write these painstaking letters, but they turn up at my door with them too. And, apparently they have some idea of my personal life too. I pick up the landline to call the cops, before remembering the CCTV I installed over the front door. If the person's stupid enough to drop the note off themselves, they might be stupid enough not to hide their face.

Opening the app on my mobile, I scroll back an hour and watch the footage on fast-forward. The only person that came to the door was the postman, with Kerry's brochure. It's possible the sender dropped this off last night, and I walked straight by it this morning in my distracted state.

I scroll back through twelve hours' worth of CCTV footage on a speed setting, pausing only to grab a cup of tea and get comfortable at the table.

There! I freeze the frame. I'd know that figure anywhere and the sweeping gesture of pulling the hair from her face is one I've seen a million times since we were seventeen. A tell-tale rash dots her neck, further confirming my suspicion – it's Clodagh! I see her as clear as day, despite the enormous sunglasses she wears. The tiny square envelope is clear in her hand. I watch as she double-checks the surrounding vicinity, before slipping it through the box. What the fuck? She's supposed to be on a cruise ship, on her way back from New York.

My brain fuzzes with a thick fog, clouding everything

before me. How? And why? Did she get back early? And why is she sending me ridiculous notes like we are still in high school? Then the answer dawns on me, loud and clear – to her we still are in high school – she never grew up.

Jesus, I can't comprehend the calculation of the entire situation. Did she ever leave at all, or was the last three months some elaborate lie? And what was the purpose of it all? I have a million questions and no answers, but the only thing I am one hundred per cent sure of is that I will be applying for sole custody of Millie asap, because clearly Clodagh is not in a good place. Jesus, I thought things were bad before this.

Flipping the letter over in my hands, I contemplate what to do. Whatever else she is, Clodagh will always be Millie's mother. And right now, I have time on my side because we *aren't expecting her home* for another week.

God, I have one woman jumping a plane to avoid me, and another pretending to board a ship to avoid me, what does that say?

CHAPTER THIRTY-NINE

KERRY

The following morning there's a gentle tap on my door. I know it's Mam, my father wouldn't even consider knocking, plus he'll have left for work by now, like clockwork, his schedule hasn't changed in thirty years. I remain fixed in my position, staring up at the magnolia ceiling. When I don't answer, the door opens a fraction. As ever, my timid mother is afraid to put a foot out of line.

'Are you ok, Kerry?' She takes a step in, closing the door behind her with a gentle click.

'I'm fine.' I'm not, I'm a mess, but she wouldn't understand.

'You're not, pet.' She braves a few more steps towards the bed and when I don't send her away, she sits tentatively on the edge, wringing her hands.

'I'm sorry about the baby. About everything. We had no idea.' She shakes her head, a sad little gesture of remorse. I don't need her sympathy but I wouldn't mind a bit of support.

'It's ok. He's probably right, I couldn't even mind a hamster, so I'd barely be able to manage a child.'

'You can manage a child. Didn't you spend the summer minding one? It worked out well.' She scooches up the bed closer to me. My eyes remain fixated on the ceiling.

'It really didn't work out well, to be honest.' I swallow the lump forming in my throat. Being here has somehow reverted me back to my childhood, where my mam was my world and the two of us used to pray together that Dad would be in a good mood when he got home. Something about the memory of us once being confidantes makes me want to share my troubles with her, but I can't because the second I do, I know the tears will come flooding out of me.

'I know we haven't been close the last few years, but I'm your mam and I love you. There's nothing you can't tell me. This idea of travelling and going off on your own, it's not really your style, Kerry. I wonder if perhaps you're running from something? From someone?'

My timid, mousy mother is way more astute than I gave her credit for, she's pretty much hit the nail on the head. The thought of exploring the world alone may be exciting to some people, but to me it is terrifying. But I'm so determined to do something with my life, to find myself and my purpose, and if I'm honest I wanted to do the complete opposite to her.

'Do you ever wish you went travelling?' I sit up, resting my elbow on the pillow and my head in my hands.

'Me? No, what on earth would give you that impression?' She covers her mouth with her hard-working hands.

'I just wondered if you wish you did anything differently?'

'No. My life mightn't be what you might choose. I see the way you look at me, almost pityingly. But truly, I'm happy. I like being at home. I like looking after your dad. I like the security of it. You know I grew up in the countryside with absolutely nothing. There were ten kids in our family living in a two-bedroomed cottage. We basically reared ourselves. I vowed when I had children one day, I'd do it differently. Your dad gave me love, security and a safe home to raise you. I wouldn't change a thing. Well, I'd have liked a bigger family, but it wasn't to be. It doesn't make me any less of a person though.'

Her words swirl through my brain like a heavy smoke seeking every corner.

'I know he's hard on you, Kerry, but it's because he loves you. He has a funny way of showing it, I know. Do you want to tell me about him?'

'Who?'

'The man who broke your heart? That's why you're here, isn't it?'

Silence fills the air between us, as I remember Nathan telling me I didn't have to go. He said something stupid, but it wasn't his fault that it hurt as badly as it did. It was all on me. Even when Clodagh announced she was coming home, still he wanted me to stay, but I was too pig-headed to listen. Wallowing in all my brokenness.

'I think I might have broken my own heart, actually.'

'Tell me. I'm your mam, you can tell me anything and I won't judge.' I nearly laugh because in this moment, despite my beliefs about my judgemental father, I almost believe her.

A huge sigh falls from my lips. I've got nothing to lose in confiding in her because whatever happens, I'm not staying here either way. For once, thanks to my summer job, I have enough money in my bank to enable me to choose the next step in my life, whether it's travelling or college. That knowledge alone is more empowering than I thought.

'I fell in love with my boss Nathan. I didn't mean to, but he's the sweetest, gentlest, caring, tattooed giant that I've ever met in my life. He was so good to me and way too good for me, but he had this way of making me feel like I was more than enough when I was with him.'

Mam takes my hand and squeezes it. 'You are more than enough. You're everything to me and your dad, even if he has a funny way of showing it. Did Nathan not feel the same?'

'He said he did. He asked me to stay on, as his girlfriend. I didn't want to take his money for minding his child, it felt so wrong when he gave me so much already. But then we were out and I couldn't get hold of the babysitter, and when I said I wanted to leave, he reminded me that she wasn't my child. I didn't want to be her mother, but I wouldn't have minded my role eventually evolving into stepmother. Then I realised that would mean I'd amounted to nothing and fallen into a role no different to yours. Sorry, Mam, but I don't want to be at a man's beck and call.' I wince, even saying the words.

To my surprise, Mam laughs a deep heartfelt belly laugh.

'Is that what you think, honey? That I'm at your father's beck and call?' She wipes a stray tear from her eye but she's still chuckling.

'Well, aren't you? Even if you say you're happy to do it?'

'To your young impressionable eyes, it might have looked like it. The man's a stickler for routine. But come evening time, when he's let the stress of the day go, what you don't see is when he runs me a hot bath, or sits with me while I watch *One Born Every Minute* and wipes my tears when I wonder what I did so wrong that you barely visit.'

'Jesus, Mam, I'm so sorry. I always thought I was such a disappointment. I was staying away, hoping to get my shit together, so I could for once return here and make you both proud with my news.'

'Oh, honey, we are so proud, whatever you do. Your dad just wants to see you utilise your potential.'

'Potential to fuck up everything,' I scoff.

'Language, lady!' Mam scolds, in a gentle voice. 'From today, this self-bashing stops. You're our daughter, we love you and we are so proud of you. I see why you couldn't fulfil your original plan, but let's get our heads together and see what you actually can do, because I don't think disappearing round the world drinking is going to give you any insight at all to be honest.'

'You're probably right.'

'Can I have that in writing?' She nudges me. 'Let's go bake a cake for your dad. He'll be delighted to see you're still here when he gets home, and you can tell me all about this Nathan chap.'

As the sweet comforting smells of Mam's home baking fill the familiar country kitchen, I tell her about Nathan's remarks and his remorse, and that what I really can't get over, is myself.

'Maybe you need to talk to a professional? The loss of a baby is hard enough, believe me, I know. The loss of the ability to ever have babies is devastating.'

'I'm starting to see it, now I'm not out partying five nights a week. I'll call Abby, she'll be able to recommend someone.' I glance at my phone, where it sits on top of my handbag. I dropped it in a puddle on the way to the Trailblazer office and haven't been able to get it to turn on since. I figured it was a sign – the end of that chapter of my life. At least with a new number I won't have to worry about ever hearing from Craig or Mags again. Not that I expect to, but just in case.

'Do you love him?'

I don't need to ask who she's referring to. 'Yes.'

'Does he know?' She glances at me from where she's whipping cream into soft fluffy spirals.

'That I can't have children? Or that I love him?'

'Both.'

'I told him the first, but I couldn't bring myself to say the latter.'

'Well, perhaps it's time you did. At this stage, what have you got to lose?'

I never thought I'd see the day, but I think my mother is right.

CHAPTER FORTY

NATHAN

The hole Kerry's absence has left in both our lives is a raw, gaping wound that not even the prospect of a trip to Disney can plug. As I pack a bag for Millie, and for myself, I can't help but think she should have been here, just as excited as my five-year-old princess.

The front door opens. Barbie runs from her position on the landing, leaping down the stairs.

'Stupid bleeding dog.' My mother's raspy voice travels up the stairs. 'Where are you, son?'

'Up here,' I call, shoving the last few items into a holdall and zipping it shut.

'You all set for tomorrow?' Mam stands in the bedroom doorway, eyeing the hastily packed bag.

'Think so. Hopefully this will cheer Millie up.'

'Hopefully, it will cheer you both up. I still can't understand it, you know? Kerry was obviously infatuated with you. I can't believe she'd go at the first fight.'

'It wasn't even a fight. I said something stupid and insensitive that opened a deeper wound of her own. But still, if she runs at the first sign of trouble, she's probably not right for me anyway.'

'You don't believe that for a second, Nathan.' Mam's clenched fist rests on her hip, her weathered face creases further into a frown.

'I thought she was. She's broken, just not in the way that she thinks.'

Mam huffs and rolls her eyes. 'We're all feckin' broken!'

'I know that.'

'So why didn't you tell her?'

'I tried.'

'Huh.' She scoffs. 'Not hard enough. Remember how badly you wanted to make the under-eighteen rugby team? Remember how hard you fought for that? I had to work three jobs to pay for your one-on-one coaching, and you used to kick that ball about the nearest green from dawn till dusk. That's what fighting is: carrying on when your body begs you to stop. Did you do that with Kerry?'

I pause, debating on confiding in the only person I know will understand, even though it means breaking Kerry's confidence.

'Kerry can't have children of her own.'

Mam looks at me, her face unchanged. 'And? You don't want any more children. You said it yourself a hundred times.'

I stare at the intricate pattern of the thick carpet under-foot, silently contemplating.

'Don't tell me you didn't feckin' reiterate that fact? No wonder she feels broken. You're such a brilliant father, regardless of what you may have said the poor girl probably assumed you want to fill the house with children. No wonder she got out before she fell any deeper. Because she did fall for you, Nathan.'

'If she did, she never said it.'

'Well in that case, if I were you, I'd be doing a detour by wherever she's gone on the way to the airport to see if the two of you are ready to tell each other some honest truths.'

'I would, if I knew where she was. I always kind of figured that because she'll never have to be tied down with her own kids, she couldn't truly be happy being tied down with me and mine.'

'That's the most ridiculous thing I ever heard.' Mam takes a cigarette out of her bag and rolls it between her index finger and her thumb.

'Well, you couldn't manage to persuade anyone to stick around to help rear me. Why should it be any different for me?'

Mam takes a step towards me, drops the unlit cigarette and swipes me across my arm in jest. 'You bloody cheeky fecker!' A look of indignation infiltrates her lined face. 'Don't be so daft. It wasn't that I couldn't keep them! None of them were good enough for me, or my son! I refused to settle for anything less than the real deal and I was happier that way.'

'Seriously?' All these years I'd truly believed she couldn't keep a relationship going because nobody wanted to take on another man's child, now she tells me this.

'Seriously. Your dad was a first class bollocks, but my god, did I love him. I couldn't think straight when he was in the room. My love for him made me dizzy. When he left, there was no way I could settle for anything less than that. And if I never find it again in my whole life, I won't settle. Why do you think I scour the pubs and the bookies of Dublin city? You know as well as I do, I don't belong to that life anymore. Stupidly, I can't help hoping I'll bump into him again one day. I don't know whether I'd wring his neck or throw myself at him, but I'd love the opportunity to find out.

'Now, tell me, is that what you feel for Kerry Walsh? Because from where I'm standing, that's exactly what it looks like. She's a great girl, so wholesome, down to earth. Ok, she mightn't be as flashy as some of the girls you dated, or as poised as Clodagh was, but she is real, raw and she adores you and Millie. You two were made for each other.'

I perch on the bed, dumbfounded by this ridiculously obvious revelation. All these years I made assumptions, assumptions that were completely unfounded.

'Speaking of Clodagh, there's something I need to tell you.'

'Oh, Jesus, what's she done now?'

'Nothing, that's the whole point. She hasn't done anything, she hasn't been anywhere. It looks like she's been lying about the whole cruise ship trip and been here the whole time.' I pass Mam the phone with the screenshot of Clodagh, and pass her the letter, which I'd kept in my bedside drawer.

'The poor girl.' Mam clutches the necklace over her heart. 'She never did get over you. She probably thought by disappearing from yours and Millie's life would show you both how much you need her.' A huge sigh echoes round the room, I'm not even sure if it comes from her, or me.

'What are you going to do about it?'

'I'm going to show her the evidence and apply for full custody of Millie. I can't allow this kind of behaviour, no matter how troubled or hurt she is by our split.'

'I think it's for the best, son. Clodagh will still see Millie, but if she can disappear for months at time with such an elaborate plan, maybe she won't want to. Poor Millie. At least she has you.

Where is she by the way?' Mam picks up the cigarette she dropped.

'Downstairs. Watching *Frozen*, eating lollipops. I haven't had the heart to stop her. She's missing Kerry like crazy.'

'You both are, by the look of it. The real question is, what

are you going to do about it?' She stalks out, leaving me to
wonder the same thing.

CHAPTER FORTY-ONE

KERRY

When Dad arrives home to see Mam and me setting the table together, a smile breaks out on his habitually serious looking face.

'I'm sorry, Kerry. I was angry for you, not at you, and even more angry at myself for not knowing and not protecting you. I'm so sorry. I said some awful things, I lashed out. It wasn't fair.' He crosses the room, places his briefcase down and pulls me into the tightest hug.

My tense shoulders relax under his embrace, and a stray tear falls from my face.

'I'm sorry, Daddy.' I squeeze him back with all my might.

'I know I have an unusual way of showing it, but believe me when I say I only ever want the best for you. You have so much potential, you always were the quickest, smartest kid in your class. I only ever wanted to see you utilise it. Let your mam and me help you for once. Instead of rebelling against us, tell us what we can do to support you.'

Mam pulls out Dad's chair for him and gestures for him to

sit. This time, instead of viewing it as another chore that she has to do, I see it for what it is – a gesture of love.

How could I have gotten it so wrong for all of these years? I've been completely delusional, lying to myself rather than facing the truth, letting my own hurt and disappointment taint every aspect of my life and contort the way I see the world.

'You could start by teaching me to drive. I started learning over the summer and I think I'm almost ready to sit my test.'

'Well, that's fantastic news.' Surprise strikes my father's crinkled eyes.

'And that's not all,' Mam chips in, placing a plate of sizzling, steaming stir-fry in front of him – it is Monday after all. 'Kerry's thinking of going back to college.'

'I am. I can't pursue a career in childcare, but I can learn how to teach what I know. I'm going to do a post-graduate in teaching, pass on my knowledge to those that can.'

'That's absolutely fantastic news.' Dad beams from ear to ear, apparently he's not as hard to please as I'd built him up to be all these years. 'You're tight for time, that's the only thing. The new term starts mid-October, but I know the dean at Trinity, might be able to pull a few strings. Get your application in online tonight, and I'll make a few calls.'

It seems I've found exactly what I'd been looking for – a sense of direction, in the last place I'd have expected to – right back at the very beginning. I'm not sure how I veered so far from home all those years ago, but I'm so glad to be back. Facing the ones I've been avoiding has helped me find where I'm meant to be heading, at long last.

The only thing I haven't found, is a way to plug the massive Nathan and Millie sized hole in my heart. But one day at a time.

Mam places my dinner at my old spot, in the middle, with

them heading up each end of the table. I sit and begin to eat, even though I'm not awfully hungry.

'And what about the travelling idea? Have you abandoned it completely?' Dad asks between mouthfuls of tender chicken.

'Truthfully, the only place I really want to go is Euro Disney. I know I'm supposed to be growing up, at long last, but I'm still a massive child at heart.'

'Ha. That's ok, even your mother and I would love to get to Euro Disney. We went to Paris on honeymoon, but of course it wasn't open then. Bet you didn't know that now, did you?'

I swallow a mouthful of tender spicy chicken before answering, 'Turns out there's a lot I didn't know.'

'Why don't you go to France for week or two? Before school starts? Once you get into the thick of lectures and assignments, you won't get much of a break.'

I'd love to. I even have a ticket to go, leaving tomorrow afternoon, with the very people that make up the final pieces of my broken jigsaw.

'Would you think I was really irresponsible if I went tomorrow?'

'Not at all,' Dad says, 'as long as you get that application form in tonight. Now you've committed to something you want to do, I'm determined to see you follow it through.' The authority in his tone is coated with an underlying affection that I'd previously failed to notice.

'Can I use your computer?'

'It's in the study.'

I'm in for a long night, even more so because once I submit my application, I spend the remaining few hours of darkness wondering if I have the balls to do what I'm thinking of doing. The thought that I might no longer be welcome, is one I can't bear to consider for too long.

CHAPTER FORTY-TWO

NATHAN

When Mam left yesterday, I contacted my solicitor immedi-ately to begin proceedings to apply for full-time custody of Millie. Keira, Eddie's sister, is one of the best lawyers in the city. I will never deny Clodagh access, but I can't chance her unpredictable behaviour, even if I can sort of understand her hurt.

I realise, in her own way, she probably wanted to show us how much we'd miss her if she was gone. Sadly, it showed us the opposite. When Kerry moved in, we saw light, sunshine and laughter.

Even though it didn't work out, Kerry showed us what life could be like, and for that I'll be eternally grateful, even if it means spending the next decade licking my wounds in the process.

A car arrives to take us to the airport just after midday. Millie clutches Captain Barnacles under her arm, dragging her *Dora the Explorer* case behind her. The driver puts the bags in the boot and I set the house alarm. Barbie has gone to Mam's for the week, much to both their disgust.

My phone vibrates in my pocket – stupidly I still pray it's Kerry, even though I know she's long gone. It's a withheld number.

'Hello?' The caution in my tone is apparent, even Millie flicks her head round to stare inquisitively.

'Nathan Kennedy?' a deep, gravelly voice asks.

'Who's asking?' I pray it's not the press.

'My name's Marco Garcia, I represent Calvin Klein clothing brand. I wondered if you'd be interested in doing a bit of modelling with us.'

'Are you serious?' Hell, it's not number one on my bucket list, but it's up there.

'Yes, deadly. We often use sport stars to promote our clothing. I'm sure you're aware Dan Carter was with us for a number of years, but we're looking to bring some fresh flesh into the company. How would you feel about meeting to discuss the terms of our offer?'

'I'd definitely be interested in having a chat about it, at least.' How can my voice sound so calm and collected, when I'm secretly jumping for joy inside? Following in Dan Carter's shoes, it's one of the biggest honours yet.

'Would London suit? Next week. Or I can fly you to New York, if you'd prefer?' He clears his throat and the sound of a rhythmic tapping resounds across the phone line, it's either his fingers or a pen, he's impatient.

'I'm actually in Paris for the next week, do you have an office there?'

'Absolutely. I'll get my secretary to set something up with our French representative.'

'That would be ideal.'

'See you next week.' As the call disconnects, a rush of

pride sweeps through me. I scroll through my recent contacts to call Kerry, before remembering she doesn't care.

The airport is thronged with people trying to make the most of the last week of the summer holidays; families congregate, couples stroll hand in hand to their gates and people sit sipping coffee, waiting for their loved ones to arrive or depart.

I glance down at the tickets in my hand. I brought three, even though there's only the two of us. It's a stupid notion, a daft romantic one, even for me, but on the off chance she changed her mind at the last minute, I want to be prepared.

Millie's tiny hand grips mine as we walk towards the check-in desk. The queue for economy's enormous, but I booked first class, so we get to use a quicker one. There's only one person in front of us; a short brunette wearing sculpted backside-hugging jeans and a red shirt. A familiar holdall sits on the floor beside her. My feet slow to halt as the tiny hand in mine squeezes my palm. I glance down in response, certain that when I look up again, the brunette in front will have been a mad illusion.

Millie's bright blue eyes gleam up at mine, as my heart pounds erratically in my ribcage. I look up again and the brunette's turned round to face us. Her graphite eyes well with unshed tears.

'I'm so sorry I ran at the first hurdle.' Her fists clench and unclench by her side. I feel like she's fighting the urge to reach out to us, why, I don't know.

'What about the travelling plans?' I'm still not entirely convinced that her being here is not a complete fluke, and she's actually getting a plane to a different destination, an exotic child-free one.

'When I really thought about it, the only place I want to travel is with you, wherever you go. If you'll still have me?'

My arms are open in a split second and I pull her into them at the same time Millie throws her arms around her. The three of us stand in a group hug, not entirely unlike that first morning, but this time, there's nothing awkward about it.

'I missed you so much,' Millie says into Kerry's stomach, where her face nuzzles against her shirt.

'I missed you, sweetheart.'

'Are we enough for you?' I whisper into her ear. The last thing I want is for her to come back, only to leave us again. My heart couldn't take it, and neither could Millie's.

'You're everything I needed and I didn't know it. I'm sticking around, if you'll have me. I'll never be Millie's mam and I can't be your nanny anymore either. But I can be your girlfriend, if you'll still have me? I shouldn't have left, you only spoke the truth. But I couldn't handle your truths until I faced my own.'

'You're not broken, Kerry.'

'I'm beginning to realise that now. I've arranged to see a professional, to talk about what I lost, you know.' As she places a hand over her flat stomach, a newfound strength radiates from her eyes.

'And I'm going back to college.'

'Kerry, that's wonderful.' A queue's started to form behind us. I motion for them to jump in front of us.

'I might need a weekend job though.' Kerry glances up from underneath enormous glossy eyelashes.

'I have plenty of work for you, lady. You won't need a thing.' I squeeze her into my chest, with Millie sandwiched between us, but instead of my daughter being in the way of us, it's almost like she's cementing us together.

'Can we go to Disney now?' Millie jumps up and down excitedly. 'You are coming, Kerry, right?'

'If you'll still have me, I will.' Her eyes gaze almost shyly up at me and I gently cup her chin in my right hand, needing her to look at me while I tell her what I should have told her weeks ago.

'I love you, Kerry Walsh. I suspected it would happen the second you arrived on my doorstep. I love everything about you.'

'I love you too.' It's only a whisper, but its more rewarding than the cheering of a stadium filled with seventy-five thousand ecstatic fans.

The three of us walk to the check-in desk, holding hands, to begin the first adventure of our new lives. And unlike *Frozen*, I never plan to 'Let It Go'.

EPILOGUE

FOUR MONTHS LATER

KERRY

Sweat pumps from my underarms in a less than ladylike manner. Luckily, my boyfriend knows I'm no lady. I still can't believe Nathan Kennedy, Irish sports star and tattooed hottie, is actually mine.

'Are you sure I'm ready?' I smooth down the black cotton trousers I'm wearing and double-check my underwear isn't hanging out.

Nathan takes both my hands, squeezes them and gazes into my eyes. 'You're ready.'

'What about the weather?' A crisp frost has settled on the ground, dusting the pavements and the rooftops alike. Christmas lights sparkle from every house and shop window, a multitude of red, gold and green.

'It's just a little frost. Hopefully it will help you keep your cool.'

'Huh.' Tell that to my armpits, they didn't get the memo.

The driving instructor approaches from the test centre, nodding his acknowledgement to both of us. Nathan plants a firm, reassuring kiss on my lips and whispers, 'I know you can do it.'

I swallow my snort, but Nathan's reassurance grounds me.

It's my third attempt at this. If I don't get it this time, I probably never will. But one thing's for sure, I won't give up until I do. Slipping into the driver's seat, I focus, reminding myself how far I've come in a few short months and that for once, I, Kerry Walsh, am in the driver's seat and fully in control of my own future. And this time, I truly believe it.

With my first semester at Trinity almost behind me and the support of my friends and family, I am like a new woman. I've got this.

Pulling out into the dark evening, I realise I'm the last test of the day. I follow the instructions spoken to me to the exact tee – as if I'm reading a recipe. He asks me to demonstrate a parallel park and reverse around a corner. He quizzes me on changing a tyre. I tell him what he wants to hear, knowing I'll never actually do it myself. Apart from the fact the tyre is almost bigger than me, I have the best boyfriend in the world and I know if I call him any time of the day or night he would come to my rescue, whether it be a break down, or one drink too many with my girlfriends. A leopard never completely changes her spots – I still love a good blow out, but instead of trying to escape my life now, I mostly celebrate it.

The forty minutes fly by, with no major faults. Unless I've fucked up with my minors, I'm pretty sure this time I've nailed it. I indicate back into the test centre where Nathan is pacing the ground, hands tucked tightly into his coat pockets. He glances up as I park expertly in the box outside the office and wink at him.

'Kerry Walsh, I'm delighted to inform you, you passed. Congratulations.'

Before I can think about it, the instructor's face is in my hands as I squeeze his cheeks in an ecstatic, but entirely inappropriate, gesture of thanks. He inches away from me uncomfortably and straightens his clipboard.

I wind the window down at a grinning Nathan. 'I did it! Honk if you're...' I let the sound of the horn drown out the rest of my sentence.

Leaping out of the car, I jump straight into Nathan's strong arms, where he swings me round in victory. He winces, his new tattoos still raw under his thick winter coat. His sleeve is finally complete; the last marks inked are a K and an M discreetly interlinked.

He's the reason I'm here, he's the reason I was able to do this. He helped me find enough direction to ensure I never feel lost again. I am the driver of my life.

While there are some things I'll never get back, I'm happier than I ever thought possible. With my friends and family behind me, and Nathan and Millie too, I no longer feel lost. I no longer have to lie to myself about who I am. This broken girl is finally complete.

THE END

ACKNOWLEDGMENTS

Thank you so much for taking the time to read my book- without you- the readers, there would be absolutely no point in the blood, sweat, and tears involved in the process. I really hope you enjoyed Kerry and Nathan's story.

A massive thank you to the book bloggers of the world and each and every one of you who takes the time to leave a review on Goodreads or Amazon, it really does mean the world to authors.

A special thank you to my beta readers, fellow authors and to Aimee Walker, my fabulous editor.

The biggest thank you has to go to my two gorgeous kids, who put up with mammy stealing away to my computer for an hour each day. It's all for you J & A. And thanks to my fabulous husband, who is my best friend and biggest champion.

If you enjoyed book 3- turn over to find out more about book 4 in the series....

ALSO BY LYNDSEY GALLAGHER

LOVE & OTHER FORBIDDEN THINGS

Book 4 of the Professional Players Series

Physiotherapist Amy Harrington is struggling to readjust to Irish life following five years immersed amongst the cosmopolitan buzz of London. After years of being single, she'd love to find the right man, but the second any potential candidate realises who her famous rugby playing brother is, they spend more time worshipping him than her.

Irish rugby player Ollie Quinn, is newly single and ready to mingle. When he meets a brunette in the players' lounge, he promises to demonstrate Irish life can be every bit as exciting as London, before realising she's Eddie Harrington's little sister. Despite the explosive chemistry between them, it's one promise he'll never be able to fulfil; everyone knows messing with your friend's sister is forbidden.

When Amy is offered the position of physiotherapist to the rugby team, the two are forced to face the growing chemistry between them. Injuries on the pitch seem minimal compared to what Eddie might do if he discovers their dalliances.

Is it simply the temptation of tasting forbidden fruit?

Or will forbidden turn into forever?

Love & Other Forbidden Things: What you don't know, can't hurt ...https://www.amazon.com › Love-Other-Forbidden-Thi...

OTHER BOOKS IN THE SERIES

-Love & Other Mushy Stuff

-Love & Other Games

-Love & Other Forbidden Things

-Love & Other Vows

OTHER TITLES By LYNDSEY GALLAGHER

-The Seven Year Itch

-The Midwife Crisis

ABOUT THE AUTHOR

Lyndsey Gallagher is a hopeless romantic, with a penchant for swoon-worthy heroes and deserving heroines. Her first book, The Seven Year Itch was inspired from the weekend she met her husband. She lives in the west of Ireland, overlooking the Atlantic Ocean and can usually be found curled up in front of the fire with a good book and a puppy at her feet.

For more information or new releases see www.lyndseygallagherauthor.com

Instagram @lyndseygallagherauthor